SIREN
Publishing

CHOICES

SLICK ROCK 19

Ménage Everlasting

BECCA VAN

Choices

Twenty-two-year-old Jaylynn is heartbroken when she sees Brax, Ajay, and Cael Rhodes bring a woman home with them, and decides to leave. Jaylynn ends up in Slick Rock, Colorado working at the diner, and while she loves the people and the work, she's so lonely, she starts working twenty-hour days.

Brax, Ajay, and Cael choose to move when a Marine buddy contacts them and tells them about his hometown. Their pleasantly shocked to see Jaylynn in the diner and when she collapses, they're determined to take care of her. The Rhodes brothers aren't about to let Jaylynn escape since they're attracted to her, and they begin to court her in earnest.

Jaylynn can't resist the men she's fallen in love with. But an obsessed nemesis follows her to Slick Rock and manages to abduct her.

The Rhodes men aren't going to give up until they have Jaylynn back where she belongs, safe in their arms.

Genre: Contemporary, Ménage a Trois/Quatre, Romantic Suspense, Western/Cowboys
Length: 68,168 words

CHOICES

Slick Rock 19

Becca Van

Siren Publishing, Inc.
www.SirenPublishing.com

ABOUT THE AUTHOR

My name is Becca Van. I live in Australia with my wonderful hubby of many years, as well as my two children.

I read my first romance, which I found in the school library, at the age of thirteen and haven't stopped reading them since. It is so wonderful to know that love is still alive and strong when there seems to be so much conflict in the world.

I dreamed of writing my own book one day but, unfortunately, didn't follow my dream for many years. But once I started I knew writing was what I wanted to continue doing.

I love to escape from the world and curl up with a good romance, to see how the characters unfold and conflict is dealt with. I have read many books and love all facets of the romance genre, from historical to erotic romance. I am a sucker for a happy ending.

For all titles by Becca Van, please visit
www.bookstrand.com/becca-van

CHOICES

Slick Rock 19

BECCA VAN
Copyright © 2018

Prologue

Twelve months ago.

"What the fuck do you think you're doing?"

Jaylynn Freedman turned from packing her car and straightened. She cursed under her breath when she saw one of her deceased brother's Marine teammates storming toward her. Jimmy Appleby was very familiar to her. He and the other members of her brother's team had been coming over to their house for years. However, she wasn't about to let him talk to her that way. She was a grown woman of twenty-three and didn't need or want to take shit from anyone. She crossed her arms beneath her breasts and raised her chin. "What does it look like I'm doing?" she asked facetiously.

Even though she wanted to back away or sidestep to put some space between her and Jimmy, she stubbornly held her ground and met his gaze steadily when he leaned his hands on the frame of the car, blocking her in.

Jimmy was breathing heavily, his chest rising and falling rapidly as if he'd just finished PT. He shifted his gaze beyond her and peered into her car. There were a few boxes of things she and her brother had accumulated over the years, but since it had been just the two of them for almost ten years, and her brother had been away on missions on a regular basis, they hadn't needed much. She was thankful for that now, although at times she wished they had had more. Her clothes and other odds and ends were already stored away in suitcases in the trunk. She'd been hoping that she wouldn't encounter anyone before she'd made her escape, but apparently it wasn't meant to be.

"Are you getting rid of some of Seb's things?" Jimmy asked as he brought his gaze back to hers. His angry expression softened for a moment. "You should have called me, baby. I would have helped you deal with this stuff."

Jaylynn shoved at his chest, but he didn't budge an inch, which wasn't a surprise since he had to outweigh her by a good hundred pounds and topped her by five or six inches. It was like trying to move a brick wall. "I'm not your baby and never have been. Move out of the way, Jimmy."

He shook his head and took a step closer. She had to crane her neck to keep their eyes locked. Jaylynn wasn't about to let this arrogant prick intimidate her, even if she was shaking on the inside.

"You haven't told me what you're doing?"

She glanced toward the open front door and tried to remember if she'd gathered everything. If she had to, she would leave in a hurry. The only furniture she and Sebastian had been able to afford after the bank had foreclosed on their parents' house after they'd been killed, was secondhand furniture from yard sales and thrift stores. She had no qualms about leaving it all behind if necessary.

Right now, she wished that the men who'd been helping look out for her since she was fifteen were home and not away on deployment. Brax, Ajay, and Cael Rhodes had been instrumental in her teenage years' upbringing. She'd idolized them from near and afar for nearly ten years, but they had never treated her any way beyond being her brother's kid sister. She'd been thinking about moving away for six months and the decision had been clinched when she'd seen the Rhodes brothers bringing a woman into their home. Jaylynn had been devastated. It felt as if her heart had been ripped right out of her chest. On top of the grief she was still feeling since her brother had died in action, it had all gotten too much.

Hence the stuff in the back of her car.

She'd given her landlord four weeks' notice and had to be out of the rental by tomorrow. She had no idea where she was going, but she didn't care.

Jaylynn just needed to get away from it all. From the grief, the memories and the heartbreak. She felt as if she was teetering on the edge of a total breakdown and something had to give, but she was determined it wasn't going to be her.

A new place and fresh start was supposed to be as good as a holiday. At least she hoped it was.

She blinked when Jimmy grasped her chin in a firm grip. He wasn't hurting her per se, however, his clasp wasn't comfortable either, but if he put any more pressure on her chin, on her skin, she might end up with bruises.

"Answer me, baby," Jimmy demanded in a hard voice.

Jaylynn could tell he was getting angrier by the second. His fingers dug a little harder into her flesh and her bones began to ache, but she wasn't about to plead with him to let her go. She wasn't sure what to tell him because she was worried he'd end up losing control of his temper and she didn't want to be on the receiving end of whatever he decided to dish out. One punch from him could do permanent damage, or end up killing her. He was a trained Marine and could probably snap her neck without any effort.

"What's it got to do with you, Jimmy?" Jaylynn decided to go on the attack, hoping to get him off balance. Maybe if he was frustrated enough, he'd let her go and turn away. She'd already set the house key in one of the kitchen drawers like she'd been asked to.

There was nothing left for her here, in Fort Worth, Texas. Everyone who'd been important to her was gone. Things were just that and could be replaced easily enough over time. People—mothers, brothers and fathers weren't irreplaceable. "You're not my fucking brother or father. Let me go and fuck off."

His fingers gripped her so hard she nearly moaned, but she swallowed the sound back down. Just as she was about to shove at him again, he slammed his mouth down over hers. The kiss wasn't pleasant in any way, shape or form. In fact, it was so brutal, he was smashing her lips against her teeth and she felt the flesh tear. Blood dripped from her split lip and down over her chin.

Jaylynn knew it was time to fight.

She pushed against his toned chest as hard as she could, but it had no effect. She shifted her hands to his arms and raked her nails down his skin, scoring him as hard as she could. He growled as he drew back and when she saw the cold fury in his eyes, she began to quake in earnest. He wasn't going to let her get away with hurting him. He wasn't going to let her get away at all.

His large hands were cruel on her shoulders as he tugged her against his big frame. She gasped when he combed his fingers into her unbound hair and grasped the tresses at the back of her head so tightly, it hurt her scalp. His other hand moved to her breast and he squeezed so firmly she was sure she was going to be left with bruises.

This time when he slanted his mouth over hers she tried to keep her mouth closed, but she cried out with pain when he bit down hard enough into her lower lip to draw more blood.

Jaylynn knew it was useless to fight him and relaxed into his embrace. The grasp he had on her hair and breast loosened, and he lessened the brutality of his mouth against hers. When he shoved his tongue in between her teeth, she had to consciously stop herself from gagging. His tongue was slimy and made her feel sick to her stomach. He released her hair, caressing over her shoulders and down her side toward her hip. She remained pliant while she allowed him to kiss her, but she didn't kiss him back. She was waiting for him to become complacent and when he did, she was going to make her move.

When he pulled her against his erection, she realized he wasn't going to stop. He was starting to get aggressive again. He grabbed one of her ass cheeks and squeezed and then he shifted his hips away from hers, and shoved his hand between her legs. Tears of fear and anger burned the back of her eyes, but she pushed the terror aside and latched on to her fury.

When Jimmy shifted on his feet and he spread his legs wider, so he didn't have to bend down too far, Jaylynn inhaled through her nose, loosened her muscles even more and lifted her knee up hard and fast.

He released her immediately and as he bent over at the waist cupping his crotch, she brought her knee up again. This time as hard as she could under his chin.

He howled with pain as he fell backward onto his ass.

Jaylynn dove into the driver's seat of her cheap car, turned the key in the ignition and squealed the tires as she reversed out of the driveway. The back door of her car, which had still been open, slammed shut after she put the vehicle in gear and pressed her foot hard down on the accelerator.

"You're going to pay for that, bitch," Jimmy screamed. "You can run, but I'll find you."

The last thing she saw before she careened quickly around the corner was Jimmy on his feet, hunched over with his hand on his junk and blood dripping from his chin.

She'd escaped with hardly a mark, other than the torn flesh inside her mouth and she'd gotten the upper hand on a trained Marine.

Jaylynn smiled for the first time since she'd been informed her brother had died, ignoring her throbbing lip.

She could hear his voice so clearly in her head, it was like he was sitting right next to her. *"I'm so proud of you, sis."*

Chapter One

"I've found her car," Brax said as he glanced up from his laptop, meeting each of his brothers', Ajay's and Cael's, gazes.

"Finally, a lead." Ajay smiled. "We've been looking for Jaylynn for twelve fucking months. Where is it?"

"She sold it for far less than it was worth." Brax sighed and ran his hands through his hair. "She was paid cash."

"Did she buy another car?" Cael asked.

Brax shook his head. "No."

"What the fuck?" Ajay shoved his chair back, stood and began to pace.

"I don't get it," Cael said. "Why? Why would she just up and leave without telling us she was moving. Why did she leave behind all the furniture? Why didn't she leave a fucking forwarding address? Why didn't she leave us a note?"

Brax shrugged, hoping to keep his anger and sorrow from showing on his face. He hated not knowing where Jaylynn was, hated that she was out in the world all alone. He and his brothers had kept an eye on her whenever her brother was away on a mission and they were home. She'd brought so much joy to their bleak lives and now she was gone.

The only scenario he could come up with as to why she'd left without any word, was that she was in trouble. His stomach knotted, and his gut churned. For the first time in his life he wished he'd been home instead of fighting in a never-ending war in the Marines. If he and his brothers had been there for Jaylynn they could have helped her, kept her safe.

Hindsight was a wonderful or an evil thing. Right now, he couldn't decide which one. He, Ajay and Cael had been talking about retiring and settling down for nigh on twelve months. Maybe if they'd made a decision sooner, they would still be honoring their promise to her brother, Sebastian, and taking care of her.

Brax felt useless and since he'd never felt that way before he didn't know how to deal with such an emotion.

He and his brothers had moved into the rental across the street from Sebastian and Jaylynn just after their parents had died in a car accident. Seb was the reason they'd moved to the quiet Fort Worth neighborhood in the first place.

They'd been sharing a dining table at the base and had been talking about finding a house away from the inner city. Seb had piped up and told them about the house across from him which had just been put up for rent. The rest was history.

Cael had been the first of them to meet Jaylynn. Whenever they'd been home, she'd followed Brax and his brothers around if she hadn't been busy studying or doing chores. She'd brought laughter into their lives when he was sure his heart had frozen into a block of ice and grown colder each time he and his brothers had been on missions. She'd brought humor back into his world and lightened the darkness on his soul. He'd missed having that and had looked forward to hearing her joy over the simplest of things.

Now he wasn't sure he'd ever get the chance. He'd never forget the moment he looked at Jaylynn with new eyes. She'd just turned twenty-two and she'd been wearing a pair of shorts and a tank top. He'd known when his brothers saw her in that outfit they were attracted to Jaylynn, too, but they'd all kept their distance from her as much as possible while still watching over her. They hadn't been about to make a move on her even though she was over the age of consent. She was still their friend's sister.

Although Brax knew there was nothing he could do unless Jaylynn contacted him or his brothers, he was never going to give up looking for her. He just needed to know that she was all right, that she wasn't in trouble of any kind. He wasn't going to be able to settle until he knew what had happened to her.

Cael pulled his cell phone from his pocket when it dinged. When Brax saw the smile on his younger brother's face he hoped whatever the message was, was good news. They could definitely use some. Cael met his gaze and then Ajay's before glancing down at his phone. "Nash Sheffield. Says he's heard we've retired and wants us to get in touch."

Brax nodded and scrubbed a hand over his face. "Call him now."

Cael pushed the call button and then the speakerphone.

"Cael, is it true?" Nash answered the call. "Did you and your brothers finally hang up your weapons?"

"You're on speakerphone. Brax and Ajay are with me. Now, Nash, you know a Marine never puts his gun away." Cael grinned. "But the answer to your question is yes."

"Hi, guys," Nash said.

"Hi, Nash," Ajay and Brax said simultaneously.

"Do you have any jobs lined up? Have you decided what you want to do now that you're just normal American citizens?" Nash asked.

"You know we're never going to be normal citizens, old man," Ajay teased.

"Hey, watch it, asshole." Nash chuckled.

"How's life treating you in Colorado?" Cael asked. "Do you like being a deputy?"

"We love it. Wilder, Cree and I have taken to this job like a duck to water."

"Not surprising, really," Brax said. "You're all probably better trained than the sheriff and the other deputies."

"Not true," Nash replied. "There are a lot of retired military in this town."

"What's the draw?" Ajay asked. "Last I heard of Slick Rock there wasn't much there, and the population was minimal."

"That's what me and my brothers heard, too, but the town is expanding fast. There are a lot of unusual relationships around the county and the locals have no trouble accepting them," Nash explained.

"That's right." Cael clicked his fingers. "You guys moved there because you all like to share your woman. What's her name?"

"Violet Sheffield," Nash answered.

"You're married. Fuck! Last I heard, you'd just moved to Slick Rock. How long's it been?" Ajay asked.

"Three or so months. I sent you all an invitation to the wedding, but guessed you were out of the country when you didn't reply. Maybe it got lost in the mail."

"It must have, because we would have replied and sent you a gift. Shit, you and your brothers work fast," Cael said.

"Not really," Nash said. "When it's right, it's right. I remember you three sharing a woman a time or two. Have you thought about moving and settling down? This is a great place to live. All the men are protective of the women and children, those weaker than they are, and wouldn't hesitate to step into the line of fire to keep them safe."

Brax was about to respond, but Nash kept talking.

"Oh, I forgot. You were helping a friend take care of his sister. Do you still need to do that? Isn't she grown up yet?"

Brax sighed with sadness and even though Nash couldn't see him, he shook his head.

"She's grown, but she's also gone."

"What?" Nash asked. "You don't mean she passed away, do you?"

"No," Ajay answered. "She took off while we were on one of our last tours. Her brother died while on deployment twelve months ago. We don't know where she is or why she left without any word."

"That sucks," Nash sounded a little angry on their behalf. "Some people are so ungrateful."

Cael glared at Ajay and quickly changed the subject. "Are there any decent jobs going in your town?"

"Can't hire people fast enough," Nash said. "A new hospital was built not long ago, and the city has already decided to expand it. Sheriff Luke Sun-Walker and Sheriff Damon Osborn were bemoaning just this morning about not having enough men on board. Hey, why don't you apply for the job? There are plenty of new houses for sale or rent if that's what you'd prefer. Slick Rock is on a growth boom and doesn't look as if it's going to slow down anytime soon."

"Let us talk things over and we'll let you know," Brax said.

"Okay. Take care, guys, and don't keep me waiting too long. I can put a good word in for you with the Sheriffs if you decide you want to come to Slick Rock."

"Thanks, Nash. Take care. Later," Cael said.

"Later, guys." Nash disconnected the call.

"What do you think?" Cael asked as he met Brax's gaze and then Ajay's.

"There's nothing keeping us here any longer," Ajay said. "I'm in if you both are."

"Brax?"

Brax rubbed at the back of his neck. He could tell that both of his brothers were eager to move forward with their lives. He was, too, but he couldn't get Jaylynn out of his mind. Nonetheless, if he put his life on hold, he might end up looking back on his life when he was old and gray, and alone with years of regret. There was no reason for him and his brothers to remain in Fort Worth.

Everything they'd had here was now gone.

It was time to move on.

"Let's find out what we need to do to become a deputy," Brax said.

* * * *

"Are you okay, Jaylynn?" Enya asked.

Jaylynn looked up from the large bowl of blueberry muffins she was mixing to find Enya frowning in her direction.

"I'm fine. Why did you ask?"

"You look tired."

"It's only five in the morning, Enya. I'm not awake yet."

Enya shook her head. "You're a morning person. You're usually bright eyed and bushy tailed at this time of the morning, even if you don't talk much, but something's changed over the last couple of weeks."

"I was too hot and didn't get much sleep."

"That's not gonna wash with me, girlfriend. It hasn't been hot every night, and yet each morning those dark smudges under your eyes are darker. You know you can talk to me or the other women if you have a problem, don't you?"

"I do, but I'm fine. Thanks for caring though."

"Don't forget I'm here if you change your mind, and if you decide you need me to lend an ear when I'm not around, all you have to do is call me. Okay?"

"Okay." Jaylynn nodded. She quickly turned back to the muffin mix when tears of gratitude and emotion burned the back of her eyes. She'd never had any close female friends before arriving in Slick Rock. Other than her mom and a few female acquaintances at school, she'd never had any real friends. She'd spent most of her teen years around guys and wasn't sure how to act around women. She'd always been a bit of a tomboy and not a girly-girl, which was one of the reasons she hadn't really fit into any niche or clique while she'd been growing up.

Grief welled when she thought of her mom, dad, and brother. She missed them all so much. They'd been the only family she'd had, and they'd been cruelly taken from her. First her parents in a car accident and then her brother while he was fighting a war. Sometimes she wondered if the gods or the fates were punishing her for something she'd done in another life, but she didn't even believe in reincarnation.

Jaylynn had resigned herself to living her life alone. It just hurt too much to love someone and then have them snatched away. She even used to dream about meeting the man of her dreams, but that had quickly changed to men of her dreams when Brax, Ajay, and Cael Rhodes had moved into a house across the street from her. They'd been so much older and had treated her like the kid she was. That hadn't swayed her from her determination to be with them once she was grown up though.

Dreams and reality were so far apart though. Her childish dreams and heart had been shattered not long after she'd turned eighteen when she'd seen Brax leading a beautiful woman into his house by the hand. When she'd seen him kiss her right out on the front porch, she'd run to her room and cried so hard she'd been ill.

Those childish shattered dreams had put everything into perspective for her, which in a way had been a godsend. She poured her heart and soul into her studies and learning everything she could while attending the Culinary School of Forth Worth where she'd earned her Bakery and Pastry Arts Diploma.

Sebastian had been over the moon proud of her and of course, he'd loved sampling her baking, as had the Rhodes brothers. Even though she'd been helping Enya out with making the pastries, muffins and cakes for the last few months or so, she hadn't revealed that she'd had professional training. However, she didn't think she'd put anything over on Enya. She caught the speculative glances from time to time she'd given Jaylynn as she'd worked. Nonetheless, she was hoping Enya wouldn't ask any prying questions. She still wasn't ready to talk about her previous life and wasn't sure if she ever would be.

Jaylynn pushed her depressing thoughts aside and lost herself in her work, creating edible works of art. She made a fluffy light chocolate torte, some apple and custard-filled pastries, the blueberry muffins and a couple of cakes. By the time she and Enya were done, she was exhausted. As much as she would have liked to climb back upstairs to the apartment above the diner, she was also scheduled to work the breakfast shift. She, Enya and Cindy would be taking orders, pouring coffee and cleaning tables.

Normally she loved working, but over the last couple of weeks with so little sleep, her passion was beginning to become a chore. She was tired, jumpy and stressed, but worst of all, she was all alone.

Even though she'd been devastated when her parents had died she'd still had Sebastian and the Rhodes brothers to hang out with when they were home from deployment. For that last couple of years, she'd had no one. Brax, Ajay, and Cael had been on missions so often, they'd only managed to get home for a day or two before heading out again.

Her brother's team had stopped in from time to time, but most of them had lives of their own, girlfriends, wives, kids and other family members to spend time with. The only constant had been Jimmy, but he'd given her the absolute creeps.

Jaylynn had hated the way he'd stared at her, as if he could see through her clothes down to her naked body, but she'd never told Sebastian how she felt about his fellow soldier and friend. She'd been terrified of causing a rift in the team. If that had happened, the dissent could have been a distraction which could have gotten them killed. It seemed her worries weren't so far from the truth. While she'd kept her mouth shut, it hadn't prevented her brother from dying or Jimmy from trying to take what he considered his.

A shiver of trepidation skated up her spine. She'd never forget the angry resolve in his furious gaze or the intent in his tone when he'd screamed at her as she'd made her escape.

Jaylynn had been so worried that Jimmy would follow her, she'd driven for nearly seven hours straight, into the wee hours of the morning and slept in her car. As soon as she could, she'd bought another cheap car from a private seller and hadn't transferred any of the registration details, since she'd wanted to make it hard for Jimmy to find her. After she'd swapped her things from one car to another, she'd sold her car for cash and kept right on driving. She'd made sure to pay the registration well in advance before a notice could be sent out, so the previous owner wasn't alerted to the fact she'd never changed the personal information she was supposed to have. She bit her lip and hoped the Sheriffs hadn't run a check on her. If they had, they may well have alerted the asshole to her whereabouts. She mentally shook her head. None of the sheriffs or deputies had questioned her about the car she hardly ever drove anymore. They may not even know she owned a vehicle. She kept it parked in a storage shed that was on the outskirts of town. When she'd first arrived in town she'd walked the few miles from the storage facility towing a small suitcase behind her.

She hadn't been back since because she'd been making do, however, if she ever managed to save enough money to buy her own place, that might change. Her car was still packed with keepsakes from her deceased family, more clothes and other personal items. Maybe one day she would be able to look through the family photo albums and not be swamped with grief.

When she'd seen the town of Slick Rock, something had drawn her. She'd been amazed how protective the men were and how friendly everyone was and had decided to stay, but lately she'd been thinking it was time to move on.

She was starting to get paranoid and swore that she was being watched, yet whenever she surreptitiously glanced about, she never caught anyone staring at her. Maybe exhaustion was making her hallucinate.

It was hard to smile as she took orders and served customers when inside she was crying, but she was determined to get through her workday.

She glanced toward the door when Violet's men entered and grabbed a booth close to the door. Violet was an amazing woman who had survived a hellish childhood in the clutches of cult members. Jaylynn admired how loving and kind she'd remained after what she'd endured. In fact, all the women she worked with were amazing with big hearts. They'd all been to hell and back and yet had come out the other side smiling and willing to help anyone in need.

Jaylynn would help anyone, too, but she wasn't about to spill her guts and tell the other women about her life story. There was nothing harrowing in her past other than the death of everyone she'd loved, but the other women had lost people, too.

Jaylynn thought that Delta, Violet, and Enya were all wonderfully amazing, but she was no one special. She was just an average woman, living an average life and trying to get ahead. While she knew the other women would be all over her denying her claims if she voiced her averageness, Jaylynn wasn't sure she'd ever believe them.

Sometimes, she wished she'd been with her parents that fateful night ten long years ago when they'd gone to the movies. She would have been with her family if she'd have died with them.

The loneliness was becoming increasingly hard to endure, but she would continue one step at a time. If Sebastian had been alive, he would have read her the riot act for indulging in a pity party. Normally, she wasn't so pessimistic, but exhaustion was wearing her down.

It had been years since she'd had a vacation. The last time she'd had time off was after being let go from her previous job at the bakery close to her home in Fort Worth. Before that she'd been working and studying and even though Seb had sent home what money he could while he was on a mission, the rest of the money had gone to paying off the rest of her parents' debts and her school fees. Now that all the debts were paid, she was trying to save for her own home, but at the rate she was going, it was going to take years before she had enough for a deposit.

"Hi, guys, what can I get you?" Jaylynn asked as she poured coffee for Wilder, Cree, and Nash.

"You don't need to take our order, Jaylynn," Wilder said. "Violet already knows what we want."

She bit her lip and nodded. She was about to turn away, but stopped when Cree placed a hand on her arm. She met his intent gaze briefly before glancing about the diner, looking to see if anyone else needed their coffee refreshed. "Are you all right, Jaylynn?"

"I'm fine, thanks."

"You look tired, honey." Nash frowned.

"I was up at three this morning and here at four to help Enya with all the baking."

Wilder shook his head, garnering her attention. "You've lost weight and you're really pale. Maybe you should go and get a check-up."

"Thanks for the concern, but I'm fine." She turned away and hurried toward the far side of the diner, sighing with relief at her escape. She liked that the men who lived in Slick Rock and the surrounding county were protective, but sometimes they annoyed her with their overbearing, caring tendencies. Not because she didn't like being shielded, but because it always reminded her of Sebastian, Brax, Ajay, and Cael.

She sucked in a breath and hoped the tears threatening to well weren't visible. If the men in the diner saw tears in her eyes, they were likely to have conniptions.

If that happened, she wasn't sure she'd be able to keep the tears at bay.

Chapter Two

No matter how hard he tried, Jimmy couldn't get Jaylynn out of his head. She was the one who'd gotten away, and he was obsessed with her.

He'd gone back to the house the night she'd left and staked out the place, but she'd never returned. Night after night he'd wasted, hoping that she'd come back and be with him.

He'd had a thing for Sebastian's sister since she'd turned eighteen, but he'd kept it hidden, just waiting for the opportunity to pounce. When Seb had been killed and a few others of their team injured while on a mission, he'd thought he'd be able to inveigle his way into her life by consoling her from her grief. Those asshole Rhodes brothers had stepped in and stolen his opportunity.

He'd retired from the Marines with dreams of making a life for himself with the sexy auburn-haired, green-eyed witch, but his dreams hadn't come to fruition. At least not yet, but he wasn't giving up. Jimmy knew deep down in his heart and soul that Jaylynn was perfect for him and he was perfect for her. All he needed was a chance to prove it. He'd thought he'd been getting somewhere when he'd kissed her. She liked dominant men. She had to since she always seemed to do what her brother and those Rhodes bastards ordered. He'd kissed her hard, trying to show her he was assertive the way she liked and more than masculine enough to handle her sexy little body, but the slut had kneed him in the balls and then the chin. He hadn't been expecting that and she'd literally knocked him on his ass, and he'd nearly passed out.

Jimmy had done everything he could to find her. He'd hacked into the DMV, CCTVs and other avenues as he'd thought of them, but she had managed to elude him. He hated to think of her out in the world all alone, or worse, with another man. A red haze of fury slipped over his eyes and he roared with anger. She'd been gone for twelve long fucking months and still there was no sign of her.

He'd even broken into the Rhodes residence and tapped their phone, but those fuckers were gone on missions more often than not. Nothing he'd done had given him a hint as to where she'd run.

He shoved to his feet, kicked the chair across the room and then punched his fist through the wall. The pain of his knuckles splitting felt good. He'd learned to deal with pain and killing while training and soldiering in the Marines. Sometimes he wished he was still fighting in the war, holding an automatic rifle in his hands and taking insurgents down with a spray of bullets. He missed the camaraderie with his fellow soldiers, but he missed the aggressive violence, the killing more.

He'd made the decision to retire after Sebastian had died. He'd walked away unscathed but other members of his team hadn't. Although they hadn't been as severely injured as he'd first suspected, it had been too close of a call.

He paced about the room, trying to figure out how to find Jaylynn. He'd visited her house a lot over the years and while Sebastian had been earning decent money, he and his sister had lived frugally while paying off their deceased parents' debts.

He clicked his fingers and smiled. "That's it. She has to be earning a living somewhere. If I can hack into the IRS, I'll be able to find her." Jimmy shook his head. If he got caught he'd end up behind bars.

Maybe he'd do a state by state search on her name. He might just get lucky enough to find her on an employer's website or in a local paper. He picked up his seat, sat, cracked his knuckles and got to work.

* * * *

Ajay grinned as he shook first Wilder's, then Cree's and finally Nash's hand. "It's great to see you all."

"You, too." Nash slapped Ajay on the back and then greeted his brothers.

"Come in and have some coffee." Wilder held the door open.

Ajay gazed about the house as he followed Cree and Nash toward the kitchen. "This place looks great. Why hasn't our home ever looked this good?"

Brax cuffed Ajay on the back of the head. "Because we don't have a woman to make all those special little touches that make a house a home."

"Speaking of which." Cael quirked an eyebrow. "Where's your wife?"

"Violet is part owner of the diner in town with two other amazing women. She's cooking for the breakfast and lunch crowd," Cree explained.

"We're meeting her there to share a late breakfast with her since it's our day off," Wilder added.

They all sat around the dining table and sipped their coffee.

"Have you settled into your new house yet?" Nash asked.

"We have. We finished unpacking our stuff last night," Ajay answered.

"When do you start work?" Wilder asked.

"Monday next week," Brax answered. "We wanted a few days to familiarize ourselves with the town and surrounding county."

"Once a Marine…" Cree trailed off.

"Always a Marine," they all said simultaneously. "Hooyah."

"If you don't have any plans, why don't you join us for breakfast at the diner?" Nash suggested. "You can meet Violet."

"She'd have to be a hell of a woman to put up with you three."
Brax grinned.

Wilder, Cree, and Nash chuckled.

"She's amazing," Wilder said.

"Beautiful and sexy." Cree waggled his eyebrows.

"She's one of the strongest women I know," Nash said as he
tugged his cell from his pocket.

Ajay watched as his friend swiped over the screen and pulled a
photo up. He sucked in a breath. "You lucky fucking assholes. She's
fucking gorgeous."

"She is." Nash smiled as Ajay passed the phone to his brothers.

"She looks as if a stiff wind could knock her from her feet," Brax
said.

Cree shook his head. "Violet's stronger than she looks. She's had
to be."

"Why do you say that?" Cael frowned as he handed the phone
back to Nash.

Wilder sucked in a breath. "Long story short, her mom was killed
in front of her when she was very small. She was kidnapped and
raised in a cult, used as a servant with no rights. Those assholes were
training young teenage girls in the art of sex by making them watch
porn."

Cree shook his head. "The sick fucks were taking the girls'
virginity without consent once they turned sixteen."

"Son of a bitch," Brax growled.

"Motherfuckers," Ajay snarled.

"Fucking assholes." Cael clenched his fists.

"Violet managed to escape before she was raped and ended up
here. We met, fell in love and here we are," Nash said.

"I'll bet there's a lot more to that story." Brax crossed his arms
over his chest.

"There is, but we'll leave it for another time." Wilder glanced at
his watch. "We need to move or we're going to be late."

They all stood, and Ajay helped Nash take the mugs over to the sink, rinse them and put them in the dishwasher before following him to the front door.

"Are you guys going to join us for breakfast?"

"Yeah, but we need to stop in and see the boss first," Brax said.

"We'll see you at the diner then," Cree said. "We'll save you a seat."

"You'd better." Ajay grinned as he headed toward Brax's truck. "I'm starving."

"You're in for a treat," Wilder called out. "Those women are great cooks."

"We're looking forward to it." Cael climbed into the back of the truck.

"I like this town," Ajay said as he slid onto the front passenger seat.

Brax met his gaze and nodded as he started the engine and backed out of the drive. "I do, too. I have a really good feeling about relocating."

"So do I," Cael agreed.

"From what our boss Sheriff Luke Sun-Walker said, the diner isn't that far away. Once we've collected our uniforms, we can lock them up and walk to the diner," Brax suggested.

"Sounds good to me." Ajay grinned.

"Me, too." Cael nodded. "I love being out in the fresh air. This is wonderful after being in the Sandbox off and on for months on end."

"That it is, bro. That it is." Ajay hadn't been this enthusiastic about anything for a long time. He couldn't remember the last time he'd smiled before seeing the Sheffield brothers again. Even though he and his brothers were now retired Marines, so were the Sheffields, and the camaraderie was still there after months of not seeing each other.

About twenty minutes later, Ajay, Cael, and Brax were stowing their new deputy's uniforms in the truck. After Brax locked the vehicle, they started walking toward the diner down and across the street.

"This town has everything a person could need," Ajay pointed out. "There's a hotel/motel, the new hospital Nash told us about, several mechanic shops. A hairdresser, supermarket, two gas stations and the diner."

"Don't forget the clothes and lingerie shops." Cael grinned. "I wonder if Violet frequents any of those stores."

"You'd better not let Wilder, Cree, and Nash hear you say anything like that," Brax said. "They're likely to punch you out."

"Nah." Ajay shook his head and slowed his pace as they got closer to the diner. "I bet they go into the lingerie shop and buy things for her."

"If she was my woman I'd be in there every other day." Cael chuckled.

"I hope the both of you aren't attracted to Violet. It'd be a useless endeavor since she's already married."

"I'm not," Ajay said.

"Me either," Cael replied. "We're just having a little fun."

Ajay glanced in the window of the diner and stopped dead in his tracks. A loud roaring set up in his ears and his knees nearly buckled when he saw a woman who looked exactly like Jaylynn. He blinked a few times and stared intently before sucking in a surprised breath. There was no way to mistake that sexy little body, auburn hair, or jade green eyes. He'd know that face anywhere. It had starred in his dreams for the last couple of years. He grabbed his brothers' arms, spun away from the diner and walked a few paces away. He didn't stop until they were out of view from the windows.

"What the hell, Ajay?" Brax frowned.

"Have you lost your mind?" Cael asked. "We're supposed to be meeting our friends for breakfast."

Ajay's heart flipped in his chest and he was panting as if he'd just finished a ten-mile run. His palms were sweaty, there were nervous flutters in his belly and he couldn't understand how he was still standing. He felt as if someone had just sucker punched him.

"What's wrong, bro?" Brax asked. "You look as if you've just seen a ghost."

"In a way I have." He swallowed around the constrictive emotional lump in his throat. "I know where Jaylynn is."

"What?" Cael crossed his arms over his chest and scowled at him.

"How the hell could you know that?" Brax asked. "We haven't seen her for just over twelve months, and she's never once contacted us."

"Prepare yourselves, brothers."

"What are you trying to pull?" Cael grabbed Ajay's shirt in his fist.

"She's working in the diner," Ajay said hoarsely.

"Are you shitting me?" Cael released Ajay's shirt and leaned back against the brick wall.

"No. You know I'd never joke about Jaylynn."

"She's in there?" Brax asked incredulously. "Right now?"

Ajay nodded. "Yes."

"Does she look okay?" Cael asked.

"As far as I can tell, but I only got a glimpse of her." Ajay frowned. "She's very pale and looks exhausted, and I think she's lost weight."

"Fuck, she was already slim." Brax rubbed at the back of his neck. "She couldn't afford to lose any weight."

Ajay nodded. "I know, but just remember I only got a glimpse of her, so my assessment may be off. I wanted to prepare you both for seeing her."

"I'm glad you did." Cael placed a hand on his chest, over his heart. "My heart is racing and I'm not sure what I would have done if I'd gone in there without knowing she was here."

"Me, too," Brax said. "We have to keep our emotions out of this. There has to be a damn good reason why she ran off the way she did."

"And if there isn't?" Ajay asked.

"I guess we'll have to cross that bridge when we come to it," Brax answered.

"Are you both ready?" Cael glanced toward the diner. "I need to see her for myself. I just want to know that she's happy."

"Let's go." Brax nodded.

Ajay spun toward the door and took the lead with a brisk determined pace. Whatever was going on with Jaylynn, he intended to find out. Even if it took the rest of his life.

He paused outside the glass door and took a deep calming breath as he searched for Jaylynn. He exhaled slowly when he saw she was tending to some customers with her back toward them. Ajay pulled the door open and stepped inside, his brothers right behind him.

He spied the Sheffield men right away and grinned as he moved toward their booth. He took a seat, scooted over to make room for Brax and Cael, then placed a finger over his lips.

"What's going on?" Cree asked in a whisper after he leaned forward.

"Our friend's sister that disappeared has just shown up," Ajay replied in a quiet voice.

"Are you shitting me?" Nash frowned.

"Where is she?" Cree asked.

"Did she call or text you?" Wilder asked.

Brax shook his head. "No, she's right here, working in this diner."

The three Sheffield men frowned.

Wilder crossed his arms over his chest, but quickly unfolded them before glancing about the room. He turned back to meet each of his brothers' gazes before locking eyes with Ajay. "Are you talking about Jaylynn?"

"We are," Cael said.

"Shit. She's been here for around twelve months," Wilder said.

"She's a quiet little thing." Cree rubbed at his chin.

"If we'd known the name of the woman you were worried about, we could have put your minds at ease," Nash said.

"Doesn't matter." Brax leaned back against his seat. "We know where she is and that she's okay. That's what's important."

"From the way you three can't take your eyes off of her, I'd say she's very important." Cree quirked an eyebrow. "Am I right?"

"You are," Ajay replied.

"What do you know about her?" Cael asked. "Does she talk about where she's from? Why she's here?"

"We don't know much," Wilder answered. "She keeps to herself mostly. Don't you know her that well? I thought you would since you were her pseudo guardians while her brother was serving."

"We do know her, for the most part, but she changed after her brother died. She used to be so open and friendly, but then she closed up, became introverted after Sebastian's death. We hated leaving her alone, but we were called up on mission after mission." Brax shrugged. "You know how it is."

"That we do," Cree murmured.

"She's about to turn around," Ajay whispered. He kept his gaze on her and knew his brothers were watching her just as intently. She was walking toward them with a smile on her face, but Ajay realized the smile was fake because her eyes weren't sparkling.

Her steps faltered when she glanced toward the booth they were sitting in and she came to a halt. Her face paled even further and when she began to sway on her feet, Ajay wished he wasn't crammed in against the window, so he could get to her. She closed her eyes and murmured something under her breath and then opened her eyes again.

And then her knees started to buckle.

Brax jumped to his feet and caught Jaylynn in his arms before she could hit the floor. He lifted her up against his chest and frowned with concern down at her beautiful face. Cael and Ajay were on their feet seconds later, as were the Sheffield brothers.

"Shit!" Wilder squeezed Brax's shoulder. "I think you've given her a great shock."

Ajay didn't say what was on the tip of his tongue. *Nothing like stating the obvious.*

"Bring her to the office," Cree said before turning to lead the way.

"I'll get her some water." Nash followed behind. "It might be a good idea if I got Violet, too. If Jaylynn's upset when she comes around, another woman might be able to calm her. Plus, they're familiar with each other, and friends."

"Good idea," Cael said.

Ajay wished he was the one holding Jaylynn in his arms, but he was thankful it was Brax, and not another man. He didn't want any other man other than him or his brothers touching their woman.

He clenched his jaw as he gritted his teeth.

They'd been attracted to Jaylynn for a couple of years but hadn't been willing to break their promise with her brother to watch out for her. However, she was a mature woman now and it was time to make their move.

Ajay just hoped that she didn't laugh right in their faces when they told her what they wanted with her. A loving relationship that would stand the test of time.

Now all Ajay, Brax, and Cael needed to do was convince her that they were the men for her.

It would break his heart if she rejected them.

Chapter Three

Jaylynn bolted upright and gasped. Heat suffused her cheeks when she blinked open her eyes and saw the people surrounding her. She'd been lying on the sofa and she could barely draw a breath when she realized how close Brax, Ajay, and Cael were. She couldn't believe she'd fainted and was so embarrassed, she quickly lowered her eyes to her knees, gripping her hands and twisting her fingers together with nervous agitation.

She'd never fainted before, but put it down to the shock of finding the loves of her life sitting in the diner where she now worked. Had they tracked her down? How could they have found her? But the biggest question of all was why? Why had they searched her out? She was nothing to them, but her deceased brother's little sister. Someone who'd been a burden to them when they'd needed to look out for her whenever Sebastian had been away fighting in wars.

"Look at me, baby," Brax ordered.

Even though she didn't want to meet his gaze, she found herself lifting her eyes to his. He was down on his knees, so close to her she could smell the amazing fragrance of his cologne. She'd never forget the manly-spicy scent of him and of his brothers. Ajay and Cael were crouching on either side of Brax, staring at her with worried expressions, but she wasn't about to meet their gazes head on. It was bad enough being trapped by Brax's intent brown eyes.

"Are you okay, Jaylynn? Are you sick? You don't look well. Haven't you been taking care of yourself?"

She sighed with relief that he hadn't asked her the question she expected him to, but she knew by the resolute expression in those amazing chocolate brown eyes that he would eventually.

When Brax covered her hands with his, she jolted and met his eyes again. She hadn't noticed that she'd looked away from him. She nervously licked her lips and surreptitiously gazed at the other men watching her so avidly. Her face was so hot she was sure it had to be redder.

"Have you eaten anything today, Jaylynn?" Wilder asked in a firm voice.

She really, really wanted to lie and tell him yes, but for some reason the men of this town, as well as Brax, Ajay, and Cael knew whenever she was fibbing. Maybe she could redirect the concerned interrogation by asking a few of her own.

"What are you doing here?" she asked, briefly gazing at Cael, Ajay and then Brax.

Brax grasped her chin when she went to glance away again. "That's not going to work, baby. You're not leaving this room until you start answering some questions."

She sucked in an annoyed breath, turning her face away, hoping to dislodge Brax's hold on her, but he just firmed his grip, without hurting her. She threw her hands up into the air with frustration, secretly pleased when she knocked Brax's finger and thumb from her chin. "I'm fine. No, I'm not sick and yes, I've been looking after myself."

Ajay laced his fingers with hers. "And the other question you were asked."

God save her from arrogant, determined men. It didn't matter that she secretly liked the way her brother's friends, or the men of Slick Rock, looked after her. She wanted more from life than friendly concern. Tears of grief burned her eyes. She'd never have the chance to be with the Rhodes men since they still saw her and treated her like a child. What was it about her that caused men to treat her as if she was a kid?

"Jaylynn, answer the fucking question," Cael ordered.

She gaped at him. She'd never heard Cael so authoritative before. Usually it was Brax and Ajay giving her commands and expecting her to obey them without question. She wasn't putting up with their shit any longer. She was a grown woman and could take care of herself. They might think they had authority over her, but they didn't. While Sebastian, Cael, Brax, and Ajay had looked out for her, she'd been independent from a young age, out of necessity. Just because they'd looked in on her while Seb was deployed didn't mean she was useless.

She wasn't about to let them bully her around anymore. She inwardly winced over her choice of words. They'd never bullied her, but she wasn't about to let them tell her what to do ever again.

She tugged her hand out of Ajay's grip and tried to decide how she was going to make her escape. She would either need to climb over the arm of the sofa, or shove one of the men out of the way. Neither was a real option since they were all so much bigger and stronger than she was. If she tried to go over the arm of the couch, she had a feeling she'd be stopped. All Brax would have to do was wrap an arm around her waist. She wasn't sure she could stand any of them touching her again. Just having Brax's finger and thumb on her chin, as well as Ajay holding her hand, had set her body on fire.

Jaylynn felt as if she was teetering on the edge of the cliff. There were so many emotions warring inside of her heart and soul she felt sick to her stomach. Maybe she wasn't well after all.

She placed a hand over her roiling belly, inhaled and swallowed, trying to prevent herself from tossing her cookies. Sweat broke out on her brow and upper lip and even though she felt hot, she was so cold she didn't think she'd ever be warm again.

Was she reacting this way because she was in shock? Or was she sickening for something? Either way, she didn't feel so good.

"Let me up," she ordered, but her voice didn't come out as strong as she'd been hoping.

"Not until we've talked, honey." Ajay brushed her hair back from her face and then frowned. He placed the palm of his hand over her forehead. "She's fucking burning up."

"No, I'm not," she contradicted as she wrapped her arms around her waist and shivered. When saliva pooled in her mouth she realized that she really was sick.

She shoved to her feet, stumbled between Brax and Ajay and raced toward the door. As she hurried around the doorway she knocked her shoulder into the doorframe and would have cried out with pain if she wasn't scared to open her mouth. She burst into the restroom and the first cubicle, dropped down to her knees and vomited. After the two cups of coffee had been purged from her system, she ended up dry heaving since there was nothing left in her stomach.

Finally, when the spasms faded, she flushed the toilet and rose on shaky legs. She got dizzy when she turned toward the sink and had to place her palm against the cubicle wall. It took a few moments for her blurry vision to clear and while she'd known that Brax, Cael, and Ajay had followed her into the bathroom, she was hoping by ignoring them, they'd become bored with her and leave. Although she hated that they'd heard and maybe seen her being sick, there was nothing she could do about it, so she pushed her humiliation aside.

Jaylynn stood in front of the sink and after washing her hands, cupped her palm and scooped water up to her mouth, rinsing the acidity away before spitting the water out. When the horrid taste was gone from her mouth, she splashed water onto her face and murmured her thanks when one of the guys handed her some paper towels to dry off with.

"Come on, honey." Ajay moved to her side, wrapping an arm around her shoulders. "Let's get you out of here."

She wanted to tell him and his brothers to leave her the hell alone, but she just didn't have the energy and ended up nodding in agreement.

Brax held the bathroom door open, stepping aside to allow Ajay to guide her from the bathroom.

"Jaylynn, are you okay?" Violet asked as she walked out of the kitchen. "My men told me you're sick. Do you want me to call one of the docs?"

"No," she croaked. "I'm okay. It's probably just that twenty-four-hour bug that's been going around."

"Oh, you poor thing. Go on up and get some sleep. Don't you dare come in tomorrow," Violet told her sternly. "In fact, you can take the rest of next week off, too. You've got more than enough sick leave and vacation time to take a break."

"I'll take tomorrow but that's it," she replied. There was no way she was taking off more time than was necessary. She'd been taking any shift she could to save up for her own place. She'd work twenty hours a day if she had to, and had. If Violet, Delta, and Enya had noticed what she'd been doing, they would have had a fit. Luckily, so far, they hadn't twigged that she was working so much since the other women's shifts overlapped. Cindy, the young teenage waitress, had given her a few worried looks, but she was the only one. Jaylynn shrugged Ajay's arm off and then unlocked the door to her upstairs apartment.

She froze when one of them clasped her shoulder.

"What are you doing, sweetness?" Cael asked.

"Going upstairs to lie down."

"You live upstairs?" Brax asked almost angrily.

She swallowed around the constrictive lump in her throat and nodded, keeping her gaze on the door she had yet to open.

"That's not safe, honey," Ajay said. "If anyone knew you were living here all by yourself—you could be in danger, Jaylynn."

She shook her head. "Good security," she forced out from her tight throat. Already her stomach was churning again. Whatever she'd caught wasn't over yet and she needed to get upstairs before she embarrassed herself again. "Thanks," she said as she opened the door and quickly closed it behind her so that they couldn't follow her.

She engaged the lock, raced upstairs toward the bathroom.

* * * *

"What the fuck is going on?" Ajay asked frustratedly as he ran his fingers through his hair.

"I don't know," Brax answered through clenched teeth. "But whatever it is, I don't like it."

Cael led the way back toward the diner and after they were seated again, he said what worried him the most. "She hardly looked at us."

"I'm aware." Ajay sighed.

Wilder, Cree, Nash, and Violet joined them at the booth with loaded plates. Wilder wrapped an arm around his woman's shoulders. "Baby, this is Brax, Ajay, and Cael Rhodes. Guys, the love of our lives, Violet."

"Hi." Violet smiled shyly.

"Pleased to meet you, Violet," Brax said.

"Hey," Cael greeted.

"Nice to meet you, Violet," Ajay said.

Cael started eating as his mind whirled in circles. "What's she doing living upstairs?" he asked after swallowing.

"She asked if she could lease the upstairs apartment a few months ago," Violet explained. "Since I didn't need it anymore, and after talking to my partners, they agreed she could rent it."

"I can see how worried you are," Cree said, "but you have no need to be. The security system is state of the art and monitored twenty-four-seven. No one can even try to get in without someone knowing about it."

Cael relaxed a little at knowing that Jaylynn was safe, however, he was still worried about her being alone and ill. What if she passed out again and was sick while unconscious? She could end up choking on her own vomit and suffocating.

"Do you want more coffee?"

Cael glanced at the young woman holding the coffee pot.

"Yes, please, Cindy," Violet said.

Cindy immediately started filling the coffee mugs.

"I don't like Jaylynn being all alone when she's sick." Cael scrubbed a hand down his face. "She looks as if a good wind could blow her from her feet and she's lost too much weight. She didn't have any excess to begin with and is downright skinny. Those dark smudges under her eyes tell their own tale, too. She can't have been sleeping much."

"That's because she's been working nearly twenty-hour days," Cindy said and then gasped before covering her mouth with her hand.

"What?" Violet frowned. "Are you serious? Why am I just finding out about this now? Did we somehow muck up the roster? Oh god. She's sick because we stuffed up." Violet lifted a shaky hand to her chest.

"You, Enya and Delta haven't mucked up the roster, Violet," Cindy said. "Jaylynn's been volunteering for any shift she could. She's also been helping Enya with all the baking."

"She's been getting up to start work around four and then working the morning and afternoon shift?" Violet asked incredulously. "When has the woman had time to sleep?"

"I don't know," Cindy answered.

"Damn it. She's also been helping me on the late shift." Cael could see guilt and concern in Violet's troubled gaze. "If I hadn't swapped this shift with Delta today, I would probably never have known what Jaylynn was doing. Shit! We need to call a staff meeting. Can you arrange for one to coincide for around three this afternoon,

Cindy? That way all three of us will be here. What time are you working till today?"

"Five," Cindy answered.

"Good, you need to be there, too. Please call Katie and Kiara, as well. I'll make sure they get paid for coming in on their day off."

"Uh." Cindy shifted from foot to foot uncomfortably.

"Spit it out, Cindy," Violet ordered.

"Katie and Kiara were scheduled to work today. Jaylynn overheard them talking about wanting to spend the day in Monticello, Utah for a festival of some kind. She told them she'd cover their shifts."

Violet covered her face. "I can't believe what terrible bosses we are. Why didn't we notice what Jaylynn was doing?"

"Don't go blaming yourself, love." Nash leaned around Cree to caress a hand over Violet's head. "You've been too busy to keep up with everything."

Cael wished he could have spoken to agree with Nash, but he was so angry at what Jaylynn had been doing, he was worried he'd end up cursing up a blue streak. Since there were a few children present, he kept his mouth shut. Thankfully Violet had kept her voice soft when she'd cursed. He wasn't mad at Violet or the other women, but he was furious that Jaylynn had run herself into the ground. No wonder she was sick. She'd only been getting a few hours' sleep a night for god knew how long.

"How long, Cindy?" Violet asked.

Cael was glad that Violet was thinking along the same lines as he was.

"About four months," Cindy whispered and lowered her gaze. "I'm sorry, Violet. I should have said something sooner. I feel so guilty. Jaylynn's covered a few of my shifts, as well, so I could catch up on classes at school. Mom's been working so much, I've had to skip some school days to take care of my sister."

"You're not to blame, Cindy," Brax piped up. "Jaylynn's done this to herself."

"Brax is right," Violet agreed. "However, things are going to change. I think there's going to be a couple of new rules put in place. We'll talk more about this later, okay?"

"Okay." Cindy nodded and hurried to serve more customers.

"Why the hell would Jaylynn work so much?" Ajay asked.

"Is she in trouble?" Cael asked, directing his question to Violet.

"I don't think so, but I can't be certain," Violet answered. "Jaylynn's a very private person and doesn't talk about herself or her past much."

"Damn." Brax sighed. "I don't like this. She used to be an open book."

"You know her?" Violet asked.

Cael nodded. "We used to live across the street from her and her brother."

"She has a brother?"

Ajay shook his head. "He was killed in action about twelve months ago."

"What about her parents?"

"They died in a car accident when she was fifteen," Brax replied. "She has no other family. Me and my brothers used to look in on her when her brother, Sebastian, was away on missions."

"She is all alone." Violet frowned. "I had a feeling she was, but didn't want to ask in case I upset her."

"We need to get into her apartment," Cael said.

"I agree." Ajay nodded.

"Can one of you recommend a doctor who'd be willing to make a home visit?" Brax asked.

Violet nodded. "Enya's involved in a relationship with three doctors. I'm sure one of them wouldn't mind examining Jaylynn." She rose. "She should still be in the kitchen. Let me go ask."

Cael watched Violet hurry away before glancing at his brothers. "This has to stop. If we don't step in, Jaylynn is going to put herself into an early grave."

"Depending on what the doc says, I think we should bring her home with us," Ajay suggested.

"I want that as much as you do, but we can't just take over her life." Brax sighed and rubbed the back of his neck. "I know we watched over her, but that little woman has been on her own a lot since she was fifteen years old. She's independent and mature and is going to make a fuss if we try and take over."

"I get that, Brax," Cael said. "However, I agree with Ajay. She's sick, lost way too much weight and looks as if she's about to keel over. I'd rather deal with her anger than not having the chance to deal with her at all."

"Phoenix should be here any minute," Violet said as she took her seat again. "Apparently he was already on his way to the diner."

"Thanks, Violet," Brax said.

"Thanks," Cael and Ajay said simultaneously.

"How are we going to get into her place?" Brax asked.

"I grabbed the spare key from the office after I spoke to Enya." Violet held up the key. "She's worried about Jaylynn, too, and I know Delta will be, as well, when she realizes what's been going on."

Cael was so worried about Jaylynn he didn't finish his breakfast. Normally nothing could stop him from appeasing his hunger, but his stomach was too knotted with concerned tension.

He wouldn't relax until he knew Jaylynn was okay.

Chapter Four

Jaylynn had never felt so ill in her life. After throwing up yet again, she was too exhausted to get up off the floor. The cool tiles felt amazingly good on her hot face, yet she was so cold she was shivering, and her bones were aching. No, not just her bones. Her whole body was aching. The only consolation was she'd been able to grab a bottle of water from the fridge before having to rush back to the bathroom. At least she'd been able to rinse her mouth out before slumping to the floor. She really wanted to brush her teeth and gargle some mouthwash, too, but moving was way too hard.

She closed her eyes and drifted in a dream-doze like state between awareness and sleep. Every now and then she could feel and hear her teeth chattering together and her body quaking on the floor.

For a moment she wondered if she was dying and while the thought brought tears to her eyes, it was tempting just to let go. She missed her parents and brother so much, it was a physical ache. There was no one left in her life to care about her and it was alluring to just give up.

Yet she couldn't. Brax, Ajay, and Cael were in town. She wanted to see them again and wished she could go back downstairs and tell them how much she'd missed them, how much she loved them, but she couldn't. Firstly, because she was so weak she couldn't move, and secondly because there was no way she was going to humiliate herself by telling them what was in her heart. They'd never see her as anything but a kid.

Goose bumps raced over her flesh and she trembled violently as she grew colder by the second. When she felt her arms and legs go rigid before she started jerking, Jaylynn knew she was in real trouble.

Tears leaked from the corners of her eyes and just before she passed out, she wondered if she'd ever wake up again.

* * * *

"Fuck!" Brax roared with fear when he saw Jaylynn convulsing on the floor. He grabbed a towel from the rail, hurried over to her, knelt, carefully lifted her head and put the towel under her so she wouldn't give herself a head injury.

Dr. Phoenix Carter had been introduced to them by Violet before coming upstairs with him and his brothers.

"Her temperature's way too high. It's a hundred and four. If we don't get it down, she could end up with brain damage," Phoenix said after pressing a digital thermometer into Jaylynn's ear. He grabbed a syringe out of his medical bag as well as a vial of something and filled the needle. After swabbing her upper arm, he injected the medicine into her system. "I've just given her a high dosage of antibiotics to help combat whatever she's fighting. I'm also going to give her a painkiller which will help bring the fever down."

Brax and his brothers sighed with relief when she stopped convulsing.

"What can we do?" Ajay asked. He and Cael were leaning against the vanity, staring at Jaylynn with worry.

"How well do you know her?" Phoenix asked as he prepped another syringe.

"Well," Cael answered. "We used to live across the street from her."

"What I want to know is if she'll be pissed or upset if one of you saw her naked. She needs to be stripped down and put into a lukewarm bath. That's the fastest way to lower her fever."

"She can be pissed all she wants." Brax practically growled the words. "I'll do whatever's necessary to make sure she gets better."

"I could call an ambulance and admit her to the hospital," Phoenix said. He injected the painkiller, pulled a stethoscope from his bag and listened to her heart. "Her heart rate's elevated but that's to be expected." He felt along her throat and after lifting her arms to the side, he felt in her armpits. "Her glands are up in her throat, but the ones under her arms are normal size. I think she has a bad case of the flu or glandular fever.

"She's been pale for a while and from what Violet told me before I came up, she's been pushing herself way too hard. If she doesn't slow down she could end up with chronic fatigue syndrome, if she hasn't already got it."

"Shit!" Ajay crossed his arms over his chest.

Brax clasped her small hand between his two much larger ones. He hated seeing her like this, so pale and sick, but now that he and his brothers were in town to stay, they would look after her like they had when she'd been growing up. However, this time she would be in their home. There was no fucking way he was leaving her here by herself. She needed a caretaker so she could get her health back on track, and she was going to have three.

He didn't like the thought of leaving her by herself so he, Cael and Ajay could start their new jobs as deputy sheriffs. Once he knew Jaylynn was out the woods and her temperature was lower, he was going to contact one of their bosses and ask if they could delay their start date.

Nothing was more important than Jaylynn and her health. He'd tie her to a fucking bed if he had to.

"What's chronic fatigue syndrome?" Cael asked.

"Chronic fatigue syndrome, or CFS, is a complicated disorder characterized by extreme fatigue that can't be explained by any underlying medical condition. The fatigue may worsen with physical or mental activity, but doesn't improve with rest."

"Fuck!" Ajay sighed.

"The condition is also known as systemic exertion intolerance disease, or SEID, or myalgic encephalomyelitis, or ME. Sometimes it's abbreviated as ME/CFS.

"The cause of chronic fatigue syndrome is unknown, although there are many theories—ranging from viral infections to psychological stress. Some experts believe chronic fatigue syndrome might be triggered by a combination of factors.

"There's no single test to confirm a diagnosis of chronic fatigue syndrome or glandular fever. You may need a variety of medical tests to rule out other health problems that have similar symptoms. Treatment for chronic fatigue syndrome focuses on symptom relief.

"She's not going to be working for a while. It can take months for the symptoms to ease and years for them to disappear altogether." Phoenix shook his head. "I could be wrong, since I've already told you there's no way to confirm my diagnosis. I'm hoping this is flu or glandular fever."

"Why the antibiotics then?" Brax asked.

"Just in case she's fighting a severe infection. They won't harm her if she's not, but I injected them just to be on the safe side," Phoenix explained. "I'm going to leave you all, so you can get her into the tub." He stood after closing his medical bag and dug into his trouser pocket. "Here's my card. Call me anytime day or night if you need me."

"Thanks, Phoenix." Brax nodded.

"Yeah, thanks, man." Ajay proffered his hand and shook with the doc.

"Thank you," Cael said as he too shook the doctor's hand.

"Oh, I almost forgot." Phoenix crouched as he rummaged in his bag. "Here, you're going to need this."

Cael took the digital thermometer.

"If her temp doesn't lower, call me or an ambulance."

"Do you think we'll need to?" Ajay asked.

"I don't think so. I think this is Jaylynn's body's way of saying enough is enough. She's not going to be working for at least a week or maybe more. I'll let Enya and Violet know before I head out."

"Thanks again, Phoenix," Cael said as he followed him out of the bathroom.

"Sure," Phoenix replied.

Brax lifted Jaylynn onto his lap and started removing her clothes while Ajay filled the tub. If Jaylynn hadn't been so sick, he would have draped her over his thighs and spanked her ass. She'd never done anything like this to herself before and he wondered what had happened to her to cause such an about face. She'd always eaten right and made sure she got enough sleep when she was younger. It was as if she'd become a different person after moving away from Fort Worth.

When she was on the road to recovery he was going to get all the answers to the questions running around in his mind.

Cael came back into the bathroom and closed the door just as Brax finished removing all her clothes. He lifted her against his chest and then handed her over to Ajay. He stripped off quickly and stepped into the tepid water in the tub and then took her back into his arms when his brother passed her over. Brax sucked in a fortifying breath and sank into the cool water.

Jaylynn whimpered and shivered but other than that she didn't make another sound or move in any way. Brax had no idea how long he sat in the lukewarm water, but it felt as if more than an hour had passed. He took the opportunity to wash her and tried to keep his touch as clinical as possible. It was difficult to ignore his hard, throbbing cock, but ignore it he did. This wasn't the time or the place to be lusting after their woman. Not when she was sick and unconscious. Of course, he couldn't help his body's natural response. However, he could disregard it.

"Ajay, call Luke and explain to him what's going on. See if you can get us a reprieve on our starting date for our new jobs," Brax ordered. "Cael, come and take her temperature again."

Ajay exited the bathroom to make the call. Cael knelt next to the tub and inserted the thermometer into Jaylynn's ear. He pulled it out when it beeped. "Ninety-eight-point-eight."

Brax breathed out a sigh of relief. Her temperature was still slightly high, but was nearly back in the acceptable range. It was time to get their woman out of the bath, dried off and dressed. Then he and his brothers were going to pack her a bag and take her home with them.

He was so fucking glad they'd bought their own place with six bedrooms, three bathrooms, and a large gourmet kitchen. He just hoped that Jaylynn liked the place, too, as well as the location and the acre tract of land with the landscaped gardens. There was a wraparound verandah where they could sit and enjoy a drink and when they got around to buying an outdoor setting, they could eat out there, too.

If Brax had his way, and he was determined he would, Jaylynn was going to do nothing but eat, drink and sleep for a month. He just hoped that Luke was agreeable to him and his brothers starting work at a later date.

"Let me take her." Ajay had a large bath towel ready and waiting. He wrapped it around Jaylynn and then lifted her against his chest.

Brax got out of the tub, grabbed another towel, quickly dried off and dressed. He dried the moisture from Jaylynn's skin while Ajay held her and when they were done, Ajay carried her back into the bedroom.

"Put her into bed while we find her some clean clothes and pack her things," Brax said.

Cael entered the room. "When Luke heard what was going on with Jaylynn and our connection to her, he was the one to suggest delaying starting our new roles as deputies. He doesn't want us distracted while on the job. He was pretty upset he hadn't checked up on her lately, but Slick Rock is growing so fast, they can't keep up. Crime is on the rise, and he wants to nip that shit in the bud before it gets too bad.

"He also said to contact him if we need anything."

Brax was relieved that he and his brothers could concentrate on getting Jaylynn well. They didn't have to worry too much about money because they'd received an inheritance from their grandparents when they'd passed away. Plus, they hadn't had many expenses other than paying for rent and utilities when they were living in Fort Worth, but the rent had been cheap because they'd been on the outer edge of town and they were away so often, they hadn't used much gas or electricity, so they'd accumulated a fair amount of savings in their own right, as well. He and his brothers were comfortably well off and didn't really have to work if they didn't want to, but all three of them hated being idle. Him the most. Brax had loved being a Marine, as had Ajay and Cael. Their parents had instilled good morals and work ethics in all of them.

He knew that Jaylynn hadn't liked being told what to do when she was growing up, but it had been for her protection and there was no way he was going to change who he was for anyone, including her. Brax sat on the edge of the bed and brushed the hair back from her forehead and then checked her temperature by placing his palm over her forehead. It felt as if it was back to normal and hoped it didn't spike again. Fierce possessive protectiveness surged into his heart as he stared at her pale, thin face.

If he had his way, she wouldn't be getting out of bed for a week.

* * * *

Jaylynn groaned as she surfaced from sleep. She was aching all over, her throat was sore, and she felt as if she'd been hit by a truck. Even though she'd just woken up, she was too tired to move. The plus side was that she was warm and comfortable. She frowned because her bed didn't usually feel as good as this.

She forced her eyelids up and gasped when she realized she was in a strange bedroom. It was huge and nicely decorated, but it wasn't hers. She frowned as she tried to remember where she was and squeezed her eyes shut with humiliation as the memory of fainting and then tossing her cookies after leaving work. Everything was hazy after that, but she had a bad feeling she knew where she was.

Tears leaked from under her eyelids before she could prevent them. It had been shockingly wonderful to see Brax, Ajay, and Cael again, but it had also been pure torture. She loved them from the age of eighteen and it had hurt to look at them, to see them laughing and happy with other women. She'd tried to keep her emotions hidden from them, but it had hurt too much to see them building a life without any chance of her being a permanent member in it.

She had no idea what they were doing in Slick Rock, but she could hazard a guess. They liked to share women and this town was accepting of ménage relationships without too much angst. Jaylynn decided the best course of action was to move on as soon as she was feeling better.

However, first she needed to find out where she was and get the hell out of here. She wasn't going to hang around and let them treat her like their kid sister anymore. She impatiently wiped the tears from her face and opened her eyes again. After flinging the covers aside, she slowly scooted toward the edge of the bed. Even that small amount of effort left her feeling drained and her body felt as if it weighed a ton. She hadn't been feeling well for a few weeks and knew she should have backed off working all the hours she could. Now she was sick and wouldn't be able to work at all. She gave a mental "pfft". She wasn't about to let illness keep her down. Jaylynn had learned to be tough and to keep going no matter what. She'd had to when Sebastian had been on missions as well as the Rhodes brothers.

She shoved to her feet and bit her lip when her aching body protested. Taking steady deep breaths helped diminish the dizziness and when she was sure she wouldn't fall on her face, she moved toward the closed door across from the bed. A sigh of relief emitted from between her parted lips as she tried to hurry across the room to another closed door.

After doing her business she stood in front of the long mirror over the vanity and washed her hands. This place was amazing, but she kept thinking of herself sharing it with Cael, Ajay, and Brax. There were four sinks and the door-less tiled shower with the glass partition was big enough to fit six people in it with room to spare. There were multiple shower heads and the décor was fantastic. The wall tiles were large and white with gray streaks and flecks running through them, and there was a line of dark tiles running down the middle of the white to break up the starkness. It worked well. The counter was white granite and the cupboards were a dark brown. The tiles on the floor were a smoky gray hue. The combination of colors was a great contrast.

Jaylynn opened one of the cupboards and grabbed a new toothbrush still in its packaging as well as a tube of toothpaste. As she brushed her teeth she couldn't help but see how bad she looked. Her auburn hair was in a messy halo around her face, shoulders and beyond. The dark smudges under her eyes looked as if they were bruises, as if someone had punched her in the face and given her black eyes and there was no color in her cheeks at all. She looked like a skinny ghost.

Her arms and legs were much slimmer than they used to be and even though she was wearing shorts and a tank, she could see her hip bones and the bottom of her rib cage protruding starkly under the material. She looked like a skinny ghost hag.

When she was done with brushing her teeth and gargling mouthwash, she searched for and found a brush and started pulling it through her hair. It turned out to be a difficult chore when her arms were tired and as heavy as lead, but she persevered until her hair was no longer a messy nest.

"What the fuck are you doing out of bed?"

Jaylynn shrieked and startled so badly she had to grab the edge of the counter so she didn't fall on her ass. Thankfully, she'd put the brush down before Brax had shouted his question. She met his eyes in the mirror as he stormed toward her and though it was tempting to turn and face him, she kept her back to him. It didn't seem to matter that he could see her face in the mirror. She felt as if she had a little more control if she wasn't staring directly into his eyes.

"Where am I?" she asked and tried to keep from wincing when her sore throat protested. Her mouth was so dry even after brushing her teeth and gargling. Jaylynn felt as if she could have downed a gallon of water without taking a breath.

"You're in our home," Brax answered.

He was so close she could feel the heat emanating from his big, muscular body and couldn't stop from shivering. He took a step closer and wrapped an arm around her waist. It was tempting to lean back against him when she was so tired, but she remained still and tense in his embrace. If she gave in to the urges running through her body and he ended up rejecting her, her heart would break all over again.

"Why did you move here?" she asked as she briefly met his gaze before lowering her eyes and scowling at the sink. The pain in her heart at being so close to him and yet so far away made her ache, but she turned that ache into anger. It was the only way she'd be able to deal with him and his brothers and keep sane, as well as her love hidden.

"A few days ago," Brax answered as he tightened his arm around her waist.

"Why? Are you following me? Why am I in your house? I'm not a fucking child."

Brax removed his arm from around her waist, grasped her shoulders and spun her around. She blinked when her head swam for a moment or two at the fast, abrupt movement and then she glared at him.

"No, you're not a child, but you're fucking acting like one."

She poked him in the chest. "I don't give a shit what you think of me. You have no rights over me whatsoever. You're not my fucking brother." She flattened both of her hands against his chest and shoved him as hard as she could. He didn't so much as sway and that just mad her madder.

Tears threatened again, but she kept them at bay. Jaylynn was so tired and weak she just didn't have the energy to deal with Brax's shit.

"Let me go."

"Never." Brax didn't give her a chance to respond before he swept her up off her feet and carried her out of the bathroom.

"Hey." She slapped his shoulder. "Put me down. I wasn't finished in the bathroom."

"Yes, you are."

"You're a fucking Neanderthal."

"Watch your mouth," Brax ordered before letting her go.

Her cry of fear hurt her sore throat as she fell. The breath in her lungs whooshed out when she landed on the bed. She placed a hand over her racing heart and scowled at him. When he sat on the edge of the mattress she scrambled as far from him as she could. She hated the way her body was heating in his presence. Even in her weakened state her breasts had swollen, her nipples hardened, and her pussy was growing wetter by the second. Even her traitorous clit was beginning to throb as it filled with blood. She tugged at the covers angrily and pulled them up to hide her reaction to him.

"Do you have any idea how fucking worried we've been about you?" Brax asked irately. "We've spent every spare moment we've had searching for you." He rubbed at his chin with agitation. "And when we finally find you, you're so fucking sick you pass out. What the hell, Jaylynn?"

She kept her gaze lowered and plucked at the quilt. "You don't need to worry about me anymore. I appreciate everything you've done through all those years to make sure I was okay, but I don't need you to look out for me anymore."

"Bullshit!" Brax snarled. "Have you even looked at yourself? You're so fucking skinny your ribs and hip bones are showing. You look as if you've gone ten rounds in the boxing ring and you're as pale as a fucking ghost. You need a keeper, baby, and we're just the men to take care of you."

"No." She shook her head. "I don't need anyone watching over me. I'm a full grown-assed woman. Where are my clothes? Can I borrow the phone? Shit! What time is it? I need to call a cab. I'm probably late for work."

"You're not going anywhere, honey," Ajay said as he entered the room, a tray with food and drink in his hands.

Cael was right behind him and had several bottles of water.

"Yes, I am."

Brax climbed up onto the bed, sitting so close to her she could once more feel the heat from his body and smell his amazing tantalizing scent. A shiver of desire raced up her spine, but she was able to suppress it and keep it from showing. When he cupped her face between his large, warm, calloused hands, she tried to pull back, but he didn't let go. "Your clothes are in the dresser and closet, what there is of them. We moved here because there was nothing keeping us in Fort Worth anymore. We've retired from the Marines and decided to relocate when our friends, Wilder, Cree, and Nash Sheffield, called. Had we known you were living here, we would have been here faster. You have a month off with paid sick leave. You have suspected glandular fever, Jaylynn. Dr. Phoenix Carter treated you and ordered you to rest and that's exactly what you're going to do."

Ajay had set the tray on the bedside table and taken a seat on her other side. After putting the bottles of water on the other side table, Cael had climbed onto the end of the mattress near her feet. She was surrounded by her dreams and heartache and didn't know what to do.

"You have no idea how fucking sick you were, do you, honey?" Ajay asked as he threaded his fingers with hers.

She shrugged, hoping her nonchalance would make them back off. Of course, she knew how ill she'd been. She still felt dreadful but there was no way she was going to admit it. When Ajay lifted her hand to his mouth, she couldn't stop herself from following his movement and when she met his hazel eyes, she couldn't look away. He kissed the back of her hand before lowering it to his thigh. He covered her hand and kept it trapped between his denim covered muscles and his hand.

"Your temperature spiked to dangerous levels and you were convulsing, Jaylynn. You have no idea how fucking scared we were to find you that way. The doc gave you two shots, an antibiotic in case you had an unseen infection and a strong painkiller to ease the aches in your body and bring your fever down."

She shook her head because she didn't remember any of that.

"Don't fucking shake your head at me," Ajay snapped. "You were so out of it you had no idea what was going on."

She drew in a ragged breath and shifted her gaze toward Cael when he clasped her foot over the quilt. Jaylynn remembered being sick and so exhausted afterward she hadn't been able to move, but nothing else. No wonder she felt so awful. She had no idea what to do to get healthy again. She'd never met anyone who'd had glandular fever and didn't know much about it other than it was sometimes called the kissing disease. She frowned over that because she hadn't kissed anyone.

Ever.

That asshole she'd tried to neuter didn't count since he'd forced his kiss on her.

How the hell had she contracted glandular fever? Was it contagious? Could she pass her illness on to the Rhodes brothers? She didn't want to do that, but she wasn't even sure she had the disease. Phoenix could have diagnosed her incorrectly, couldn't he? She might only have a bad case of the flu. It had been making its rounds across America and from what she'd heard it was a harmful strain which had killed a lot of people.

There was no way she was going to take time off work even if her generous bosses had said they'd pay her the full month the doctor had suggested she needed off. She didn't work that way. She'd always paid her own way and wasn't going to stop now. Plus, she wasn't staying here with Cael, Brax, and Ajay. She could end up giving her feelings away and that would be a huge embarrassment. What she needed to do was leave and head back to her apartment. She'd concede to taking the rest of the week off, but then she was returning to work at the diner. She had rent and bills to pay.

"Please call me a cab."

Chapter Five

"You've always been stubborn, but this is just fucking ludicrous," Cael said angrily.

"You can bitch as much as you want to, but you aren't going anywhere." Brax sighed.

Ajay grabbed the tray of food and placed it in her lap. "You're going to stay here with us in our home, so we can look after you. Eat the damn food."

"I don't have to do what you tell me." She folded her arms beneath her breasts and instantly regretted it when she noticed Cael was staring at her chest and quickly unfolded her arms.

"You're going to eat everything on that plate, even if I have to spoon feed you while you're tied to the bed," Cael stated calmly.

Jaylynn sighed with frustrated resignation. The three brothers were staring at her with implacable resolve and she knew she wasn't going to win this round. Besides, all of a sudden, she was starving, and her belly was grumbling. She couldn't remember the last time she'd eaten a decent meal. She could have eaten at the diner when she'd been on break, but lately just thinking about food had turned her stomach. Maybe that was because she'd been fighting whatever illness she'd picked up. Why was she hungry now though? Was it because she finally purged what had been upsetting her system? Maybe she was fighting an infection and the antibiotics were doing their job. She gave a mental shrug. She might never know.

* * * *

Cael sighed with relief when Jaylynn picked up the fork and broke off a piece of the vegetable omelet and lifted it to her mouth. He thought they may have finally gotten through to her, but knew that she'd no doubt try and fight them again.

He'd never forget seeing her small, delicate body convulsing on the bathroom floor. Seeing her so ill had scared the shit out of him. He wondered if Brax or Ajay was going to ask her again why she'd left Fort Worth. They had to have noticed she'd avoided answering the question. There were so many things they needed to discuss, but what worried him the most was the sadness he could see in the depths of her beautiful green eyes. He hated seeing those deep shadows of sorrow and wanted to ask her why she was so unhappy. She was no doubt still grieving her brother's death, but he had a feeling there was more to her melancholy than Sebastian dying.

He was grateful to Sheriff Luke Sun-Walker for giving him and his brothers the time they need to take care of Jaylynn. Cael hoped by the time the month was up they'd convinced her to stay and live with them permanently as their woman.

Neither, he, Ajay or Brax said a word until she'd finished eating her meal. Ajay took the empty plate from her, set it back on the tray and handed her the steaming mug of coffee. He'd made it with milk and hoped she still drank it that way. When he remembered her taking a sip of his black coffee years ago and then spitting it out, he almost smiled. She'd been so disgusted with the way he took his coffee, she almost choked. However, she laughed at herself after she'd regained her breath. Jaylynn had been so happy, but the woman he'd remembered was nowhere to be seen.

She'd lost so much, and they'd been deployed more often than not. He wondered if their absences had brought on the change in her. If it had, he hoped to rectify the situation. Cael wasn't going to give up until the sparkle of life and laughter was back in her gorgeous jade green eyes.

"Why did you leave Fort Worth?" Cael asked.

"What did I have to stay for?" she countered with her own question.

"You had us, baby." Brax frowned.

"No, I didn't."

Cael knew she hadn't meant to say that when color crept up her cheeks and she lowered her gaze.

"What the hell does that mean?" Ajay asked.

"You were away fighting for our country, which I thank you for, but I couldn't stay there any longer."

"Why?" Cael asked.

"Sebastian was in every room. Everywhere I walked, I saw his smiling face, heard his deep laugh. I couldn't stay. There were too many memories, too much grief."

"Why didn't you talk to us, tell us how you felt?" Brax asked. "We could have helped you find a place and packed up your things. You could have stayed with us. We were worried sick about you, baby. We all had nightmares of hearing about you being found dead on the news."

"Are you in trouble, sweetness?" Cael asked. "We can help you if you are."

She frowned, bit her lip and slowly shook her head. "I'm not in any trouble."

Cael had a feeling she wasn't being quite truthful, but he would come back to that later. They needed to sort things out and tell her what was going to happen. He knew they wouldn't be able to keep her in their home against her will, but he hoped she'd agree to stay with them. When he remembered what the doc had said, he decided to tell her. "Dr. Carter said if you don't rest up and start eating properly you could end up with chronic fatigue syndrome. If you get that it will take you months, maybe even years to get over it. You need to follow his orders to the letter, so you don't end up permanently debilitated with fatigue."

"I can't afford to take a month off work, Cael. I have rent and bills to pay."

"Not anymore you don't," Ajay said.

"What?"

"We've already packed up your things and brought them here," Brax explained. "When I told you earlier that your clothes were in the dresser and the closet, I meant all of them. You no longer live in the apartment above the diner. You live here with us."

"You had no right!"

"We had every right," Brax responded. "Your brother trusted us to look after you and we're not going to go back on a promise we made him, just because you've got a bee in your bonnet about something."

As soon as Brax said those words, Cael knew his brother had hit the nail on the head because of the guilt he saw flash across Jaylynn's eyes.

"How long?" she asked.

"How long what?" Ajax quirked a brow.

"How long are you going to live here? How long do you expect me to stay here? I have a life and I'm sure you don't want me cramping your style. Ever heard of a third wheel, or should that be fourth wheel? You think I didn't see you bring women home to share between you. I may have been younger, but I'm not that fucking naïve or stupid."

"This is our house, baby," Brax said. "We own it outright. As for the other, you don't need to worry about that."

"The hell I don't," she retorted. "No woman is going to want or put up with another female staying in her house with the men she loves. It won't work. She'll be jealous, and it will cause problems. I'm not going to come between you and your girlfriend or girlfriends."

"You won't," Ajay replied.

"You don't know that. You could meet someone tomorrow and click. She's not going to want to come to your house if I'm here."

"We've already met someone," Cael said, staring intently at Jaylynn.

If he hadn't been watching her so avidly he might have missed the tears pooling in her eyes and the soft gasp of pain when she inhaled.

In that moment, he knew one of the reasons why Jaylynn had left Fort Worth. She'd had a crush on them when she was younger, but seemed to have quickly gotten over her infatuation. Maybe she had, now he suspected she was attracted to them again. His heart and soul lit up with joy and determination. She was going to be their woman. He wasn't going to let her get away from them again.

"I'm happy for you," she said in a hoarse voice, still keeping her gaze down. "I think it would be better if I went back to my apartment. What's your girlfriend going to think if she finds out I'm living in your spare bedroom?"

"It's not the spare bedroom, honey," Ajay said.

"Whatever." Jaylynn handed her empty coffee mug to Brax and shoved at Ajay.

Ajay frowned, but rolled to his feet so she could get up if she needed to. Cael could tell his brothers were concerned she was feeling ill again, but he knew differently. He stood and hurried around the bed until he was standing in front of her.

"You need to move." Jaylynn poked him in the chest.

"Do you need the bathroom, sweetness? Are you feeling sick again?"

"No. Please get out of my way."

"I'm not letting you get dressed, Jaylynn. You belong here with us."

"I do n—"

Cael leaned down as he bracketed her face between his hands and pressed his mouth to hers. She gasped and groaned, giving him the edge he needed. He licked into her mouth, rubbing his tongue along hers, before swirling and twirling in an erotic passionate dance of need. He kissed her like he'd wanted to for a couple of years. All the pent-up lust and emotion he'd had locked down tight came bubbling up as he ravaged her mouth. He growled when she melted against him, removed his hands from her face and wrapped his arms around her waist. They kissed, nipped and licked at each other as if they were starving. He wasn't sure about Jaylynn, but he was and had been famished for what felt like forever. This was the first opportunity he'd had to show her how much he cared for her. She was a mature independent woman and there was no longer any need to hide his attraction.

When he felt her nails digging into his chest he broke the kiss and panted for air. Even though she was still ill, pale and way too slim, she was the sexiest woman he'd ever seen. However, he wasn't a saint and had normal manly urges.

He, Brax, and Ajay had always made sure the women they brought home knew the score. Most of them had been eager to be with them just so they could brag to their friends about fucking a Marine. He hadn't cared at the time, but he had a feeling their woman was inexperienced. When he'd first started kissing her, she'd been hesitant, tentative as if she didn't know what to do. As soon as she stopped thinking, let go so the passion could take hold, she'd burned him up from the inside out. His cock was as hard as a spike and aching so much he was almost in pain, but if he was right, they were going to have to go slow with her. Plus, she was still fucking sick.

"What did you do that for?" She covered her mouth and looked utterly horrified.

Cael's heart sank, and he wondered if he'd just fucked up all their chances to have a long-lasting relationship with Jaylynn. She shouldn't have kissed him back if she wasn't interested. He mentally shook his head as he peered into her hazy green eyes. There was color in her cheeks and when he glanced down her body, he saw how hard her nipples were. And from the way she had her thighs clenched together, her clit was probably throbbing with need. He finally remembered to answer her question. "Because you're ours, sweetness."

She shook her head.

Brax and Ajay, who'd gained their feet while Cael had been kissing her breathless, moved closer to her. Ajay embraced her from behind and Brax laced his fingers with hers.

"You were like a little sister to us, baby," Brax said.

"You were one of our friend's sister and we just wanted to make sure you were okay. We hated that you were alone a lot of the time, honey. You were so strong and mature," Ajay whispered against her ear. "But our feelings changed not long after Seb died. You were twenty-two and while we wanted to start dating you, we were still in the Marines. We didn't want to start anything only to be sent on a mission. We've seen some of our comrades' lives fall apart because their women couldn't handle them being away so much. We weren't about to start something only to have you walk away."

"I-I…"

"Why did you leave, Jaylynn?" Cael asked again.

She shook her head.

"Why did you leave, baby?" Brax palmed her face and locked gazes with her.

"Why did you leave, honey?" Ajay asked as he pulled her tighter against him.

"Let me go," she demanded in a shaky voice.

"Never!" Cael, Brax, and Ajay said at the same time.

"We've lost you once, Jaylynn. We aren't about to lose you a second time," Ajay said emphatically.

"You don't even like me," she wailed hoarsely. "I was a burden to you all. A promise you made to my brother, which you regretted."

"Why would you say that?" Brax asked. "You never have and never will be a burden, Jaylynn. We loved watching over you, loved spending time with you."

"Brax is right, honey. We used to hate it when we'd be called away. We'd much rather have spent all our time with you. You made us laugh." Ajay kissed the top of her head.

"You're lying. I saw you with those women. I saw you laughing as you looked over to our house. You were probably lamenting with your latest fuck about how annoyed you were for making that promise to Seb."

"Do you think I go around kissing every pretty woman?" Cael asked.

"How should I know? I can't read your fucking mind."

"Watch your mouth, Jaylynn. I don't like to hear you dropping the f-bomb," Brax said.

"Oh, you fucking hypocrite." Jaylynn poked Brax in the chest. "Y'all say fuck and more all the time. That is such a double standard. I can say what I fucking like, whenever I fucking want."

"You're right." Brax rubbed the back of his neck.

"What?" Jaylynn cupped her ear and tilted her head. "I'm not sure I heard you right. Can I get that in writing?"

Smack.

Cael bit his lip when Jaylynn spun around to scowl at Ajay.

"You didn't just fucking hit me. Tell me you didn't."

"No, I didn't hit you, honey. I tapped you on the ass for that smart mouth of yours."

Cael stepped in between Ajay and Jaylynn to break up their stare fest. He could tell by the slump of her shoulders that she was tired again, but knew she'd never admit it. Not even if he offered her a million bucks. He mentally snorted. She'd probably tear up the check and throw it in his face if he wrote her one, no matter how much was on it.

Jaylynn was a good person. He'd actually seen her coming out of a soup kitchen one afternoon just after she'd turned seventeen. The next day, he'd seen her come home from school and after she'd dumped her school bag, she walked out of the house eating a banana. He'd been curious when she'd locked up and started walking down the street. Cael had hurried to his truck and followed her from a distance. She'd hopped on a bus and a few miles later got off again. After walking half a block she'd entered the soup kitchen. He'd parked his vehicle in an alley beside the building and gone in the back way. Jaylynn had never even known he was there. She'd been so happy, carefree and friendly. She'd treated the homeless like she would have him, his brothers, or her own brother as she'd helped dish up food. Three hours later she'd left and gone back home, but before she'd hopped on the bus, she'd given one of the homeless Vets sitting on the stoop a five-dollar bill and a snack for his dog. Cael had never let on that he'd known how she spent some of her free time. He had no idea how she'd coped with her workload of school, study and working at a local restaurant. She was amazing in his eyes.

Nothing had ever gotten her down. After her parents had died, she bounced back to her bright bubbly self after six months, but it had been different when Seb hadn't come home. She'd sunk into a deep black hole she couldn't seem to climb out of and then she'd left.

"You need to get back into bed, sweetness," Cael said after pushing his thoughts aside. She was getting paler by the minute but was too stubborn to do anything about it. Was she worried about looking weak, looking vulnerable in their eyes? Fuck that shit. She was the strongest person he knew. What other young woman of fifteen would have helped her brother pay off the accumulated debts from her parents after they'd been killed? None of the kids he'd met in this day and age would have been so moralistic or driven to repay money they hadn't borrowed.

"I'm fine." Jaylynn shoved her hands onto her hips and sighed.

"You're far from fine, sweetness." Cael didn't give her a chance to refute his statement because he swept her up off her feet and carried her to the bed. "Do you think I didn't see your hands shaking before you put them on your hips? You can lie to yourself if you want, Jaylynn, but you can't lie to us. We know you too well."

"Stupid observant Marine."

"Get used to it, baby," Brax stated as he hurried around the bed and helped Cael pull the covers back up.

Jaylynn covered her mouth when she yawned. "What time is it?"

"Just after six in the evening," Ajay answered as he sat on the mattress near her feet.

"What? I've been asleep all day?"

"You slept for over twenty-four hours, sweetness," Cael answered as he sat next to her.

"Oh." She frowned.

"Oh? That's all you've got to say?" Brax asked. "I never want to see you that away again, baby. You about killed me with worry."

"I'm sorry, but I didn't do it on purpose. I didn't even know I was sick. I just thought I was tired."

"We need to talk about that, too, honey," Ajay said as he leaned against the headboard. "When you get the all clear from the doc and you're allowed to go back to work, you won't be taking everyone's shifts and working twenty-hour days. What possessed you to do such a thing?"

She crossed her arms under her breasts and frowned. "How do you know I've been working twenty-hour days? You've only just arrived in town. Haven't you?"

"We've been here for a couple of days, Jaylynn, but we spent most of our time setting up the house. Today is the first day we ventured out to meet up with our friends," Cael explained.

"To answer your question, baby," Brax said. "The young waitress, Cindy, told Violet how you'd been taking over the other waitresses' shifts when they couldn't work. She was concerned when you passed out."

Jaylynn didn't look happy about being ratted out, but she didn't say anything regarding the other waitress. "Did y'all know I was here?"

"No," Ajay answered and sucked in a deep breath before continuing on. "Why'd you do it, honey? Why'd you leave without sending word about what you were doing or where you were going?"

Chapter Six

Jaylynn was riddled with guilt and couldn't look any of them in the eye. She'd already told them the partial truth as to why she'd left, why she couldn't stay in the house she'd shared with Sebastian, but she couldn't tell them the rest.

How was she supposed to explain about Jimmy, one of Seb's friends and Marine teammates? Or that she couldn't stand to see them laughing and happy when they brought a woman home with them? She couldn't. If she did, they'd know that she had feelings for them. She'd tried to get over her crush after telling herself they were way too old for her and she had for a few years, but just before she'd turned nineteen, those childish feelings had come back, but they were way more than a crush.

Jaylynn was irrevocably, deeply in love with Brax, Ajay, and Cael. They'd never treated her as anything other than Seb's kid sister, and she didn't think that would ever change. She frowned when she remembered the kiss she and Cael had shared. Did he kiss her because he was angry with her and didn't know how to punish her other than using his fists? Which he and his brothers would never do because their psyche was to protect those weaker than them, not harm.

"I've already told you why," she finally answered.

"You're not telling us everything, honey," Ajay said. "If you can look me in the eye and tell me again, why you left, I might believe you."

Jaylynn pushed her hurt aside, pulled up her anger and met Ajay's hazel eyes. "I already told you I left because I couldn't deal with the memories. I missed Seb too much to stay."

Ajay nodded before glancing at Brax and then Cael. "I believe you, honey."

She sighed with relief.

He stroked a finger down her cheek. "But I also know you're not telling us everything. Spill it, Jaylynn."

She closed her eyes and concentrated on keeping her breathing deep and regular. She was too tired to battle wills with them right now. If she tried, she had a feeling they would win and get all of her secrets out of her. Would they look at her with sympathy if they found out she loved them? Would they laugh in her face?

That was something she couldn't deal with. She already felt as if her heart had shattered into a million tiny pieces and she'd never be able to put it back together again. She relaxed her tense aching muscles and prayed that she would fall asleep. It would only be a short-lived reprieve, but she would take what she could get at the moment. Nonetheless, she knew her ploy wasn't going to work when they didn't move. She could hear their steady breathing and something rustled when one of them shifted on the bed. Jaylynn opened her eyes again to find all three of them staring at her expectantly. *Damn it! Why did they have to be Marines?* They could probably see every little twitch she made. They'd have been trained to read infinitesimal movements and body language.

"I was having a few problems," she blurted out before she could censor herself.

"Like what?" Brax asked.

Cael's gut knotted into a lump of anxiety. "Someone was bothering you?"

"Fuck!" Ajay grumbled. "I hadn't even thought about that. Did you have a boyfriend who wouldn't take no for an answer?"

"I don't...didn't have a boyfriend. If you'd all been around, you would have realized that." Jaylynn mentally cursed. She hadn't meant to say that. For some reason Brax, Cael, and Ajay piqued her ire easier than anyone else she'd ever known. Including her brother.

What was it about them that got her back up, and she just spat shit out without thinking about what she was going to say first? The answer floated across the front of her mind before she could stop it. *Because you love and trust them. That's why.*

Oh, shut up! I hate a know-it-all.

Brax cupped her face and turned her gaze in his direction. He was frowning and staring so deeply into her eyes, she swore he could see into her heart, into her soul. She shifted uncomfortably and tried to look away, but he held her chin firmly. "Cael was right, wasn't he, baby. There was a man bothering you. Who was it?"

"Was it someone from the soup kitchen?" Cael asked.

"What?" Brax and Ajay asked simultaneously.

"You helped out in a soup kitchen?" Ajay's tone rose with incredulousness.

"Why do you find that so hard to believe?" she asked grumpily.

"Hey." Ajay held his hands up, palms out in the classic "I surrender" or "I didn't mean anything by it" pose. "I wasn't trying to offend you, honey."

Jaylynn decided attack was the best defense and said a little vitriolically, "I liked to help out. Do you know how many retired veterans are homeless, living on the streets? Our politicians should be strung up by the toes. Those poor men and women have suffered untold injuries and are now dealing with mental issues such as PTSD, depression and anxiety, but do they care? No! They sit up in their ivory towers making all their bullshit rules, patting each other on the back, all the while lining their own pockets and making their own lives easier. They don't give a shit about anyone but themselves."

"You're preaching to the choir, sweetness," Cael said.

"Avoidance isn't going to work, baby. We're not leaving this room until you've told us who hurt or scared you." Brax frowned at her.

"Jimmy Appleby," she murmured.

"What did he do, honey?" Ajay asked through clenched teeth.

"You know what?"

"What?" Cael asked.

"I'm tired. I can't cope with the third degree right now. I'd like to go back to sleep."

"You can sleep as soon as you've told us what Jimmy did," Ajay said in a firm voice.

"I don't want to deal with this now."

"Too damn bad, baby. Start talking," Brax commanded.

"You're like a dog with a bone. Do you know that? Once you have your mind set on something you won't let go." Jaylynn was still hedging, but she knew it wasn't going to work.

Brax settled more comfortably on the bed, his stare never leaving hers. He lifted his hands up behind his head and sighed. "We have all night, baby. I can tell you're exhausted. If you want to sleep, you'd better start explaining."

"After Seb died and the rest of the team came home, they'd pop in from time to time unannounced to see how I was doing."

"We saw them a few times," Cael said. "Go on, sweetness."

"Jimmy started coming around frequently by himself. Nearly every time he visited he'd ask me out. I didn't have the time or the inclination to date anyone and I kept refusing, but he just kept coming back. He used to look at me...in a creepy way, I guess. Maybe I was imagining things, but he made me uneasy.

"He was totally different when the others were around, but when we were alone he'd breach my personal space and touch me often."

"Did he fucking grope you?" Ajay asked angrily as he sat up straighter.

"Not until the last day." Jaylynn shivered, her breath hitching. "When he found me out front packing my things into my car, he stormed over and blocked me against the vehicle. The door to the car was open and he had me caged in so I couldn't get away.

"He asked me what the hell I was doing, or something like that and when I didn't answer he assumed I'd packed up Seb's things and was going to take them to a thrift store. He told me that I should have called him to come and help me. I wasn't about to tell him I was leaving because I was so scared he'd fling me over his shoulder and carry me into the house.

"When he started kissing me I knew I was in real trouble. I tried to fight him off, but it was like trying to move an elephant. He was too big and strong, so I changed tactics. I relaxed into him, waiting for an opportunity to make a move. He grabbed my ass." A sob escaped before she could stop it.

"Fucking asshole," Cael growled.

"Motherfucker," Ajay snarled.

"He's a dead man," Brax said in a hard voice.

Jaylynn didn't acknowledge their outbursts. Now that she'd started, she wanted to finish so she could go to sleep. Weariness was tugging at her and if it wasn't for the adrenaline running through her system as she remembered how scared she'd been, she probably would have already been asleep. "I knew he was going to leave bruises on my ass and breast, but I pushed the pain away and waited. He became distracted when he pushed his hand between my legs. I kneed him so hard in the balls he let me go and as he bent over holding on to his junk, I brought my knee up again. This time under his chin. He fell backward onto his ass. I dove into the car, reversed so fast out of the drive the tires screeched and then I took off.

"He yelled at me that he would make me pay and that I could run, but he would find me." Jaylynn swiped impatiently at the tears that had rolled down her face. She hated to cry but she was too tired to stop them.

"Come here, baby," Brax ordered, but before she could move, he reached over and tugged her into his arms. She sighed with contentment as she rested her cheek in the crook of his shoulder and chest and closed her eyes.

"Did you ever go back?" Ajay asked as he rubbed a hand up and down her back.

"No," she murmured as her muscles relaxed. "I'd already packed everything I wanted to take. I didn't care about leaving the furniture behind. It was all secondhand and starting to fall apart anyway."

"Why'd you sell your car, sweetness? How did you get here?" Cael asked.

"I didn't want Jimmy finding me through my license plate. I sold it for cash and then bought a cheap wreck. I never changed the registration details, but I made sure to pay the fees before they came up, so the previous owner didn't get any bills or debt collectors after him."

"Do you still have the vehicle, baby?" Brax asked.

She nodded. "I've leased a storage shed on the outskirts of town. Most of my things and Seb's are still in it. I just brought a small suitcase and then walked the few miles to the town proper." She lifted her gaze to Cael's, Ajay's and finally Brax's. "He's going to find me. Jimmy had this crazy look in his eyes. Every time he came over he was more possessive. He treated me like I was his girlfriend. I didn't lead him on. I tried to avoid him, but he seemed to pop up everywhere I was. When he started showing up at the soup kitchen, I stopped going. I didn't want anything to do with him, but he was fixated, obsessed with me. He was so angry that I bested him and escaped. I don't think he's going to give up until he has what he wants."

Brax brushed the hair back from her forehead and then kissed it. "You're safe with us, baby. He'd have to get through us to get to you. Put your head down and rest, Jaylynn. We can talk more in the morning. Okay?"

"Okay." She snuggled into Brax and closed her eyes again. "Will you stay with me? I don't want to be alone anymore."

"Wild horses couldn't pry us away, honey." Ajay stroked a hand down her back.

* * * *

"I want to find that fucking prick and rip him a new asshole," Ajay said in a quiet seething tone as soon as Jaylynn's breathing deepened.

"I'll be right alongside you," Cael said.

"We should see if we can find him," Brax suggested. "I want to know where the fucker is at all times."

"I do, too, Brax, but he's a Marine. He has the skill to fly under the radar for as long as he wants." Ajay sighed.

"We can start looking," Cael said. "Is he still serving?"

"No," Brax answered. "He and the rest of the team retired after Seb died."

"Do you think he has mental issues from what he's seen and done?" Ajay asked. "From what I remember, Jimmy was always laughing and joking around."

"It might be a good idea to contact some of the other team members," Cael suggested. "They probably know that man better than his own family does. If there's something off with him, they'll be able to tell us."

"Good idea," Ajay agreed. "We can start tomorrow. I don't think she got it."

"Got what?" Cael asked.

"I don't think she realized we were staking a claim on her," Ajay clarified.

"We can spell it out for her tomorrow," Brax said. "Right now, I'm just going to enjoy having her in my arms."

"We need to feed her up." Cael frowned. "She's far too skinny."

"Don't go telling her that," Ajay said. "We don't want to give her a complex. What we need to do is encourage her and reinstate all that self-confidence she used to have. I want to see that lively sparkle back in her eyes and hear her laugh."

"It might take a while." Brax rubbed his stubbled chin over the top of her head. "She's dealt with a lot of loss in her life. I think Sebastian's death was the hardest."

"Yeah," Ajay said. "Do you think she still has feelings for us?"

"I'm not an expert, but, yeah, I think she does." Cael smiled. "We broke her young heart when she saw us bringing a woman home with us. From that day on she became more introverted. I hated that we hurt her, but she was so young, I thought of her as my sister."

"Yeah, I know. I think we did too good of a job keeping her at a distance. She may have taken our disinterest as her being a burden to us. We're going to have our work cut out for us to get her to open up with us," Brax said.

"You're a lucky bastard." Ajay nudged Cael with his foot. "You got to kiss her. Does she taste as good as I imagined?"

"Better." Cael grinned. "She's so fucking innocent, but also passionate. I've been walking around with a hard-on ever since I spotted her in the diner."

"We all have, Cael." Brax shifted down the bed and settled his head deeper into the pillow.

Ajay kissed Jaylynn's cheek and then rolled to his feet. He clapped Cael on the shoulder. "Help me do a search for this fucker. If we don't find anything, then we can start calling Seb's team."

"How are we going to deal with him when we find him?" Cael asked as he followed Ajay from the room.

"We can decide that once we find the prick," Ajay replied. He was going to beat the shit out of Jimmy Appleby.

He and his brothers were the right men to teach him a lesson.

Chapter Seven

"Got you, you fucking bitch." Jimmy laughed with glee.

For nearly twelve months he'd been searching for that beautiful slut and he'd found her by pure chance. He couldn't believe he'd found her. He rubbed his aching cock through his jeans as he stared at her gorgeous face in the background of a photograph in a local newspaper.

He'd changed tactics only about four weeks ago and his patience was finally paying off. He'd found nothing on CCTV cameras, or through his contact at the DMV. So, he'd started searching through the food network. He'd remembered Seb bragging about what a fantastic cook Jaylynn was, how she'd been at the top of her class in culinary school, and he had to agree. Jimmy had sampled her cooking more than once.

He'd been frequenting the local library whenever he wasn't working at his day job at the firing range. He'd been flipping through headlines of restaurant reviews when one had piqued his interest. The headline was, "Hearing impaired chef puts small town on the map."

He'd been amazed to see all those stunning women smiling for the camera and after reading the article of how three women partnered up and bought the place, and how well they were doing, he studied the photo again. When he'd seen Jaylynn's profile in the background, his heart had stopped beating. At first, he thought he'd been seeing things because he was so desperate to find her, but he'd have known her face anywhere. However, he hadn't gotten excited until he'd pulled out his magnifying glass to make sure it really was her. There was no denying it.

She was working in a diner in a small town in Colorado, called Slick Rock. There was also a short expose on the unusual ménage relationships prevalent in the area.

Jimmy seethed with rage as he imagined all those country hicks trying to get into his woman's pants. He'd been so furious he'd put his fist through a wall. It had taken him a few minutes to calm down and think rationally. Jaylynn wasn't like other women. That was one of the reasons he was so attracted to her. She was so sweet and innocent and yet had a body made for sin. He was the man to teach her all about sex. When he found her, and got his hands on her, he would show her what it was like to be with a real man. He was dominant and liked to be in control of every aspect of his life. Jaylynn was his. They were meant to be together. Once he had her in his life, he was going to tame that independence right out of her. By the time he was finished with her, she would be kissing his feet and doing whatever he ordered her to.

He tugged open his jeans and groaned with relief. As he stared at her beautiful face he started stroking up and down his hard, aching dick. He licked his lips as he remembered the heat of her pussy through her jeans, of how toned her sexy ass felt in his hand, and how soft her breast had been.

He gasped as cum shot out the tip of his dick, and shuddered with ecstasy.

Tomorrow morning Jimmy was going to take a leave of absence from his job and hit the road. He had a long trip ahead of him. It would take him two days to drive from Fort Worth, Texas, to Slick Rock, Colorado but he was eager to get started. Now that he knew where she was, he might even take some time out and see a few of the sights along the way, because once he had Jaylynn with him, he was going to need all his energy to train her to be the submissive sex slave he knew she kept hidden down deep.

Jimmy was excited for the night to be over.

* * * *

Brax had spent all night cuddling with Jaylynn. He'd never been happier, and he hoped that she still had feelings for him and his brothers. He also hoped that her schoolgirl crush had deepened to something more.

Today was the day he, Cael and Ajay were going to explain how much they wanted, needed her in their lives. He was nervous, which was a surprise to him because he was usually so sure of himself. Being a trained Marine had gone a long way to teaching him life skills as well as boosting his confidence. When he first signed up he'd still been wet behind the ears. He'd sure grown up quickly.

Protecting those weaker than him had always been something he'd never had to think about thanks to his mom and dad, but the Marines had taught him and his brothers how to get the job done as quickly and painlessly as possible. He hated killing, but some people were just so evil they didn't deserve to walk the earth.

The military had also ingrained in him, Ajay and Cael how important it was to fight for what you believed in. Even though he was glad they were now retired, he wouldn't change anything. Every step in his, *their* lives had led to this moment. The chance to have a long-lasting loving relationship with the woman of their dreams.

He wished Seb was still around. Jaylynn's brother had known how they'd felt about his sister just after she'd turned twenty-two, a couple of weeks before he'd died. He'd pulled them aside on one of the rare occasions they'd all been home from deployment and made them promise to give her time to experience life and find her way in the world before trying to court her. Brax, Cael, and Ajay had agreed immediately. They hadn't wanted to clip her wings before she'd flown. Even Brax had known that she was way too young to be tied down in marriage. She might have been independent, but she'd just been starting to live her life.

While Jaylynn had been very mature for her age, in other ways she'd been as innocent as a newborn babe. She'd needed a couple years to live and learn and see what life was all about, not that he really knew either.

No one knew what the meaning of life was, but he knew what was important. Love, family and living each day to the fullest. Things didn't matter worth a damn when it came down to it. Although it did make life easier to have a little money to fall back on as well as a roof over one's head and food to eat.

His and his brothers' parents had been so in love with each other, Brax knew he'd wanted to have a relationship as strong as theirs when he was ready to settle down. Playing the field had grown old quickly and while he and his brothers had hooked up with willing women, he'd always imagined having more.

Jaylynn had the biggest, kindest heart and he wanted to have all the love locked away in that organ directed at him. Sure, he was no saint and had had his share of women to slake his lust, and while sex and attraction were important in a relationship, the physical aspect wasn't as important as love, respect, and friendship.

Wooing Jaylynn was the most crucial thing they were ever going to do, and it was imperative they succeeded in their goal.

Brax wasn't sure what he'd do if they failed to win her heart. Just thinking about it caused an ache in his chest. He pushed his thoughts aside and stared at her gorgeous face. His heart swelled with warm emotion and he pulled her tighter into his arms.

She fit perfectly. Not just against his body. Brax couldn't quite explain it to himself. She just felt so right. Everything about her was right. She made him feel complete and he didn't want to face the rest of his life without her in it. She was his light and happiness, every beat of his heart and every breath he took.

She was their woman, even if she didn't know it yet.

* * * *

Jaylynn blinked her eyes open when she felt movement next to her. She lifted her head to find Brax staring down at her. "Hi," she greeted hoarsely.

"Hi yourself, baby. How are you feeling?"

"Uh, I don't know yet. I'm still half asleep," she answered honestly as she sat up. "I'd kill for a shower though. What day is it?"

"Sunday," Brax answered.

She grimaced as she pushed her hair out of her face. "I can't believe I just slept away two days."

"You needed it, Jaylynn. You were exhausted. Please, promise me you won't push yourself that hard again."

She nodded her acquiescence. "I won't. I promise."

"Thank you, baby. You scared the hell out of us."

"Sorry."

"Don't apologize, baby. Just start taking better care of yourself."

"I will." She watched Brax stand and stretch. He'd taken his T-shirt off and she couldn't help staring at all his bulging muscles in his arms, shoulders, and back. She gulped when he turned to face her. He was so damned sexy, she almost swallowed her tongue. She was of average height, standing at around five foot six, but Brax, Ajay, and Cael all towered over her by a good half foot or more.

She licked her dry lips when he rubbed a hand over his chest and belly, following the path with her eyes. He had broad shoulders, muscular pecs and defined washboard abs. When she realized her gaze had drifted down lower, she quickly glanced up and then looked away when she saw that Brax was watching her with a grin on his face.

"I'm going to shower in the other bathroom so you can use this one. When you're done, come on out to the kitchen for breakfast."

She nodded and smiled when he winked at her before turning away and leaving the room. Now that he was gone she could concentrate once more. After gathering some clean clothes, she hurried toward the bathroom.

She'd never been one to linger in the shower or getting ready. She'd never really been bothered with make-up or other girly things. Of course, she liked to dress up and apply light make-up if she was going somewhere, but she'd never been a socialite. She was more interested in helping people out than spending hours on her appearance. She'd never forget her mother's motto which she passed down to her. "People can take me the way I am, or not at all. It's their choice." She'd liked how confident her mom had been and had tried to emulate her over the years.

Jaylynn entered the kitchen fifteen minutes later.

"Hi, sweetness." Cael hurried over and pulled her into his arms.

"Hi," she replied. She watched his brown eyes peruse her face before he locked eyes with her again.

"You're looking a little better. How do you feel?"

"I'm okay," she said. "I'm still a little achy, but my throat isn't sore anymore, and I don't feel as tired."

"That's good to hear, honey." Ajay came up behind her, bent down and kissed her on the cheek. "You're not as pale today."

"The color in her cheeks could be from the hot shower she just had," Brax stated as he entered the kitchen. "Take a seat, baby. We'll get you something to eat."

"I can cook."

"No!" Ajay said sternly as he guided her toward the stools on the other side of the kitchen counter. "Doctor's orders are for you to rest and you're going to follow them to the letter."

"Bossy." She frowned at Ajay as she crossed her arms over her breasts.

"Yes, I am. Deal with it."

Jaylynn scowled at Ajay, but he wasn't perturbed in the least. He laughed as he turned toward the coffee pot.

Cael was already getting ingredients for breakfast out of the fridge and Brax was pulling mugs from the overhead cupboard.

She was about to protest about the number of calories in the bacon and eggs, but decided to keep her mouth shut when she noticed Cael watching her from the corner of his eye. Brax placed a mug of white coffee on the counter in front of her and then collected the ingredients to make pancakes. "I can help."

"Not happening, sweetness."

"I don't think I've got glandular fever. I feel much better. There was a bad strain of flu going around which I probably caught. Even though I'm not coughing or sneezing, I had a sore throat and threw up. Maybe I had a diluted strain of flu, or I was able to fight off the effects quickly."

"You don't know that for sure, baby," Brax said. "We're not letting you do anything until you've been cleared by the doctor, so stop pushing."

Jaylynn decided to take matters into her own hands. She slid from the stool and hurried back toward the bedroom. She'd seen her purse on the top of the dresser and was hoping her cell phone was in it, too. She smiled when she pulled her phone out. The battery had half a charge. More than enough to make a phone call or two. She swiped her finger over the screen to activate it, scrolled through her contacts and hit the call button.

"Jaylynn, what are you doing calling. You're supposed to be resting. Are you okay?" Enya asked.

"I feel much better, Enya. Thanks for asking. Can I ask you a favor?"

"Of course," she replied without hesitation.

"Would you please call one of your men and set up an appointment for me, or give me their numbers so I can do it?"

"Are you sure you're all right?"

"Yes. Promise. I just want a follow-up appointment because I don't think I have glandular fever. I think it was the flu."

"I'm glad to hear that." Jaylynn could hear Enya smiling through the phone. "I'll call you back in a minute."

"Thanks, Enya."

"Don't thank me. That's what friends are for." Enya disconnected the call.

Jaylynn sat on the bed and stared at the empty doorway. She was sure that one of the men was going to come looking for her at any moment, but she hoped to have a doctor's appointment set up before they did.

Thirty seconds later her phone rang, and she answered instantly.

"Is this afternoon at two okay?" Enya asked. "Phoenix can fit you in before he does his hospital rounds."

"Shit! I didn't think about his other patients. I can see him another time, or go and see someone else."

"You will not," Enya replied. "He was glad to do it and he saw you when you were really sick. He'd want to do the follow-up exam to make sure you're on the road to recovery."

"That'd be great. Thanks again, Enya."

"No problem, honey. Let me know how everything goes."

"I will. Bye."

"Bye."

Jaylynn hung up just as Cael entered the room.

"Who were you talking to, sweetness?"

"Enya. I'm going to see Phoenix this afternoon at two."

Cael frowned as he sat beside her and draped an arm around her shoulders. "Are you feeling sick again, Jaylynn?"

"No, I feel fine. I'm going to prove it to you lot that I'm on the road to recovery and can go back to work and return to my apartment. I can't afford to not work, Cael."

He rose and held his hand out to her. She clasped it and let him guide her back down the hallway, through the large living room and into the kitchen.

"Where'd you get to, honey?" Ajay asked as he pulled a chair out for her. When she sat he pushed it in and then sat down next to her. Cael took the seat on the other side of her and Brax sat across from her.

"Jaylynn has a doctor's appointment at two this afternoon," Cael said.

She frowned at him, but he ignored her and continued on. "She says she can't afford not to work and wants to go home."

"Eat," Brax pointed at her loaded plate. "We'll discuss this after you've had breakfast."

"There's nothing to discuss."

"Oh yes, there is," Ajay said. "But you're going to eat first."

Jaylynn stared at the food mounded on the plate. There was two pieces of toast loaded with scrambled eggs and bacon, as well as a five stack of pancakes smothered in maple syrup. There was enough food to feed an army—or should that be a Marine?

Jaylynn ate one piece of toast with eggs and bacon and was comfortably satisfied. She was about to push her plate aside and pick up her coffee, but decided against it when she noticed Brax watching her. With a sigh of resignation, she ate one pancake, too. By the time she was done, she was so full she wasn't sure she'd be able to move. She moved the plate aside and raised an eyebrow at Brax, daring him to comment, but when he remained silent she wrapped her hands around her coffee and sipped at the fortifying brew.

"I'm glad you're going to see the doc again," Ajay said after swallowing. "It definitely can't hurt to have your health checked out."

"You don't need to go back to work, baby," Brax said. "We have more than enough money to live comfortably on. However, if you want to, that's fine, but not unless the doc says you can."

"You have no say in what I do, Brax." She glared at him and then at each of his brothers. "I've been mostly on my own since I was fifteen. I always pay my own way."

"You're not going to be on your own any longer, sweetness. You're living in our house." Cael crossed his arms over his chest.

"I've already told you why that won't work."

Brax finished off his last bite of pancake, chewed, swallowed and then shoved to his feet. He walked around the table and stopped behind her. He pulled her seat away from the table, bent and scooped her up into his arms. She hooked an arm around his neck and turned to look over his shoulder. Ajay and Cael had both risen and were following. He carried her into the living room and sat on the huge, dark blue leather sofa, placing her in his lap.

Jaylynn was about to slide off his thighs, but he grasped her hips, turned her and lowered her until she was straddling his hips. Ajay and Cael sat on either side of them. "What are you doing?"

Chapter Eight

Brax framed her face between his big hands and inhaled deeply. He and his brothers were about to tell Jaylynn that they wanted a relationship with her. He was excited and nervous all at the same time. He could feel the heat from her ass on his thighs and his dick was rapidly filling with blood. He shifted slightly, trying to keep her from feeling his erection, but he wasn't sure he'd succeeded. Jaylynn glanced away nervously, licked her lips and exhaled with a noisy whoosh.

"Please, look at me, baby," he said.

Her lips twitched, and he wondered if she was surprised over him using the word please. He normally didn't bother, because when he gave an order he expected it to be carried out.

"You're going to stay here in our house where you belong. We want a relationship with you, Jaylynn."

"You do?" she whispered.

"We do, honey," Ajay said.

"We're attracted to you, sweetness," Cael said. "We think we can have something special."

She clasped Brax's wrists and tugged his hands away from her face. "I'm not like one of those women you used to bring home. Please, don't lie to me."

Brax snagged her around the waist so she couldn't get up off his lap. He pulled her tighter against him to prove to her that he found her attractive. She was more than attractive. She was stunningly sexy with her slim curvy body, auburn hair and gorgeous green eyes. She shoved against his chest with the flat of her palms and wiggled on his lap. She froze when she felt his hard dick pressing against her denim-covered pussy.

Brax combed his fingers into the hair at the back of her head and held her still. "Have I ever lied to you before?"

"How would I know?"

Cael stroked a finger down her cheek. "You know, sweetness. I can see the answer in your eyes."

"Those women meant nothing to us, honey," Ajay said. "We're normal healthy men who had needs we couldn't ignore. They were only with us so they could brag to their friends about fucking a Marine."

"Ajay's telling the truth, baby. Those women were just a hookup. There were no emotions involved."

"But you don't even like me."

"Yes, we do," Brax whispered. "Let me show you how much I like you."

He lowered his mouth to hers and brushed his lips back and forth. She gasped and moaned, her lips parting, giving him the opening he craved. Brax slowly delved into her mouth with his tongue, rubbing along the length of hers before swirling and twirling with her in an erotic dance. She whimpered, her fingers—which were clutching at his shoulders—dug deeper into his flesh, turning him on even more. The kiss deepened, turning hot, wild and passionate. He caressed his hands up and down her back, getting lower and lower with each pass until he smoothed his hands over the denim-clad cheeks of her ass. He grabbed her butt cheeks, squeezing and kneading the soft, yet toned flesh. She moaned and shifted on his lap, causing him to growl as she pressed against his hard, throbbing dick. She felt so good, tasted amazingly right and was so delicious he never wanted to stop kissing her. Nonetheless, he slowed the kiss down until he was sipping at her lips and finally lifted his mouth from hers, so they could gasp air into their burning lungs.

Brax nibbled and licked his way from her mouth over her jaw and up her neck. When she cried out and arched against him as he suckled on the skin under her ear, he knew he'd found a sweet spot. He lapped and nipped at the skin and tendon until she started rocking on his lap. He groaned with hungry approving need and nipped at her earlobe before soothing the slight sting with his tongue.

He lifted his head and perused her beautiful face. Her eyes were closed, the dark lashes standing out in stark relief against the paleness of her skin, and yet there was a pink flush tinting her cheeks. Her lips were red and swollen from his kisses and she was breathing heavily.

Brax moved his hands from her ass and edged his way up under her T-shirt. He caressed the soft, warm skin of her belly with his fingertips, giving her time to protest or back away if she wanted to, but she didn't. Her eyes fluttered open and his dick twitched against his zipper when he noticed her green eyes were hazed over with desire. He couldn't resist another second. He needed his mouth on hers again. Lowering his head and opening his mouth over hers, he growled with hungry need. Jaylynn moaned as she licked into his mouth. Brax suckled on her tongue until she was gasping for breath and whimpering at the same time. He smoothed his hands over her belly, up her sides and paused on the outside of her breasts. When she bowed her chest toward him, he realized she was giving him silent permission to go further, but as much as he wanted, needed to feel her breasts in his hands, he had to make sure she knew what they wanted with her.

Brax broke the kiss and panted until the desirous fire coursing through his blood slowed somewhat. He tugged his hands out from under her shirt and palmed her cheeks with them.

"Baby, we want you. We want to have a relationship with you. Don't you want that, too?"

When he saw the tip of her pink tongue peeking out from between her lips, he had to close his eyes. He could very well imagine how sexy she'd look with his cock in her mouth. He heard her inhale raggedly and opened his eyes again.

"For how long?" Jaylynn asked.

He frowned. "For how long, what?"

"How long do you think you'll want me?"

Ajay smoothed a hand over her shoulder, down her arm and laced his fingers with hers. "We want everything with you, honey. The whole nine yards."

"We want you to live here with us, sweetness. We want you to move in and never leave." Cael lightly tapped her on the end of her nose.

"We want forever with you, baby," Brax explained.

"That's what you say now, but what if you find out you don't like me as much as you think you do? What if I have bad habits that annoy you so much you want me to leave?"

"That'll never happen, Jaylynn," Brax answered. "We know you, baby. How could we not when we were watching out for you for nearly ten years. We like everything about you, baby."

"You can't know that because you've never lived with me."

"We do know, honey," Ajay reiterated. "You're the sweetest, sexiest woman I've ever met. You have the kindest heart and would do anything for anyone even if you have to go without yourself."

"What's it going to be, sweetness?" Cael asked. "Are you willing to give a relationship with us a try?"

Brax held his breath when he saw the wheels turning in her mind. A frown appeared between her brows and he could see hesitancy in her gaze, but that wasn't all he saw. There was an eagerness underlying that indecision and he hoped she would give them the chance they wanted, needed with her. If she accepted, he and his brothers would do everything within their power to make sure she was happy and felt loved.

"Yes," she finally answered after what seemed a lifetime had passed.

Brax wanted to stand, carry her to the bedroom and strip her off so he could feast himself on her sexy little body, but he didn't want to scare her with his eagerness.

Jaylynn must have been of the same mind because she leaned up and planted her lips on his. He wrapped his arms around her waist, pulled her tighter against him and ravaged her mouth.

* * * *

Jaylynn was so excited she was shaking. She couldn't believe she was about to start a relationship with the men she'd loved for ten long years. She gasped air into her lungs when Brax lifted his mouth from hers and she clung to him when he stood and started walking toward the bedroom.

She shivered with excited nervous anticipation.

This was it!

This was the moment she'd been dreaming about forever. She was about to have sex with Brax, Ajay, and Cael. She shuddered with hungry need and tried to regulate her breathing, but she was too eager for that to happen.

Her insides were on fire and she was aching between her legs. Her pussy was wet, and her clit was throbbing. Every now and then her internals clenched with an empty yearning she was enthusiastic to have appeased, but she wanted to touch Brax, Cael, and Ajay more. She wanted to run her hands over every inch of their bodies. Wanted to explore all those ridges and bumps she'd glimpsed through their T-shirts. They were so big, strong, muscular and handsome but it was their personalities that attracted her, that she loved. They were older than her and had spent years making sure she was okay. They could have told her brother to fuck off, but they were Marines and protectiveness seemed to be instinctive with them.

Her legs trembled when Brax lowered her feet to the floor and she hoped that she could remain upright. The last thing she wanted or needed was to look like a besotted fool in front of these confident alpha men.

"Are you sure about this, baby?" Brax asked, once more cupping her cheeks between his hands. "You've been really sick, and we don't want you having a setback. I think maybe we should wait until after you've seen the doc later this afternoon."

That was the last thing she wanted. She wasn't going to wait another second. She lowered her eyes, gazing over his body as she went and paused on the prominent bulge in the front of his jeans. He was so damn big, and she wanted to see him and his brothers totally naked. She didn't even realize she was moving until she saw her hand was hovering inches from his crotch. After taking a fortifying breath, she placed her hand over his hard cock. He groaned and while she wanted to glance up and look at his face, she was mesmerized by what she was doing. She curled her fingers around his hard, thick cock and couldn't believe how much heat was emanating from behind his jeans. If he was this hot while still covered, he was going to singe the skin from her hand once they were skin to skin. What was he going to feel like when he was deep inside of her?

Brax grasped her wrist and tugged her hand away from his dick. She was disappointed to have her curious exploration cut short, but when she met his eyes, the dissatisfaction dissipated. His pupils were so blown out, there was only a slim rim of brown showing around them. He was breathing heavily, and he was clenching his jaw. When she lowered her gaze and saw that his knuckles were white from how tight he was clenching his fists, Jaylynn began to think she'd done something wrong.

Something in her body language must have portrayed her thoughts, because Brax nudged her chin up with the tip of a finger until she was once more looking into his eyes.

"As much as I want to have your hands on me, baby, I'm too triggered to last. You can touch, explore my body any other time, but right now I'm so hot for you, I'm likely to explode before we've even started. Okay?"

She opened her mouth to reply but when nothing came out she quickly closed it again, and nodded. Movement from the side drew her attention and she glanced over just in time to see Ajay pull his T-shirt up over his head before dropping it to the floor. She couldn't help eying his body over because there was so much to see. She gasped when she noticed a puckered scar on his right shoulder and hurried over to him. "What happened? Is that a bullet wound? When were you shot?"

"It's nothing, honey. No permanent damage was done." Ajay shrugged.

"It's not nothing," she whispered, blinking rapidly as she tried to quell the tears burning the back of her eyes. She hated to think of Ajay, Cael or Brax hurting. Agony pierced her heart at what she imagined they'd all suffered. They'd been Marines for ten years. Had lost teammates, had to kill the enemy and had seen god knows how many horrors. She turned to glance at Cael and Brax. "Were either of you hurt?" Jaylynn swallowed around the emotional constriction in her throat. It was hard to breathe because her throat felt as if it was closing up. Nevertheless, she inhaled deeply and pushed her emotions aside. This wasn't about her. This was about her men, what they'd been through, what they suffered.

"We're fine, sweetness," Cael said as he came up behind her. "We were never seriously injured and we're home safe and sound. We won't ever have to worry about being shot at by the enemy again. I'm sorry, but we can't talk about what we were doing when we were serving, but it's all in the past now. Okay?"

She nodded and sighed as Cael wrapped his arms around her from behind. She leaned against him and shivered when she felt his hard dick pressed against her lower back. A shudder wracked her spine when his fingers brushed against the skin of her belly, under her shirt.

"Arms up, sweetness," Cael rasped out.

She raised her arms above her head and gazed at Brax. He was staring at her chest and licking his lips. She couldn't help but moan at the tantalizing action. She tried to imagine what it would feel like having his tongue lapping and sucking at her hard nipples.

"You're so fucking beautiful, baby," Brax said in a hoarse voice.

"Gorgeous," Ajay said as he moved closer.

"Stunningly sexy," Cael whispered against her ear.

She shivered as the breezy warmth of his breath caressed her flesh. Brax stroked the tip of his finger down her neck, over her collarbone and then between her breasts. When he stopped at the front clasp of her bra, she held her breath.

Ajay cupped a cheek and turned her head toward his. She exhaled and inhaled just before he bent down and covered her mouth with his. Jaylynn moaned as he thrust his tongue into her mouth, dancing and dueling with hers as he devoured her. She felt Brax flick her bra clasp open but was too caught up in Ajay's kiss to be embarrassed or concerned.

Cael smoothed the bra straps over her shoulders and down her arms, and then he clasped her wrists in a loose manacle of thumbs and fingers before raising her arms above her head once more.

She whimpered when Ajay released her lips and groaned when he started licking and nipping up and down one side of her neck while Cael did the same to the other side.

A cry of need escaped from between her parted lips when Brax cupped her breasts and strummed his thumbs over her nipples. Jaylynn thought they'd been hard and achy before, but that had been a tantalizing tease compared to what she was experiencing now.

The areolae ruched and her nipples were so hard they almost hurt. She sobbed with pleasurable surprise when he pinched the nubs and gasped as he lowered his head toward her chest. Hot, wet heat seared first one nipple and then the other as he laved over each sensitive peak with his tongue. When he sucked one tip into his mouth and started suckling on it, her knees buckled. If Cael hadn't been holding on to her she would have sunk to the floor at their feet.

Brax released her nipple with a pop, met Cael's gaze over her shoulder and nodded. Cael kept one arm at her waist, bent and swept her feet from the floor. He carried her to the bed and gently lowered her to the mattress before standing up straight again.

She gaped when she noticed that Brax was standing at the bed in only his boxers and she would have had to have been blind to miss the long, thick pole in his underwear. When the bed dipped beside her, she turned her gaze and stared at Ajay. He was similarly clad—or should that be unclad?

Cael got up on her other side and she turned her gaze his way and licked her dry lips. Her greatest fantasy was about to become a reality and while she was trepidatious since she'd never had sex before, she was also impatient to get started.

Brax climbed onto the bed and pulled the button open on her jeans before lowering the zipper. She trembled when he hooked his thumbs under the waistband of her jeans and panties and then tugged them down. Jaylynn lifted her ass from the bed so her clothes came off easily, and glanced down shyly at the hand she had resting between her breasts.

Her heart was thudding hard and rapidly against her sternum and she was once more panting shallowly.

The mattress moved as Ajay maneuvered to a more comfortable position and she moaned when he cupped her breast in his hand, raising and lowering the soft globe as if he was weighing it.

"I love your breasts, honey. They are so fucking perfect with these dark, rosy, hard nipples." Ajay lowered his head and swirled his tongue around and around her nipple. She cried out when Cael tweaked the other nipple between his finger and thumb and groaned when Brax began to caress up and down her legs.

When he got to her knees, he pushed her thighs apart and then shimmied down onto his belly between them. He lowered his head toward her pussy and inhaled deeply through his nose. "You smell good enough to eat, baby."

That was the only warning she got.

Brax lowered his mouth the last couple of inches to her pussy and then licked from bottom to top. She jolted, and her belly muscles jumped when he lapped over her engorged sensitive clit. Her internal muscles convulsed on emptiness and cream dripped from her pussy.

A low groan bubbled up from her chest and out from between her parted lips when Cael and Ajay both began to draw on her nipples firmly. Shards of pleasure zipped down from her breasts and centered in her wet pussy.

Brax groaned as he swirled his tongue around and over her clit before licking back down through her folds. She shook when he dipped his tongue into her creamy well and then started fucking her with it.

Jaylynn combed her fingers into Cael's and Ajay's hair, clutching handfuls as if trying to keep herself grounded. Her insides were on fire and she felt as if she was about to break apart, and she needed to anchor herself in the tumultuous passionate storm.

Cael lifted his mouth from her breast and kissed his way back up toward her mouth. She didn't even notice she still had ahold of his hair until he clasped her wrist and tugged her hand away. He threaded his fingers into her hair and kissed her hungrily.

Jaylynn was on sensation overload. Her insides were melting with the fiery heat coursing through her veins, her blood. She wasn't sure she could handle much more without splintering apart.

Heat seeped into the palm of her hand, causing her to realize she was touching Cael's chest. She tangled her tongue with his and began to caress over his hot, toned body. His pectorals were hard and strong, and she loved the hair on the flesh over his sternum. It was soft and yet coarse, but felt so good against her palm, her fingers.

Jaylynn smoothed her hand down lower, loving the way her hand undulated over all those toned sexy ridges. When she got to the delineated muscles in his abs, she mapped the dips and hollows with the tips of her fingers. The back of her hand brushed against the tip of his hard dick and when she felt moisture on her skin, she realized he was very, very excited. She might have been a virgin, but she wasn't totally naïve. She'd read some romance stories to while away free time, which wasn't that often, so she didn't have to interact with other people over the years. When a man leaked pre-cum he was really turned on.

Her heart flipped in her chest and awe filled her soul. They'd told her how attracted to her they were, and this was definite proof that they'd been telling the truth. She wondered if Ajay and Brax were leaking pre-cum, too.

Jaylynn pushed Cael's boxers down and wrapped her hand around his shaft. He growled as he bucked his hips toward her and then broke the kiss. "That feels so fucking good, sweetness. I love having your hands on me."

She twitched when Brax laved her clit and cried out when he lashed at the sensitive nub with his tongue. A moan emitted from between her lips when he rimmed her soaked pussy entrance with the tip of his finger and she groaned when he pressed the tip inside.

Ajay scraped the edge of his teeth over her nipple, sending streaks of pleasure shooting down to her core.

She panted and puffed as Brax slowly worked his finger deeper into her wet pussy. Nerve endings sparked to life each time he glided his digit in and out of her cunt, and the pressure began to build.

Liquid desire pooled low in her belly and her legs began to tremble. Brax wrapped his arms around her thighs, spread her legs farther apart and lapped hard and fast at her clit while he thrust his finger in and out of her pussy.

The internal walls began to gather closer and closer. The wet frictional slide of Brax's digit sent pleasure deep into her cunt and womb. Tension invaded every single muscle in her body and she rolled her head back and forth on the pillow.

And then she held her breath.

Her wet delicate tissues stretched as Brax added another finger to her wet pussy and he began to stroke in and out, harder, faster and deeper.

Ajay pinched and plucked at a nipple as he slanted his mouth over hers, kissing her voraciously. When she felt Cael's erection throb in her hand, she realized she'd stopped stroking him and pumped up and down again.

Each time Brax drove his fingers in and out of her pussy, more juices dripped out and the walls were so tight, she wondered how that was possible.

All thought fled when the fiery friction melted her insides into a puddle and Brax sucked her clit into his mouth.

She arched her neck back, breaking the kiss with Ajay, gasped in a breath of air and screamed.

Jaylynn shook and shivered as the internal walls of her pussy clenched down hard around Brax's fingers before releasing and clamping down again. Her whole body quivered and quaked as nirvana washed over and through her. Just as the rapture began to dissipate, Brax did something inside her that sent her hurtling up to the stars again.

She opened her mouth on a soundless cry as her body convulsed with ecstasy. Cream gushed from her pussy, spurting onto her thighs and dripping down over her ass. She trembled and quaked as euphoria swept her up in its carnal wave and she saw stars. The stars fragmented in front of her eyes and faded away until she saw nothing but an inky blackness. Just as she thought she was about to pass out, she gasped in a breath and the darkness began to wane.

She trembled and twitched with aftershocks until finally she slumped into a boneless heap on the mattress. Awareness came back slowly, and she realized that Brax, Ajay, and Cael were all caressing their hands up and down her body, over her stomach, arms and chest, soothing her back down from her ecstatic pinnacle.

When the last quake ceased, she forced her heavy eyelids open and stared with wonder at the loves of her life. She'd read about sex in her romance novels, but nothing had prepared her for the reality. Jaylynn had experienced so much pleasure and yet none of them had penetrated her with their cocks as yet.

She was enthusiastic for the next step, but wasn't sure she'd survive it. They'd blown her mind in more ways than one. When she'd climaxed, she'd fragmented into tiny little pieces she wasn't sure would ever coalesce again. Would she be able to put herself back together after making love with Cael, Brax, and Ajay?

It sure was going to be fun to find out.

Chapter Nine

Brax was so hot for Jaylynn he wasn't sure he wouldn't come before he got inside of her. It had been a near thing when she'd come so hard she'd ejaculated into his mouth. He still had the sweet delicious taste of her cum on his tongue and would definitely be making her come like that again. But not right now. Now, he needed to be inside her, needed to be connected to her physically as well as emotionally.

He'd never been so eager to make love with a woman that he ended up trembling with need, but he'd never made love to Jaylynn before. He loved her so fucking much and while he was aching to be inside of her, he was worried he wasn't going to last the distance.

Brax took a few deep breaths as he rose to his knees between her legs and caressed his hands up and down her thighs. He smiled when he felt and saw goose bumps race over her bare skin and hoped she was ready for more. He couldn't wait any longer.

He was going to have to take his time when he breached her hot, wet cunt with his dick, because she was so fucking tight, he was concerned he'd hurt her.

"Are you okay, baby?" He cleared his throat when he heard how raspy his voice was. "Did you like that?"

"Hell yes!" she answered with immediate emphasis.

"Are you ready for more, Jaylynn?"

"Yes, Brax. Now! Please?"

Brax nodded and swallowed as he grasped the base of his aching dick and aligned the head with the entrance. He caressed up and down her belly, over her hip and down her thigh toward her knee. He hooked his hand under her knee, lifted and moved her right leg out until her foot was flat on the mattress.

He drew another deep breath and began to press in, watching her face the whole time, so he could gauge when he needed to stop or continue. He glanced at Ajay and Cael and gave them a nod. Cael nodded back just before he lowered his head toward Jaylynn's chest and lapped at her nipple.

Ajay was lying on his side close to their woman with his head resting in his hand. With his free hand he massaged and kneaded her breast before tweaking the hard peak between his fingers and thumbs.

As soon as the head of his dick popped through her slick entrance, Brax paused, giving her time to adjust to his thick intrusion. He and his brothers were big men all over and while he wanted to surge into her wet heat until he was buried balls deep, he needed to give her time to get used to his breaching. He didn't need to ask if she was a virgin. He'd figured that out all on his own when he felt a partial membrane inside her wet cunt.

When she moaned and bowed her hips up, Brax knew she was ready for more. Ajay released her nipple, skimming his hand down over her ribs, torso, and belly until he got to her mound. Just as his brother sifted his fingers through the hair on her mound, reaching toward her clit, Brax pressed in further.

Jaylynn groaned as her internal muscles clenched around him and when they loosened again, he inched in deeper.

Ajay dipped the tip of his finger into the top of her folds and rubbed over her clit.

"Oh!" she moaned. "So good."

Brax would have agreed if he'd been able to, but his jaw was clenched so tight, his teeth were aching. Sweat had beaded on his brow and was dripping down his back. It was taking all of his self-control to keep himself from driving into her hot, tight, wet cunt, hard, fast and deep.

"More, Brax. Give me more."

He nodded as he drew back and then inched forward again. Even though it seemed to take a long time to embed himself in her heat, he savored every stroke, ripple and sensation. He was finally making love to his woman. When the back of his eyes pricked with grateful tears at having found her again, he pushed his thought aside and concentrated on Jaylynn.

Brax nudged his brothers aside by tapping them on the shoulder and then blanketed her smaller, sexy body with his larger one, making sure to keep his weight braced on his knees and elbows. He kissed her throat and licked at her flesh before lifting his gaze to hers. "Did I hurt you, baby?"

"No." She wrapped her arms around his neck, leaned up and pressed her lips to his.

Brax groaned as he delved into her mouth with his tongue, gliding along before dancing and dueling with hers. He eased his cock out of her pussy until he was just resting inside her entrance and then shoved back in.

Jaylynn tightened her arms around his neck and hooked her legs around his hips. When he slid back into her again, he growled as he sank in a little deeper. Each time he advanced and retreated he increased the pace of his pumping hips, his cock rubbing along her wet walls.

She began to move with him and Brax knew he didn't have long until he was falling over the edge into ecstasy. The base of his spine was already tingling, and her lower belly felt as if it had melted. If any of the heat touched his balls, his cock, he would be done for.

Brax broke the kiss and suckled on first one nipple and then the other, before sitting back up between her splayed thighs. He reached back, grasped her ankles and unhooked her legs from around his hips before lifting them high and wide.

When the heat moved around to his groin and his scrotum, Brax shifted higher onto his knees and surged down into her hard and fast, making sure the head of his dick rubbed over her G-spot. Jaylynn moaned as she writhed under him, so he did it again and again.

"Oh, oh, oh," she chanted, and her legs began to tremble as she got closer and closer to orgasm.

Brax again nodded at his brothers, who'd moved toward the edge of the mattress. They instantly scooted back closer to their woman and began to caress and stroke her. Ajay kissed her gluttonously and Cael suckled on one nipple while squeezing the other one.

Brax felt the muscles and sinew in his neck standing up as tension invaded his body. He was so close to orgasm he could taste it. He hooked one of her ankles over his shoulder, reached down and rubbed her clit with firm strokes.

She seemed to stop breathing and moving as she hung on the precipice. Ajay released her lips and she gasped in a breath just before she cried out.

Brax powered in and out of her clenching drenched cunt, growling like a man possessed. His balls crawled up closer to his body and they turned to stone just before he started coming.

He drove into her deeply on a roar and stayed buried in her as she ground his pelvis into hers. He shook and shivered as cum spumed from the tip of his cock over and over again. His dick jerked and pulsed, and his balls felt as if they'd turned inside out until he had nothing left.

Brax had never felt anything so orgasmic in his life. Love and happiness welled into his heart and he wrapped his arms around his woman. He hadn't even noticed he was covering her body with his until that moment and while he knew he should move, lift some of his weight from her, he didn't want to. He loved how they were skin to skin, so intimately connected, he wanted to savor each and every cherished moment he had with her.

He opened his eyes, kissed her neck, her shoulder and lifted his head to look at her beautiful face. Her cheeks were flushed, her eyes were closed, and damp tendrils of hair clung to her forehead. She had never been so stunning. Her eyelids fluttered open and her lips curved up into a soft smile. "That was amazing." Jaylynn kissed him softly on the lips.

"It was better than amazing, baby," Brax panted between words, still trying to catch his breath. "It was out of this world special."

"Do you really mean that?" she asked.

Brax kissed her passionately before letting her up for air again. "Have I ever said anything to you I didn't mean?"

"No," she answered and then she smiled so brightly, Brax was sure she was lit up from the inside. The sound of her following laughter was music to his ears.

He held her for as long as possible after rolling until she was draped over him. His softening cock had slipped from her hot, wet cunt minutes ago, but he didn't want to let her go. He loved being able to hug her after watching her from a distance for so long. Having her in his arms was a priceless gift he was going to relish as often as he could.

Jaylynn might not know it yet, but she was his whole world.

* * * *

Jaylynn glanced at Ajay and Cael when Brax rolled from the bed and headed toward the bathroom. She hadn't forgotten they were there, but she'd been so intent on just being with Brax, she hadn't noticed them move away. She was surprised to see them both sitting on the small window seat with their legs splayed apart and their elbows resting on their knees. Ajay was looking her way, but Cael was glancing anywhere but her.

"What's wrong?" she asked.

Cael lifted his head to meet her gaze. "Nothing's wrong, sweetness."

"Why do you look angry?" She studied his tight features and when she realized he was digging his fingers into his forearms, she scrambled to her feet and walked toward them. She stopped within touching distance and glanced from one to the other and back again.

Ajay shifted on the seat and she took a step back when he rose. She looked up into his hazel eyes and her breath hitched in her throat. He was gazing at her with such heat in his eyes, her body instantly responded.

He reached out and clasped her hands in both of his. "Cael's not angry, honey. It was difficult for us to move away to give you and Brax the time you needed to make love and bond. We want you so damn much."

She swallowed and nodded. If she'd had more experience she might have been okay with taking them both at once, but she wasn't sure what to do. Not because she didn't have any carnal knowledge, but because she'd just had her first time making love.

Ajay released one of her hands and tugged her to the side when Cael rose. Ajay pulled her into his arms and Cael pressed his front to her back. She shivered as the heat of their bodies permeated her own. "You don't need to worry, sweetness." Cael kissed her temple. "We don't mind waiting our turn. You're not ready to make love with more than one of us yet."

Jaylynn sighed with relief at Cael's understanding. If she'd had more confidence she would have asked him to join in. She loved it when they were all touching her at the same time, but she was nervous at the thought of having more than one hole filled. She leaned against Ajay, rested her cheek on his chest and listened to the steady beat of his heart. It was faster than normal, but she guessed that was because he was turned on. She shivered as her nipples hardened and her pussy clenched, sending moisture out onto her folds.

She needed them no matter how nervous she was.

Jaylynn reached back toward Cael's groin and grasped his long, thick, hard cock at the same time she pushed up off of Ajay and wrapped her fingers around his hot, throbbing dick.

"Sweetness," Cael groaned. "You're playing with fire."

"What are you doing, honey?" Ajay asked in a low raspy tone.

"If you can't figure that out, then I can't be doing it right." She squeezed both their cocks and pumped her hand up and down through the cotton of their boxers.

"You're gonna get burned, Jaylynn," Ajay said in a growly voice.

"Maybe I want to," she replied breathlessly.

Both men clasped her wrists at the same time and pulled her hands away from their dicks. She whined with disappointment but quickly ended up gasping when Ajay scooped her up into his arms. She clung to his neck as he hurried over to the bed and then laughed as he dropped her on the mattress.

Cael came to stand next to Ajay and after a quick look at each other, they hooked their thumbs into the waistband of their underwear, shoved them over their hips and down their legs before kicking them away.

Jaylynn didn't notice she wasn't breathing until her lungs began to hurt. She exhaled and then inhaled quickly. She eyed their hard cocks and licked her lips when she saw clear beads of moisture glistening in the tips and she wondered what they'd taste like.

"You're killing me, honey."

She glanced up at Ajay just as he placed a knee on the edge of the mattress and started crawling toward her. Cael skirted the end of the bed and dropped down next to her. He cupped her face and turned her toward him. Jaylynn had only enough time to suck in a breath before he slanted his mouth over hers.

She groaned as their tongues twined and twirled before rubbing together and swirling in a carnal duel of passionate hunger. She shivered when Ajay began to caress up and down her legs, but he didn't start at her shins the way Brax had. He started at her knees, nudging them apart and smoothing his warm, callused palms up the inside of her thighs.

Cael released her lips as he cupped a breast in his hand, molding and kneading her flesh before strumming his thumb over the hard, aching peak. She moaned and arched up higher, looking for more. Cael must have read her need, because he licked his way down her neck toward her breast. He latched on to the nipple closest to him, suckling firmly on the nub while pinching and plucking at the other one.

She cried out when Ajay stroked a finger up through her wet folds before rubbing the pad of that finger in tight circles over her clit. Cream dripped from her pussy when the internal walls clenched.

"So fucking responsive," Ajay rasped out. "So hot and wet. I need you, honey. So fucking much."

"Please? Now, Ajay!"

"In a minute, Jaylynn."

She shook her head on the pillow in denial. Her whole body was on fire and she needed him to quench the flames, needed him filling her aching pussy, making love to her. Just as she was about to demand he get inside of her, he pressed a finger up into her pussy. A deep groan bubbled up from her chest and out of her mouth.

"Fuck, honey. You're so tight. Are you sure you're ready for me?" Ajay asked.

"Yes!"

She opened her eyes and watched as Ajay shifted on his knees closer to her. Jaylynn wanted to loop her legs around his waist and pulled him deep into her, but she also wanted to savor each slide and glide of his cock penetrating her pussy.

When she felt the head of his cock against her entrance, she held her breath and as he started to breach her, she exhaled slowly. She whimpered when the thick, broad bulbous head of his dick stretched her tissues and groaned as he popped through her tight folds.

A sudden carnal thought struck Jaylynn. One she'd read about in one of her romances and the urge to try the new position was too strong to ignore. She pushed against Cael's shoulder. He released her breast and frowned at her as he rolled to his back, away from her.

"What's wrong—"

Jaylynn cut Ajay off as she shifted on the mattress, causing them both to moan as his cock slipped from her body. "Give me a minute," she said quickly before Ajay and Cael could ask her what was wrong again.

She rolled over onto her stomach and then got up on her hands and knees. "Come here." She crooked a finger at Cael. He was still frowning, but he slid across the bed until he was in the middle and flopped down onto his back. Jaylynn crawled over Cael, pleased when he spread his thighs farther apart and she braced her hands on his muscular legs. She glanced back over her shoulder at Ajay and smiled when she saw he was staring at her ass and pussy.

She wriggled her hips enticingly as she wrapped her hand around the base of Cael's dick.

"Fuck, sweetness. Are you trying to kill me?" Cael groaned.

She shook her head as she grinned up at him before lowering her gaze back to his cock. When she realized she couldn't brace her weight on her elbows on the mattress with Cael's legs on the outside of her body, she sat back on her bent legs. "You need to close your legs for this to work."

Cael's brown eyes hazed over with more heat as he figured out what she wanted. He brought his knees up toward his body, so he wouldn't kick her, and then he straightened them out again. Jaylynn moved back onto her hands and knees, this time straddling Cael's legs.

As soon as she was comfortable, she got back onto her hands and knees. Bracing her upper body weight on one hand, she wrapped her fingers around Cael's cock again. Large, warm hands caressed up and down her back after Ajay moved in closer behind her. She didn't glance back when Ajay grasped her ass cheeks and squeezed them because she was too intent on pumping her hand up and down Cael's dick.

Cael made a growly sound in the back of his throat, and when she gazed up at him another surge of heat coursed through her blood. His eyes were closed, his head was tilted back with the veins and tendons in his neck standing out starkly under his skin. She wondered what he'd look like when she took his hard dick into her mouth. Jaylynn didn't waste another minute. She lowered her head down toward his dick, all the while keeping her eyes on his face and lapped over the head of his erection. He groaned, and she moaned. His sweet salty essence caused saliva to pool in her mouth as she craved more of his wonderful taste.

Jaylynn opened her mouth and sucked the head of his cock in between her lips, swirling and twirling her tongue around the head.

She froze when Ajay dipped a finger into her folds, caressing and spreading all her creamy juices around until he got to the top of her slit and pressed against her clit.

She whimpered as her blood heated even more and liquid desire pooled low in her belly.

"So fucking hot and wet," Ajay rasped out, giving her clit a final caress before dipping into her soaked entrance. "So fucking tight."

When Cael combed his fingers into her hair and grasped the tresses at the back of her head, Jaylynn realized she'd closed her eyes and wasn't doing what she'd set out to do. She wasn't sure she could open her eyes since her lids were so heavy with passion, but figured she didn't need to. All she needed to do was feel and go with her instincts.

She began to caress up and down Cael's shaft again and took him further into her mouth. Once she'd measured the depths she could take him without gagging, she began to bob her head up and down, suctioning her cheeks to add to Cael's pleasure.

She gasped in a breath when Ajay blanketed her back with his front and moaned when he cupped both of her breasts in his hands. He molded and kneaded the soft globes before strumming his thumbs over the aching peaks and then pinching and plucking them.

Her pussy clenched on emptiness, sending another slew of cream dripping onto her folds and she shifted on her knees, wiggling her hips as she tried to get Ajay to ease the carnal ache slowly building inside her womb and pussy. She sucked Cael back into her mouth and groaned when Ajay's cock shifted from between the crack of her ass to between her legs and started rocking her hips. She gasped with pleasure when the tip of his cock rubbed against her clit.

Smack.

What the fuck?

Chapter Ten

"Behave, Jaylynn," Ajay ordered as he grasped the base of his dick and squeezed. The little minx was so fucking sexy and responsive, he'd nearly lost his load. The only way he'd been able to stave off his embarrassment was by swatting her ass and grabbing his erection. He sighed with relief when the heat in his blood, dick, and balls subsided somewhat.

"What the hell was that for?" Jaylynn asked after lifting her mouth from Cael's dick and meeting Ajay's gaze over her shoulder.

"I was getting too close, honey, and I'm not even inside of you yet."

"Well, hurry the hell up," Cael groused in a deep, hoarse voice as he tightened his grip in her hair. "Our woman is a natural. I'm not fucking coming in her mouth."

Jaylynn shook her head over that statement and before Ajay and Cael could do anything else, she took him deep into her mouth. Ajay figured she'd taken him to the back of her throat when he heard her gag, but she didn't ease off to breathe. He heard her drag air in through her nose and was about to push down further, but Cael tugged on her hair.

"No, sweetness. You're not going to make me come in your mouth," Cael stated emphatically.

Jaylynn pulled off of Cael's cock and was about to protest but ended up gasping instead. Ajay pushed against her entrance until the broad head of his dick penetrated her wet folds. Even while the urge to drive into her fast and deep was strong, he remained still and concentrated on his breathing, giving her time to get used to his penetration.

When her cunt muscles clamped around him, he gritted his teeth, but when she did it again and tried to push back against him, he realized that she was deliberately trying to entice and tantalize him. The leash he held himself on broke free and he powered into her hard and fast.

She whimpered, causing him to freeze. He was panting fast and shallowly, as if he'd just run a mile in a minute flat. Contrition filled his heart and soul at what he'd done. "Are you all right, honey? Did I hurt you?"

"No," she gasped. "You didn't hurt me, Ajay."

He sighed with relief and when she flexed her inner muscles around his hard, throbbing dick again, he began to move. Ajay withdrew until just the tip of his cock was resting inside of her hot slick entrance, and then he shoved forward again. He gazed at Cael through narrow eyes when his brother maneuvered his legs out from under Jaylynn and shifted onto his side so that he was lying crossways over the mattress.

Ajay started a slow rhythmic slide and glide as Cael slanted his mouth over Jaylynn's while reaching up to cup one of her breasts. His jaw ached from gritting his teeth so hard. Each time he pumped his hips, sliding his cock in and out of her hot, tight, wet cunt, he increased the pace. The hot wet frictional glide of her soaked walls along his dick was the most amazingly pleasurable experience of his life. He'd never felt such nirvanic bliss or such a strong emotional connection while making love to a woman in his whole life. Jaylynn was the be all and end all of his existence. She was deeply entrenched into his heart, soul, the very psyche of his being and he never wanted her to leave.

He tightened his grip on her hips and pounded in and out of her wet cunt. The heated friction on his dick was bliss personified and he never wanted to stop. Ajay panted air in and out of his lungs, uncaring of the sweat dripping from his brow as he made love to his woman for the first time. Each gasp, sigh, moan and groan that emitted from her mouth ratcheted his need, his famishment for her up another notch.

Their flesh slapped together as he pistoned in and out of her hot, wet cunt. Warm tingles formed at the base of his spine and began to move around his hips toward his groin. Ajay once more blanketed her back with his front, wrapping an arm around her waist, splaying his large hand over her belly to hold her in place and dipped into the top of her folds.

Cael released her lips, ducked his head under her chest and suckled firmly on one of her hard, little nipples.

"Oh," Jaylynn moaned, rocking her hips forward and back in counterthrust to him.

Ajay growled when her internal walls rippled around and along his dick. Every twitch from her was sending him faster and faster toward the edge of reason, toward the pinnacle of climax. Molten heat pooled in his belly and the warm tingles crawled toward his balls, making them firmer and harder as if they were turning to stone. They felt swollen and heavy between his legs and so full of seed he wasn't sure how much longer he could hold out, but he was determined to hold on as long as necessary. He wasn't climaxing before Jaylynn, but he was hanging on by the tips of his fingers.

Cael released the nipple he'd been suckling on, shifted out from under Jaylynn and kissed her passionately. Her cunt tightened, gripping his shuttling length so hard he was sure he was going to topple, but he managed to hold out.

The second Cael broke the kiss, Jaylynn collapsed onto her shoulders. The angle made her pussy so much tighter and Ajay knew he wasn't going to last. He released one of her hips, caressed over her ass and then lifted his thumb to his mouth. After coating his thumb with saliva, he lowered it to her star and caressed over her pucker.

"Oh my—"

Jaylynn didn't finish whatever she was moaning because Ajay delved his thumb into her ass.

"Oh, oh, oh," she groaned.

Just as Ajay drew back his balls crawled up even closer to his body. He shouted as he plunged into her cunt before retreating and shoving in again as he pushed his thumb deeper into her back entrance.

Jaylynn cried out as she started to climax.

She sucked the cum right out of his balls. He groaned as he ground his hips into her ass. Her pussy quaked and quivered around and along his dick, massaging his length and sucking on the tip of his cock. Stars exploded in front of his eyes as spume after spume of cum erupted from his cock. She shook and shivered beneath him while he trembled and twitched. Each time her pussy muscles clamped down on and around his dick, another load of cum shot up his cock deep into her cunt and womb.

The orgasm was so strong, he felt as if the top of his head was about to blow off. Every time Jaylynn's smaller frame was wracked with another aftershock, another load of jism surged from his balls. By the time the last euphoric palpitation faded away he felt as weak as a newborn babe. Air sawed in and out of his burning lungs and he tried to blink the rapturous haze away from his blurry eyes. His arms and legs were shaking with ecstatic fatigue and he wasn't sure he was going to be able to keep himself upright. He tightened the arm he had around her waist and then flopped onto the bed onto his side, taking Jaylynn with him.

Ajay had no idea where Cael was but right at that moment he didn't care. All that mattered to him was in his arms. He kissed Jaylynn's neck after brushing the hair away from her skin and caressed a hand up and down her side, taking note of every shiver as well as mapping every delectable curve.

He was so in love with her, he felt as if they were connected on every level a human being could be. His softening cock was still locked into her tight, wet pussy but it was the love, the overwhelming emotion entrenched in his heart and soul that had tears stinging the back of his eyes.

Ajay had dreamed of this moment and now that it was here, he was totally overcome.

Jaylynn was his world and he was going to do everything within his power to make sure she was happy and felt loved. He hated the time they'd lost with her and even though there was no way to make up for it, he was just grateful she was in their life again.

His and his brothers' lives would have been dismal existences if they hadn't found her.

Ajay wondered if Sebastian was looking down from heaven and smiling. Maybe he'd even orchestrated them meeting up again. Whatever and whoever it was that had brought them together again, was too good to question. He was hoping to spend the rest of his life with Jaylynn at his side.

Losing her would absolutely devastate him.

* * * *

Cael had rolled from the bed to give Ajay and Jaylynn the room they needed to love one another. It had also been necessary for him to get out of the way. She was so fucking beautiful, sexy and responsive, he'd almost climaxed three times. He'd loved the sounds she'd made as he suckled on her nipples and kissed her passionately. He more than loved having her mouth sucking on his cock. He closed his eyes and tried to think of something other than what it had felt like to have her lips wrapped around his dick. He couldn't believe he'd been close to coming after such a short time and while she'd been tentative at first, as soon as she'd let herself be swept up in the passion, in the hunger, she'd been a natural.

He shivered as another wave of heat raced through his blood and over his skin. Goose bumps erupted over his flesh and his cock twitched. He opened his eyes and stared down at his aching cock when pre-cum bubbled to the tip. His balls were hot and heavy between his legs and he was sure just one brush of skin would send him careening over the edge into climax.

He pushed his lustful thoughts aside and turned his gaze toward the bed. Ajay was murmuring something in Jaylynn's ear and while he couldn't hear what his brother was saying, it made their woman happy. She was smiling. She was so fucking gorgeous, his heart flipped in his chest and his breath hitched in his throat.

He sighed out a breath when Ajay kissed her softly, lovingly on the lips and after another hug, rolled away from her before sauntering from the room. Jaylynn rolled over to her back and gazed about the room. As soon as her gaze locked with his, she held her hand out toward him.

Cael didn't hesitate to shove to his feet and hurry toward her. He was eager to make love with and claim the love of his life, but he was also nervous. He'd spent nearly two years dreaming, imagining and fantasizing about making love with Jaylynn and hoped he didn't do anything to fuck things up.

He laced his fingers with hers as he sat on the side of the mattress and stared at her beautiful face.

"Are you okay, Cael?"

He nodded but then shook his head.

"Come lie down with me." She tugged on his hand.

Cael swung his legs up onto the bed, rolled onto his side so that he was facing her, lifted her hand to his mouth and kissed the back of it.

"Are you...angry with me?" she asked hesitantly.

"No sweetness, I'm not angry with you."

"You look angry." She frowned.

It took a moment for Cael to realize that to his inexperienced woman his stark hunger could be misconstrued as anger. "Jaylynn, I'm so turned on I'm not sure it's a good idea for me to make love with you right now. I don't want to hurt you, sweetness. I'm a lot bigger and stronger than you are. I'm worried that if I hold you too hard, or move too fast and deep, I'm going to leave bruises and cause you pain."

She reached out with her free hand and cupped his cheek. "You might feel that way, Cael, but I know you. You would never hurt anyone, least of all me."

"I'm still not sure—"

She placed a finger over his lips, rolled from her back to her side and then pressed her lips to his.

His heart pounded so hard and fast against his ribs it hurt. Blood roared through his ears and he was millimeters away from snapping. He drew his mouth away from hers, rolled over to his back and stared at the ceiling.

She sat up beside him and when she covered her breasts with her arms, he knew he'd fucked up. He sat up quickly and grasped her upper arms before she could move away from him. "I don't know how to explain in words how hungry, how needy I am for you, sweetness. I'm scared."

Her green eyes softened, and she smiled at him. "Do you trust me, Cael?"

"Yes," he answered without any hesitation.

"Good." She moved, tugged her arms from his hold and shifted away from him. "Scoot into the middle of the bed."

He maneuvered on the bed until he was in the center and closer to her again. Although he tried to keep his gaze from wandering, it was an impossible feat. She was just so fucking beautiful to him with her long auburn hair, amazing green eyes, and slim, curvy body.

One day soon he hoped to be able to spend hours feasting on every inch of her skin.

As soon as he settled, Jaylynn straddled his hips with her hands braced on his chest for balance. He sucked in a breath and she bent toward him and he groaned when she pressed her mouth to his. He growled when she licked over his lips and immediately gave her access by opening his mouth.

She stroked her tongue in to dance and duel with his, before rubbing along it. He slanted his mouth and kissed her back hungrily. They devoured each other with a wild carnal intent.

Jaylynn broke the kiss and began to lick and nibble her way down his neck. He groaned when she scraped the edge of her teeth over the thick tendon and artery down his neck. She licked over his collarbone and down his chest toward his nipple.

Cael held his breath and then groaned gustily when she swirled her tongue around the areola. The skin around his nipple crinkled and hardened, as did the tiny bud. He was surprised that his nipples were so sensitive. No other woman had ever touched him this way or bothered to find out what he liked. He quickly pushed thoughts of other women from his mind. No female before Jaylynn was worth thinking about.

She was the most important person in his world other than his brothers.

When she nibbled at his nipple gently with her teeth, he gasped and threaded his fingers into her hair. His dick twitched and flexed and another drop of pre-cum rose to the tip. Every muscle in his body was taut with sexual tension and his legs were trembling.

"Sweetness, I can't wait any longer. Please, let me love you?"

She flicked his nipple with the tip of her tongue and lifted her head to meet his gaze.

There was so much to see in her amazing green eyes he couldn't sort out what he was seeing. And then he wasn't seeing anything.

Jaylynn lifted higher onto her knees, reached back and clasped his cock in her soft, warm hand. He gritted his teeth when she caressed the tip of his cock through her soaked folds and then began to sink over him.

He squeezed his eyes closed and clutched at the sheet. The blood raced through his system and his heart pounded so hard and fast he could feel it in his head, but that wasn't the only place. His cock was pulsing and throbbing as if it had a heartbeat of its own.

Cael wasn't sure how long he'd be able to remain still, but he was going to try for as long as possible. He wanted Jaylynn to have control so he didn't hurt her. He forced his heavy lids up so that he could see her through the narrow slits and groaned when he saw the pleasure etched on her gorgeous face. She had her head thrown back, her long auburn hair draping down around her shoulders and flowing in a silky wave down her back. Her lips were parted, and her eyes were closed.

He clutched at the sheet so hard his knuckles hurt but he wasn't, couldn't let go. Cael knew as soon as he did he'd grab her hips, flip her over and pound into her hot, slick cunt.

She moaned as she lowered down further over him and when she lifted up again, the wet frictional slide of her taut muscles sent shards of bliss deep into his lower belly, over his cock and down to his balls.

Each time she rose and lowered she increased the pace, taking him deeper and deeper until she was bathing his hard, aching dick in her wet cream. Her breasts moved up and down when she did and without conscious thought he reached toward them. He palmed her breasts, molding and kneading the warm, soft, silky skin before flicking the hard, rosy tips with his thumbs.

She whimpered and when she lowered onto him, Jaylynn ground her crotch into his. After opening her eyes, she leaned forward and braced her hands onto his chest. She was so fucking small compared to him and his brothers, he barely felt her weight and yet having her hands on him while she made love to him was the best thing he'd ever felt.

Cael spread his legs wider and as she sank down over him, he raised his hips toward hers, stroking his cock as deeply as he could into her hot, tight cunt.

"Oh," she groaned as the head of his dick rubbed against her G-spot and his shaft brushed against her clit. Her short blunt nails dug into the flesh of his chest and she picked up the pace again.

Cael growled with hungry frustration when the base of his spine began to tingle with heat. He was getting close to coming but he couldn't let loose yet.

He wrapped his arms around her slim body and pulled her down over him. As soon her breasts were pressed into his chest, Cael rolled. As soon as she spread her legs and wrapped her arms around his neck, he drove his cock into her until he was embedded all the way.

She moaned and then kissed him with greedy carnality.

Cael ravaged her mouth, their tongues dueling and rubbing together in an erotic carnal dance.

Jaylynn combed her fingers into his hair and held on tight as their bodies slapped together. The heat at the base of his spine moved around toward his groin and when his balls started tingling he groaned.

She broke the kiss and gasped air into her lungs, panting heavily as she rolled her head back and forth on the pillow. Her wet walls rippled around and along his dick, causing him to moan as he drove his cock back into her balls deep.

He could feel the tension growing in her, the same as him and hoped that they both fell together. There would be nothing sexier or satisfying than to have his woman coming with him.

Cael bent his head toward her chest, laved one of her nipples with his tongue and then sucked it into his mouth. He drew on the sensitive nub firmly and was rewarded with more soft sounds from Jaylynn. He released that nipple and quickly moved to the other one, scraping the edge of his teeth over her hard peak before suckling on it strongly.

She froze, and she was so tight with tension he knew she was about to climax, and so was he.

Cael shuttled in and out of her cunt like a man possessed, his rhythmic thrusts gone as they both reached toward ecstasy.

And then they were both falling.

Jaylynn screamed softly. He roared a second later, drowning out her cry of rapture as he followed her into bliss.

Her pussy clamped and released around his palpitating cock. Searing nirvanic heat shot up from his balls, through his shaft and out the tip of his dick. He jerked and shuddered as cum spurted from the tip of his cock over and over. Each time her internal walls convulsed around his dick, she drew another spume of cum from his balls.

Cael had never felt such profound ecstasy in his life. His arms and legs were trembling with rapturous weakness, and yet he was so full of love and joy, he felt as if he could take on the world and win all by himself.

The euphoria began to wane, leaving him in a breathless heap of feebleness. It took a few moments to notice he was slumped over Jaylynn and pushed up on shaking arms to give her room to breathe. He opened his eyes and stared with incredulous, but grateful wonder at the woman who'd stolen his heart so long ago, still finding it hard to believe that she was finally here, where she was meant to be.

Cael pushed an arm under her shoulders, tightened his hold on her and rolled until she was sprawled out on top of him. He caressed his hands up and down her smooth, soft back as he tried to get his equilibrium back.

He smiled happily when she sighed and nuzzled her cheek on his pectoral, not in any hurry to move. He was going to hold her as long as he could and savor every minute she was in his arms.

Jaylynn Freedman was the love of his life.

He would do anything for her.

Chapter Eleven

Jimmy scoped out the town as he drove through the main street. He'd read on the internet that the town had grown quickly over the last few years. The population had almost tripled. The shop fronts all looked as if they had fresh coats of paint and the windows were sparkling in the early afternoon sunshine.

A smile of anticipation curved his lips as he drove past the diner, and he wondered if his girl was working. The smile slowly slid from his face as anger replaced his excitement. He took a few deep breaths, trying to control the rage heating his blood. He still couldn't believe Jaylynn had run from him. They'd been through so much together and she'd turned away without so much as a phone call.

He had no idea what he'd done to make her leave him, but he was going to find out.

Jimmy slowed his speed as he came toward the end of the street. When he spied the motel, he put his indicator on and turned into the parking lot. After parking and turning off the ignition, he got out of his truck, pocketed his keys and walked toward the motel office.

"Hi, how can I help you?" the young woman greeted him with a friendly smile.

He smiled in return. "I'd like to rent a room, please?"

"Sure." She grabbed a clipboard with the paperwork and then asked to see his ID. Jimmy had no qualms about handing his information over. He was a law-abiding citizen who'd been a Marine. No one would look at him twice. After removing his wallet from his pocket, he retrieved his license, handed it to the woman and tugged a credit card out in preparation. He filled in the paperwork while she entered the details into the computer. "How long will you be staying for?"

Jimmy glanced at her name tag and gave her the smile that women seemed to go gaga over. She blushed and smiled back. He flexed his biceps as he leaned on the counter and almost laughed when her gaze widened as she ogled his muscles. "I'm not sure yet, Lucy. I'm here to do some sightseeing and catch up with a few friends I served in the Marines with."

"Thank you for your service." The blush on her cheeks deepened.

He shrugged as if it was no big deal, but he loved it when people, especially women, kowtowed to him with gratitude. As far as he was concerned they all should be kissing his feet for keeping them and America safe. "Just doing my job."

She nodded and shyly glanced away. Jimmy studied her face as she finished up entering the data into the computer. She wasn't beautiful like Jaylynn, only passably pretty, but he would have no trouble fucking her. If he closed his eyes and imagined it was his woman, he'd get off with no problems. He licked his lips and winked when he caught her staring at his mouth. Jimmy loved how females watched him. He was a good-looking guy and didn't hesitate to use his looks to get what he wanted. He'd never had any trouble getting a woman for the night, but none of the sluts had been Jaylynn. There was just something about her that drew him and while he knew he was obsessed with her, he couldn't just let her get away with turning her back on him.

Jaylynn Freedman was his, had been for a lot of years and he wasn't giving up until he had her in his arms, in his bed, under him while he fucked her. However, first he had to find the bitch.

"Okay, so you have room two, which is near the back of the lot. Meals are served in the motel dining room between 6 a.m. and 9 a.m. Lunch is 12:00 till 2 p.m. and dinner is 6 p.m. till 9:30 p.m. There are other establishments you could eat at in town if you wish. We have a diner, a pizza place which only opened up a month ago and a small café. The café is only open from 6 a.m. till 6 p.m. The hotel, or pub, whatever you want to call it, serves lunch and dinner, but their fare is simple like burgers, chicken wings and such. The diner serves the best meals in town besides our kitchen."

"Thanks, Lucy." Jimmy accepted the room key and the pamphlets she handed over to him.

"I hope you enjoy your stay and have fun with your friends."

Jimmy smiled, winked and turned away. He hurried out of the office and after locating his room went back to his truck to park the vehicle in front of it. He didn't want to worry about finding a carpark as he drove about the busy small town and figured he'd see more if he walked. He was eager to stretch his legs after being cooped up in his truck for so long, and search for Jaylynn. He wasn't sure how he was going to convince her to come back with him, but he wasn't giving up until he had what he wanted.

Jimmy grabbed his bag and whistled as he entered the motel room. It looked as if it had been updated recently, was clean and roomy. He just hoped he didn't have to stay too long, before he found Jaylynn. He didn't like spending money on frivolous things, but this wasn't what he'd called frivolous.

In his mind, it was a necessity.

* * * *

Jaylynn sighed with relief and smiled at Dr. Phoenix Carter. "So it was just that horrible flu virus?"

"Yes. I'm sorry if I scared you with the other things I said."

She raised an eyebrow in question.

"The suspected glandular fever and chronic fatigue syndrome. With how swollen your glands were and the excessive temperature, I thought for sure that's what you had. There's no way we can test for the Epstein-Barr virus."

"I'm really happy you were wrong, but also thankful you were being cautious. So, when can I go back to work?"

Phoenix nodded and then frowned down at the paper on his desk before meeting her eyes with a serious gaze. "You were really sick, Jaylynn. I was ready to admit you to the hospital. I heard about how many hours you've been working. You're still too pale and you've lost too much weight. Even though you might feel better, you still have the dark smudges under your eyes and you look tired. You're on the verge of exhaustion. That's why you had such a hard time fighting off that virus. If you don't slow down, you're going to end up collapsing in a heap and having a relapse. I want you to take a week off to rest and relax. Come back and see me and we can discuss you returning to work then."

"Oh, but—"

Phoenix shook his head. "I'm not clearing you and don't think you can ignore me either. I will be letting Delta, Violet, and Enya know you aren't allowed back without giving them any other information."

Jaylynn frowned, sighed and twisted her fingers together in agitated frustration. She'd thought for sure that Phoenix would have cleared her for work, but she should have known better. Most of the men in this growing rural town were protective to the point of being overbearing. Why she thought he would be any different she didn't know.

"I'll have your bloodwork sent to the lab and call you if there are any problems. Do you need anything else?"

She swallowed and hoped her face wasn't as red as it felt. "I need another contraceptive prescription."

Phoenix nodded. "Have you had any side effects? Bloating, fluid retention, headaches?"

"No."

"Good." Phoenix wrote out the script and then wrote on another piece of paper before he handed them over, after he rose and moved around his desk. "Please take the week off to rest. I've given you a medical certificate as well as the prescription. Eat properly and sleep. I'll see you in a week from today, same time if that's okay?"

"Fine," she huffed out.

"Don't get pissed, Jaylynn. Although I'm currently your treating doctor, I hope I'm also a friend. If you'd seen you the way I had, you'd be worried, too."

Jaylynn gave him an apologetic smile. "I know. I'm sorry for the attitude. It's just…"

Phoenix held up his hand with his palm out toward her. "You don't have to explain, honey. I know you're an independent grown woman." He rolled his eyes and then smiled at her. "I've heard it all before."

Jaylynn giggled. "I'll bet you have."

Phoenix hurried toward his office door and opened it for her. He glanced out in the waiting room and when he saw Brax, Ajay, and Cael shoving to their feet, he blanked his expression, but she could tell by the twinkle in his eyes he was up to mischief. "No heavy lifting and definitely no strenuous activities."

Jaylynn rolled her lips to try and hide the smile wanting out.

Brax rushed over, grasped her hand in his and frowned at Phoenix. "What do you mean by strenuous activities?"

When she saw guilty contrition in Brax's, Ajay's and Cael's eyes, she couldn't hold her mirth in any longer and burst out laughing.

Phoenix joined in and he pointed at her guys. "You should have seen your faces. Y'all looked so guilty."

"You're an asshole." Brax grinned.

"That's Dr. Asshole to you, soldier."

Jaylynn shook her head as she chuckled. She loved how her guys and the other men living in the Slick Rock area were always bantering back and forth. And while she and the other women bemoaned their overprotective attitudes at times, she also liked it because she'd never felt safer.

She shivered as a frisson of apprehension skated up her spine as Jimmy's angry determined face flashed across her mind. She quickly pushed him out of her thoughts. She didn't want to think about that abusive asshole ever again. Jaylynn was happy for the first time in a long while and didn't want to do anything to jeopardize that happiness.

After thanking Phoenix and waving good-bye she, Brax, Cael, and Ajay headed out of the hospital.

Ajay laced his fingers with hers, and Brax slung an arm around her shoulders. Cael walked behind them.

"Where are we going?" Jaylynn asked as the guys steered her away from the parking lot where the truck was parked and down the street toward the shops.

"We're going to have a late lunch at the diner and then we're going shopping," Ajay answered.

"Do you need groceries?" she asked.

"No," Brax answered without further clarification. She glanced up and him and decided that maybe she didn't want to know when she saw the determined look in his brown eyes.

"I'm not very hungry," she said, almost to herself. She had a large breakfast and didn't feel hungry in the least. Normally Jaylynn didn't eat breakfast at all.

"I don't care whether you're hungry or not, baby," Brax said. "You're going to eat something. You need to gain the weight you lost."

"You're so bossy," she groused.

"You keep saying that, Jaylynn. It doesn't matter how many times you do, we aren't going to change just because you don't like being told what to do," Cael said.

"We're only trying to look after you, honey." Ajay lifted her hand toward his mouth and kissed the back of it. "We're going to get you to eat as often as possible until you're back to your normal healthy self."

"I'm not sick." She sighed with exasperation. "Phoenix said other than signs of being tired, the virus has mostly run its course."

Brax stopped walking, nudged her chin up with a knuckle and locked gazes with her. "He also said he wants you to relax and rest. We're going to make sure you do that to the letter, baby."

"You're so annoying." She huffed out a breath as she turned her head away, dislodging his hold on her chin. She hurried ahead but didn't get far before they caught up with her.

Ajay clasped her wrist and pulled her to a stop. He guided her backward until she bumped into a brick wall and couldn't go any farther. Ajay stood in front of her while Brax and Cael stood beside him, but angled toward her until she was surrounded. "Why are you so annoyed, honey? We care for you and want to keep you healthy and happy. What's so bad about that?"

She lowered her gaze and bit her lip. She knew that, but they could be so darned arrogant sometimes, and yet that was one of the traits that had attracted her to them in the first place. She might be independent and while she wasn't submissive, she liked knowing they had her back. What scared her the most was that she had no idea how long this relationship would last. Every single person she'd ever loved had ended up leaving her. Although she knew they hadn't left by choice, she couldn't help being scared that Cael, Ajay, and Brax would leave her, too. "For how long?"

"What?" Cael frowned.

"For how long what, Jaylynn?" Ajay asked.

Brax cupped her face between his hands and brought her gaze back to his. "Shit, Jaylynn, we've already been through this. Do you honestly think we would leave you, baby? We want to spend the rest of our lives with you. Unless we're killed in an accident which is totally out of our control, we want to grow old with you. What did you think we meant when we asked if you would have a relationship with us? Did you think that once we'd made love with you that we wouldn't want you anymore?"

Tears burned her eyes and she tried to blink them back, but two welled over and rolled down her cheeks.

"I'm right, aren't I?" Brax asked. "You honestly thought we'd ditch you after getting you into our bed." He released her cheeks, his arms dropping back to his sides as he sighed. He glanced about before looking in her direction without meeting her eyes again. "We'll talk about this when we get back home. This isn't the time or the place."

Jaylynn swiped impatiently at the moisture on her face and sighed with despondency.

She still wasn't sure where she stood with the Rhodes brothers. There was physical attraction there between them, but for all she knew they might have been with her as an obligation to her brother. If that was the case, their relationship was doomed to failure. Her heart gave a painful lurch, but she ignored it. She was used to living with and hiding pain. She'd had years to perfect the image she portrayed to the outside world, when inside she was screaming in agony and dying a little each day.

She wasn't sure she'd be able to deal with life if Ajay, Brax, and Cael didn't want her for the long haul. Jaylynn pushed off the wall and turned toward the diner. It was going to be difficult to get through the rest of the day as she tried to portray that everything was right in her world, when inside she was a mass of pain and anxiety.

Getting through the next few hours was going to be sheer torture.

Chapter Twelve

Jimmy almost tripped over his own feet when he caught sight of Jaylynn walking down the street, but rage quickly replaced the excitement coursing through his blood when he noticed the men she was with.

He'd heard that the Rhodes brothers had relocated to another state, but he hadn't known where. He should have realized that those fuckers would follow his woman to wherever she was. Those assholes had always hung around Jaylynn and her brother.

A red haze of fury colored over his eyes when one of the pricks wrapped an arm around her shoulders as another of the bastards held her hand. Thankfully, he was quite a ways behind them, and he was wearing a Stetson to shield his face from the sun and mirrored sunglasses. If they turned and spotted him, hopefully having his face in shadows and the shades over his eyes would be enough of a disguise so they didn't recognize him. Plus, they wouldn't expect him to be in Slick Rock

When the quartet stopped in the middle of the street Jimmy moved closer to the hardware shop window and made it look as if he was perusing something through the glass, but all the while he kept his gaze on his woman and those motherfuckers from his periphery.

He almost smiled when she pulled away from them and crossed her arms over her chest. Of course, he couldn't see her face but from hers and their body language, they were arguing about something.

He almost took a step toward the pricks when they backed his woman into a wall and surrounded her, but he clenched his fists instead. Whatever was going on had to be good for him. If she was angry with those fuckers, he would more than likely have a better chance to court her attentions his way. Not that he really cared. She was just angry with him over some imagined infraction.

Jaylynn loved him as much as he loved her and knew they were meant to be together. She was just playing hard to get, but he'd tame all that willfulness away once he had his hands on her.

He rubbed his hands together when they started walking again. Two of the assholes tried to hold her hands again, but she wasn't having any of their attentions. She jerked away and hurried ahead of them.

The assholes glanced at each other with puzzled expressions on their faces. He could have told them they didn't stand a chance in hell of courting her when it was him she loved.

Jimmy meandered down the sidewalk at a leisurely pace, keeping distance between them, peering with feigned interest into shop windows every now and then so it didn't look as if he was watching his woman and the three bozos. They entered the diner and as much as he would have liked to go in there just to fuck with their minds, he decided keeping a low profile was in his best interests. After gazing about, he spotted the cafe diagonally across the street and after checking for traffic, crossed the road. He'd order an early dinner and once they were finished eating at the diner, he was going to follow them. When he knew where Jaylynn and the bastards were holed up, he could reconnoiter later and make some plans.

He'd brought his black-market sniper rifle with him as well as a few other weapons and necessary items.

While he was eager to get to his woman, he'd learned to be patient when he was serving as a Marine. Even though he begrudged wasting more time, time that would be better spent taming his woman to be biddable and obedient, he couldn't just go all gung-ho and make a move before he was ready. Tipping his hand would fuck up all his chances of getting what he wanted. The Rhodes brothers were Marines like he was, and he suspected they were also black ops soldiers. There'd been a few rumors flying around Forth Worth base to that effect, but of course, with everything so hush-hush, he'd never had the rumors confirmed. Not that he gave a fuck.

He was just as good as they were, if not better.

After ordering his pizza at the counter, he took a seat next to the window and kept an eye on his girl.

* * * *

Even though Cael chatted with his brothers as they waited for their lunch order, he kept a close eye on Jaylynn. She'd hardly said a word since they'd surrounded her on the street and she kept her gaze lowered.

He wished he knew what was going on in that pretty little head, but he wasn't a mind reader. He'd thought that he and his brothers had laid all their cards on the table before they'd made love with their woman, but it seemed there were still quite a few issues to iron out.

Cindy took their orders after enquiring what they wanted to eat and then hurried away after making sure they all had coffee.

Cael's gut was knotted up and while he wanted to grill Jaylynn, he didn't. There were too many people about and he didn't want anyone else knowing their business. Plus, Jaylynn was and always had been a very private person and he knew she'd be pissed if he started a deep and meaningful conversation in the diner. She'd be mortified if the conversation turned into a heated debate. He had a feeling he and his brothers were walking on eggshells right now and one wrong step would send Jaylynn scurrying away. He gazed over at Ajay and caught him frowning in Jaylynn's direction, and he wasn't the only one. Brax was trying to be surreptitious as he gazed at her from the corner of his eye.

Cael was determined to have every misunderstanding sorted out before nightfall. He just hoped that Jaylynn didn't decide to leave in a fit of pique.

* * * *

"Jaylynn, how are you feeling?" Violet asked as she hurried toward their table. "I didn't expect to see you in here so soon. Are you sure you're okay?"

"Hi, Violet. I'm fine. Apparently, I just had that flu virus that's been going around."

"You still look tired and pale." Violet glanced at the guys before looking back at her. "Are you sure you should be up and about so soon?"

"I've just been to see Dr. Phoenix Carter." She shrugged.

"And?" Violet asked.

Jaylynn sighed with frustrated resignation. The women were becoming more and more like the men, badgering her until she answered, even though she didn't really want to.

"He's given me a week off work."

"Scoot over," Violet said.

Jaylynn shifted toward Brax and hoped he'd move over so she wouldn't be plastered against his side. She wasn't sure she could deal with the physical attraction while she was in so much turmoil. And yet there was no way to deny how her body reacted whenever she was close to or thought about Cael, Brax, and Ajay. She loved them so much and it was just natural for her to lust after them, too.

"Why do you hate that so much?" Violet asked as she clasped her shoulder.

She shrugged. "I need to work, Vi."

"I get that. I really do. What I don't get is why you were working everyone else's shift as well as your own? Are you in financial trouble?" Violet whispered.

"No," she answered just as softly. "I don't want to talk about it, Violet."

Vi nodded. "Okay, but just know that I'm here if you ever want to talk about what is going on with you. All right?"

"Yes, thanks."

Violet stood. "Feel better, Jaylynn."

"Thanks." She swallowed around the constrictive lump in her throat and blinked back the tears in her eyes. She'd never normally been quick to tear up, but she was so tired and emotional lately. Hopefully after another good night's sleep, she'd have her feelings under control again.

* * * *

Brax glanced in the rearview mirror and mentally cursed when he couldn't see Jaylynn's face. She'd been quiet, too quiet at lunch, hardly speaking unless asked a question and then her replies had been one-word answers. He hadn't missed how she'd been whispering with Violet and while he wished he'd heard what they'd been talking about, his hearing wasn't that great. While serving as a Marine, he'd fired weapons, as had the rest of the team, as well as been close to explosions and other loud noises. While he wasn't deaf, he now had a hard time filtering out background noise when there was a lot of it and the diner was a prime example.

The chatter and clank of cutlery on dishes had been too loud for him to hear the women's conversation and from the way his brothers had been frowning, they'd been having the same problem. It wasn't that he didn't want to give Jaylynn privacy to talk to her friends, because normally he wouldn't have batted an eye over the way they'd been whispering. However, since there was something going on with Jaylynn, he'd been curious and hoped to get an inkling as to what was going on in her mind. Although he had a pretty good idea already, he'd just wanted his supposition confirmed.

He slowed the truck and pulled into the garage after the door came up remotely and turned off the ignition. Jaylynn's deep even breathing filled the cab and he realized she'd fallen asleep. "Let's get our woman inside and into bed. We can talk to her when she wakes up."

Ajay and Cael nodded.

Ajay and Brax got out of the truck while Cael carefully lifted Jaylynn into his arms and then maneuvered them both out the open door. Brax opened the internal door and led them inside and took the lead toward the bedroom. He and Ajay pulled the covers down and Cael lowered her to the mattress. She sighed and rolled onto her side before curling up into a small ball. Cael removed her shoes and then pulled the cover up over her body.

Brax nodded toward the door and followed his brothers out. He pulled the bedroom door almost all the way closed and hurried toward the kitchen.

"Thanks," he said as he took the beer Ajay handed him, popped the top and took a sip.

"You think she's scared?" Cael asked, scrubbing a hand over his face.

"I don't think, I know." Brax sighed.

"We told her what we wanted with her." Ajay pointed his beer bottle in Brax's direction. "Why would she be scared of that?"

"Everyone she's ever loved has died, left her. She's scared that if she loves us, too, that we'll die," Brax explained.

"Shit!" Cael leaned against the kitchen counter. "I understand why she'd feel that way, but we're safer than we've ever been now that we've retired from the Marines."

"Do you think she'll be able to handle us being cops?"

"She's tough and as long as we're always aware of our surroundings and alert while we're on the job, we shouldn't have any trouble staying safe," Brax said.

"I'm glad she fell asleep," Ajay said. "She was having trouble keeping her eyes open but was fighting the fatigue and would never admit that she was exhausted."

"I don't think she totally trusts us yet," Cael said. "If she did, she wouldn't be holding back. She used to just blurt out anything she was thinking, but not anymore. I hate that she's closed that part of herself off, or holding it back."

"We all do, Cael, and while I think you're right about the trust issue, it'll come," Brax said. "It's going take time for her to get used to us being around again."

"And if she doesn't?" Ajay asked.

"Doesn't learn to fully trust us and open up?" Brax quirked a brow.

Cael nodded and sipped his beer.

"We'll cross that bridge when we come to it," Brax answered. "We can't borrow trouble before we're facing it, because if we do, we could end up fucking everything up."

"We need to get her talking, Brax." Ajay drained his beer and then put the bottle in the recycle bin.

"You think I don't know that?" He sighed with frustration and ran his fingers through his hair.

"She's not leaving us," Cael snarled.

"You're right. She's not," Ajay agreed.

"We have at least a week to work on her and gain her trust." Just thinking about Jaylynn walking out the door nearly brought him to his knees. His brothers were right. Jaylynn wasn't going anywhere and tomorrow morning, or hopefully sooner, they were going to sit down with her and talk things through.

"Do you think she's going to wake up for dinner?" Cael asked as he walked toward the fridge.

"You can't be hungry." Ajay squinted at Cael. "You just ate."

Cael glanced at his watch and then met Ajay's and Brax's gazes. "I could eat."

"You're unbelievable." Ajay snickered as he took the ingredients that Cael passed him.

"You're both just as bad. We need to keep our strength up to deal with our woman. Once she stops hiding, she's going to keep us on our toes."

"I fucking hope so," Brax said.

"What are we making?" Ajay asked as he and Cael started to chop and dice.

"If I remember correctly, Jaylynn was always partial to our chicken and vegetable casserole." Cael smiled.

"She was more than partial." Brax chuckled. "She was obsessed with it."

"That's because she couldn't figure out what our secret ingredients were." Ajay laughed.

"There isn't anything special about Dijon and wholegrain mustard," Cael said.

"What about the mixed herbs and the paprika?" Brax asked.

Ajay shook his head. "Nah, it's probably the chicken stock and the sour cream."

Brax didn't think it was any of those things. He had a feeling that Jaylynn liked the casserole so much because it tasted good, was healthy and she didn't have to make it. Whatever it was, he and his brothers would make it for her as much as she wanted. He loved the appreciative sounds she made while she ate food they'd made for her.

Brax was glad that the atmosphere wasn't as fraught with tension as it had been. He liked seeing his brothers laughing, smiling and having a good time. He hoped that once they got through to Jaylynn and she realized they weren't stringing her along, and they wanted a lifetime with her, that she would want that, too.

She was his heart and soul, the love of his life, and he wasn't willing to let her walk away again.

Chapter Thirteen

Jaylynn knew she wasn't alone as soon as she surfaced from sleep. She could feel Brax, Ajay, and Cael watching her and while she wasn't sure if she should let on she was awake, she quickly dispelled that idea. She'd never been a coward and wasn't going to start being one now.

She forced her eyelids up and inhaled the wonderful aroma of coffee.

"Hey, baby." Brax, who was sitting next to her with his back against the headboard, stroked a finger down her cheek. "How are you feeling?"

She covered her mouth when she yawned and then shoved up so that she was leaning against the headboard, too. She blinked the sleep haze from her eyes and gazed at Ajay and Cael before looking at Brax again. "I'm good. What time is it?"

"Seven a.m."

She frowned. "I slept the whole afternoon and night through? I've never done that before. Well, besides when I was sick."

"You're still recovering from your illness and exhaustion, honey." Ajay was propped against the headboard on her other side and he handed her a steaming mug of coffee.

"Thanks."

"We need to talk, sweetness," Cael stated resolutely.

Jaylynn lowered her gaze and sipped at her coffee. She needed a kick, so she wasn't so fuzzy minded. She had a feeling this…discussion was going to be intense.

After drinking half of her coffee, she felt more alert and hoped her brain wasn't still sluggish. She gazed at Cael and nodded. "What do you want to talk about?"

"We want to know why you're scared of this relationship," Ajay said in a calm low voice.

Jaylynn jerked and was glad that she'd drunk enough coffee so it hadn't sloshed over the rim of the mug and burnt her. She should have known that Ajay, Cael, and Brax would get right to the point. They'd always been like that and although right now she was feeling vulnerable, she was glad they were. There was never any second guessing with them. They always said what they meant. She cleared her throat and lowered her gaze to the quilt. "I'm scared," she whispered.

Brax took the mug from her hand, placed it on the bedside table and then laced his fingers with hers. "We know you're scared, Jaylynn, but of what?"

She tugged her hand from his and wrung her fingers together. "What if this doesn't work out? What if you all find someone else you want to be with?"

Ajay grasped the hair at the back of her head and turned her gaze toward his. He leaned down until he was so close he was blurry and out of focus. She could feel his breath puffing against her cheek. "What kind of fucking question is that? We've already told you we want to have a lasting relationship with you. Another woman isn't going to turn our heads, Jaylynn. We want to be with you and only you."

"How can you know that?" she cried out. "I'm just me, Ajay. There are a lot of other beautiful women in this country. I'm no one special."

"Sometimes you make me so fucking angry."

She closed her eyes when he pressed his forehead to hers and swallowed around the emotional constriction in her throat. She hated making any of them angry and while they'd said they wanted a relationship with her, she was scared of laying her heart on the line. Would they laugh in her face if she told them she loved them and had done so for years? Would they even believe her or still think she was a silly schoolgirl with a childish crush? She wasn't sure she could handle them looking at her with sympathy, especially if they didn't return her feelings.

"Back off, Ajay," Brax ordered.

She sighed with relief when Ajay released her hair and moved away. They were all so much older than her. Brax was thirty-five years old. Ajay was thirty-three, and Cael thirty-one. Jaylynn hadn't turned twenty-five yet, and while sometimes she felt as if she was eighty, other times she felt so young and inexperienced.

When she felt the mattress dip she opened her eyes to see Ajay rolling to his feet. He started pacing and running his fingers through his hair with agitation.

"Why do you think we asked you to have a relationship with us, baby?" Brax asked.

She glanced at Cael and quickly averted her eyes when she saw how angry he looked. His jaw was clenched so tight the muscles on either side were flexing. Brax cupped her cheek and brought her gaze up to his. She drew a deep ragged breath and answered his question. "Because you feel responsible for me. Because Sebastian asked you to look after me."

"Wrong," Brax replied with immediate emphasis. "We used to feel responsible for you, but you were never a burden, Jaylynn. We liked having you around because you were always so happy and fun. Yes, we promised Seb we'd look after you whenever we could, but that wasn't a chore. You brought laughter into our lives when there was so much violence. You were the little sister we never had.

"However, that changed not long before Seb died, and while you were in your early twenties, you were still mourning your brother. We'd planned to start dating you because we were, are still attracted to you. There was no way in hell we were going to begin courting you while you were grieving, because we didn't want to add to your pain if things didn't work out."

"We hated that we were being sent away so often after Seb's death," Cael said. "We wanted to be with you and help you through your grief, but that was out of our control."

"Why did you fucking leave?" Ajay asked as he spun toward her, locking eyes with her. "Do you have any idea how fucking worried we were. I felt sick to my stomach."

"I didn't think there was anything to keep me in Fort Worth. I've already told you this. Everyone I've ever loved is dead or was gone. Jimmy was creeping me out. There were too many memories. I couldn't stay anymore. I saw you with those women. What did I have to stay for?" Jaylynn sucked in a breath when she heard how strident her voice had become. Tears burned her eyes and while she tried to keep them at bay, it was a losing battle. She hated looking so weak, so vulnerable in front of them when they were so strong and confident. She didn't know what to say. They'd hashed all this out before. She was terrified that if she revealed what was in her heart, she'd end up with it broken into pieces.

Brax shoved the covers aside, lifted her into his arms, turned her until she was facing him, before lowering her into his lap. She clung to his broad, muscular shoulders and he cupped her cheeks between her hands. "Do you have any idea how much I fucking love you? I, *we*, were devastated when we returned home only to find you gone."

"You love me?" she asked softly. Her heart was pounding in her chest with hope and while she was elated, she was also in shock.

"Of course, I love you, baby. Why the fuck did you think I wanted to have a relationship with you?"

"Physical attraction," she answered.

"Yes and no," Brax replied. "You're gorgeous, Jaylynn, but that wasn't the reason I fell in love with you. You're the strongest woman I've ever met and you're generous to a fault. You'd leave yourself short of food, money, whatever, just to help someone else."

"I'm not strong."

"Bullshit!" Ajay snapped as he climbed back on the bed and knee-walked closer to her and Brax.

She saw Cael move in her periphery as he moved closer on her other side. He threaded his fingers with hers and squeezed to garner her attention. "How many teenagers do you know who would have survived being left alone for days, weeks, months on end while her brother was off fighting for our country after their parents had died? You had phenomenal courage back then and even more now."

"You worked and studied hard," Ajay said as he clasped her other hand. "When you weren't working you volunteered at the local soup kitchen and you helped Seb pay off your parents' debts. I don't know any other teenager who'd take on so much responsibility. What's more, you were alone more often than not. You're strong, honey. Stronger than we are. That strength has shaped you into the woman you are today. You're an amazing woman, Jaylynn."

Jaylynn didn't try to hide the tears rolling down her face. This, right here, was all her dreams, Christmas gifts and birthdays presents being given to her at once. Happiness and love flowed into her, filling it where there'd been emptiness, pushing her fear and anxiety away.

"I love you, too." She met each of their gazes in turn. "I love all of you so much and I have since I was eighteen years old. The schoolgirl crush I had on y'all was pale in comparison to what's in my heart now."

"Thank God," Ajay breathed out.

"Halleluiah," Cael all but shouted.

"You're our world, baby." Brax palmed her face between his hands again, swiping the tears from her cheeks with his thumbs. He slowly lowered his head toward hers, causing her breath to hitch in her throat. Jaylynn quickly licked her lips, grasped Brax's thick wrists with her fingers and met him half way.

She moaned as he slanted his mouth over hers. When he swiped his tongue over her lower lip, she opened to him and gave herself into his care. The kiss was hot, wild and passionate and quickly set her blood on fire. Their tongues rubbed and dueled with erotic carnality, stealing the breath right out of her lungs, but she didn't care. She didn't care if she never breathed again as long as Brax kept kissing her, loving her. He nipped at her lip before soothing the sting by lapping at it. She groaned and suckled on his tongue.

Brax drew back, grasped the hem of her T-shirt and started tugging it up. She held her finger up in the air. "Hold that thought." Jaylynn scrambled from his lap and crawled over the bed to the edge.

Ajay got to his feet, held his hand out to her and when she took it, helped her to her feet. "Thanks." She grinned at him.

"Wait! Where are you going, sweetness?" Cael asked, concern evident in his town.

"I need the bathroom," Jaylynn said over her shoulder. "I'll be back." She laughed and hurried across the room. After using the facilities, she gazed at her rumpled state in the mirror while she washed her hands and decided a shower was in order. She felt sticky and grimy after sleeping in her clothes. She was surprised that her men hadn't taken them off but maybe they'd been worried about upsetting her more than she'd already been. They had such good hearts and always tried to do the right thing by her.

She brushed her teeth and hair, put it up in a clip and turned toward the shower and stripped. When the water was the perfect temperature, she stepped in under the hot water and quickly washed herself. Stepping out onto the bathmat, she grabbed a clean towel, dried off and wrapped it around her body. She was so excited she was shaking. She wanted to make love to all three of her men, but she was also a little nervous. Not because she was worried they'd hurt her, but because she'd never made love to three men before. She wasn't naïve and knew what to expect, but since this would be another first for her, she was worried she'd cry or something. The love in her heart was so strong and overwhelming she felt as if she was on the verge of tears again. However, this time they were happy tears, but she didn't want to put her men off by inadvertently bawling.

Jaylynn pushed her thoughts aside and hurried toward the bathroom door. Her hand trembled as she reached for the door handle and turned it. Her heart flipped, and she gasped when she spotted Brax, Ajay, and Cael reclining on the bed. They were all totally naked. She couldn't help but feast on them with her eyes. They were so handsome, sexy and muscular, they took her breath away. When she noticed their damp hair, she realized they'd showered when she had.

She took a step toward the bed, almost stumbling as her knees weakened. Ajay must have seen the hesitancy in her step because he shoved to his feet and walked toward her. Jaylynn eyed his body up and down and stopped at his hard cock. He was long, thick and hard, and his erection swayed and bobbed as he moved. He stopped a couple of feet from her and offered his hand once more.

Jaylynn didn't hesitate to take it and let him guide her back to the bed. He released her hand, clasped her hips and lifted her onto the mattress. She shifted toward the middle of the mattress and when the towel started to slip, she did nothing to prevent it. Cael, Ajay, and Brax didn't say a word as they perused her body over.

Cael was the first to move. He grabbed her ankles and tugged her down the bed as he scooted backward. He slid to his knees on the floor, pulled until her ass was near the edge of the bed, wrapped his arms around her thighs and spread her legs. "I've been dreaming about tasting all that sweet honey."

He lowered his head between her legs and licked her from bottom to top. Jaylynn closed her eyes and moaned.

Ajay and Brax shifted beside her. She opened her eyes just as Brax cupped one breast while lapping over the nipple of the other with his tongue. Ajay covered her mouth with his, delving in with his tongue to tangle and caress with hers.

The blood racing through her veins heated and thickened. Liquid desire pooled low in her belly and she whimpered with arousal.

"You taste so fucking delicious, sweetness. I want you to come in my mouth," Cael rasped out.

"Oh!" she moaned.

Cael lapped at her clit before licking his way down to her soaked pussy and dipped his tongue in her entrance. She gasped and groaned, her hips bucking up reflexively, to get more and closer to the pleasure.

Ajay sucked and lapped his way down her neck toward her chest. When Brax released the breast he was kneading, Ajay drew her nipple into his mouth. Two hot, wet mouths suckled on her sensitive nipples, sending sparks of bliss shooting down toward her pussy.

Cael rimmed her cunt with the tip of his finger and as he pushed it up into her, he lashed her clit with the tip of his tongue. She shook and shivered as the pressure began to build slowly and juices dripped from her pussy.

She cried out when Cael began to thrust his finger in and out of her entrance, moving faster and deeper each time he surged inside.

And then Cael added another finger.

He drove both digits in deep before twisting them around inside of her. It felt like he crooked them, and he pressed against a spot inside that was so sensitive, she cried out as her whole body jerked,

Brax released her nipple, leaned up and covered her lips with his. Their tongues glided together before twining and twirling around. She gasped in air and moaned. Ajay clenched her nipple between his teeth, biting down lightly as he squeezed the other hard peak between his finger and thumb.

Jaylynn combed her fingers into Brax's and Ajay's hair and held on tight as the coil inside her womb and pussy grew tauter.

Cael licked and nibbled on her clit, all the while continuing to massage that hot spot deep inside her pussy. Her internal walls rippled around his fingers and the heat began to melt her insides.

The muscles in her legs and arms began to quiver as the tension grew higher. Her blood was so hot she wondered why it wasn't boiling, but the thought was only fleeting.

Brax broke the kiss before nipping and sucking on the skin just under her ear. She cried out when he scraped the sensitive flesh with the edge of his teeth and gasped.

Ajay took her mouth with his, the kiss they shared was greedily carnal as their tongues frolicked and played together.

Jaylynn shivered as goose bumps raced over her flesh and when Cael pressed and rubbed firmly over her G-spot, everything inside her seemed to freeze as she hung on the precipice.

Ajay lifted his mouth from hers before he and Brax both drew her nipples into their mouths and suckled firmly. At the same time, Cael sucked her clit into his mouth and flicked it with the tip of his tongue.

Jaylynn screamed as she toppled over the edge. Her whole body quivered and quaked, her pussy clenched down around Cael's fingers before releasing, and clamped down again.

Cream gushed from her pussy in spurts of ecstasy and stars burst apart in front of her eyes. She shook and shivered as ecstatic bliss washed over and through her, holding her in its grip of euphoric release.

Aftershocks wracked her body as she gasped air in and out of her lungs, trying to get her breath back. Cael eased his fingers from her pussy, causing her to groan with sensitivity and she jerked when he gave her cunt a final lick. Ajay and Brax caressed their hands over her shoulders, down her arms, and over her breasts, murmuring soothing noises as they brought her back down from her rapturous pinnacle.

She blinked her eyes open just as Cael released her legs and kissed the top of her mound. When she met his hungry brown-eyed gaze, she shivered in reaction as her just satisfied libido perked up with interest.

She watched him lift the fingers he'd used to fuck her with to his mouth and suck them clean. "Fucking delicious, Jaylynn. I could eat that pussy out for hours."

"Oh," she moaned and closed her eyes again. She felt so replete she didn't want to move, and yet she was eager for the next step.

Jaylynn wanted Cael, Brax, and Ajay inside of her, and she wanted that right now.

She had no idea how she could feel so needy, so horny for her men when she'd just had the most amazingly strong orgasm, but she didn't care.

All she cared about was having her men filling her, loving her and claiming her.

Chapter Fourteen

Cael shoved up from his knees and nodded to his brothers. Ajay and Brax grasped Jaylynn under the arms and tugged her up the bed. He was so hungry for his woman he was shaking, but he loved hearing her screaming as she came.

As he climbed up on the bed he sucked in a deep breath and tried to get his lust under control. This was a big moment for all of them, but especially for Jaylynn. He and his brothers were about to make love to her all at the same time, and she had to be nervous.

Once he was in position on his knees between her splayed thighs, he grasped the base of his cock and he dipped a finger into her hot, wet cunt to make sure she was ready for him. He sighed with relief when he found her soaked. He caressed her flat belly to get her attention. "Are you ready for me, sweetness?"

"I've been ready for a long time, Cael. Please, make love with me."

"My pleasure, Jaylynn." Cael kept his gaze locked with hers as he aligned the head of his hard dick with her wet pussy and pressed forward. Her eyelids lowered until he could barely see her gorgeous green eyes, but she didn't look away or close them. He gritted his teeth as he slowly eased his cock in her tight, hot, wet cunt, rocking his hips, sliding his dick forward and back until he was buried in her to the hilt. Making sure to brace his weight onto his elbows and knees, he lowered himself down until they were touching from chest to groin. He closed his eyes to savor the skin to skin contact and tight wet grip she had on his dick. Cael knew his brothers were waiting for him to roll himself and Jaylynn over, but he needed a moment. The urge to pound his cock in and out of her hot pussy was almost too strong to ignore. He didn't realize he was grinding his hips into hers until she moaned.

"Wrap your arms around my neck, sweetness," Cael ordered in a raspy voice. She looped her arms around his neck and when she went to hook her legs around his hips, he stopped her by taking hold of one of her knees. "Stay still, Jaylynn." He shoved an arm under her upper back and the other under her slim waist and rolled.

He groaned, and she moaned when his dick pressed in further. When Jaylynn shifted, bringing her knees up next to his hips and braced her hands on his chest, Cael held his breath. His cock twitched and throbbed as if urging him to move, but he held still. He saw Ajay moving from the corner of his eye and when he saw the bedside drawer was open, he realized his brother had already grabbed the tube of lube.

Cael hoped he didn't shoot off before Ajay and Brax had prepared her, but it was going to be fun trying. He loved having his hard cock buried so far up into her cunt he could feel the entrance to her womb. Jaylynn didn't seem to mind having him in so deep. In fact, she loved it. She was grinding down on him as if trying to take more, but she had all of him and he wasn't a small man. None of them were.

"Lie on top of Cael, honey," Ajay said as he pressed a hand on Jaylynn's back between her shoulder blades.

She licked her lips and lowered onto his chest. Cael grasped a handful of hair and tugged her mouth up toward his. She moaned as he kissed her with love and passion and hoped like hell he could last the distance.

* * * *

Ajay maneuvered in between Cael's spread legs and caressed his hands up and down Jaylynn's back. He needed to prepare and stretch her ass, before he could fuck her without hurting her.

He glanced at Brax and nodded to his brother, who was sitting on his haunches near Jaylynn's hip. Brax nodded back before reaching over to grasp her ass cheeks with his large hands. She whimpered and moaned, the sounds muffled as she kissed Cael.

Ajay opened the tube of lube, squeezed a good dollop onto the tips of two fingers and then caressed over her ass. She gasped and moaned, and he growled when her star opened to him. He tried to ignore his aching cock, racing heart, and hot blood. He'd need to take his time so that Jaylynn didn't feel too much discomfort. He continued to rub his wet fingers over her pucker, dipping the tip of one finger into her back entrance whenever her muscles loosened enough.

He glanced up when Jaylynn broke the kiss and shoved up from Cael's chest. Her movement caused his finger to breach her ass a little deeper. "Are you okay, honey?"

"Yeah," she groaned. "Feels so good."

Ajay grinned at Brax. Brax released one of her ass cheeks and cupped her face, turning her gaze toward him, before leaning down and kissing her passionately. Cael cupped both her breasts in his hands, kneading and molding her soft skin, before pinching and squeezing at her hard nipples.

Ajay slowly and carefully worked his two fingers in and out of her ass, spreading his fingers and stretching her tight muscles. When she started rocking her hips, he realized she was ready for more. He removed his fingers, squeezed more lube onto the tips and pressed three up into her ass.

He paused when she tensed and waited for a sign to continue. Brax licked his way down her neck, nipped and then suckled her earlobe. Cael leaned up, took one of her nipples into his mouth and reached between their legs. Ajay knew the second he began to caress her clit because she moaned and the tension in her ass muscles eased.

He sighed out a breath of relief that he didn't have to stop and began to slowly thrust his fingers in and out of her rosette.

"Do you like having Ajay's fingers in your ass, baby?" Brax asked just before he lashed her other nipple with his tongue.

"Yes," she groaned. "So much...to feel."

Ajay would have smiled at the surprise in her voice if he'd been able to, but he was too busy concentrating on Jaylynn and trying to keep his own hunger on a leash. He'd never been so hard in his life. His dick was throbbing along with the beat of his heart and he was continuously leaking pre-cum.

Finally, after what seemed like forever had passed but was probably only minutes, Ajay knew she was ready. He eased his fingers from her ass, grabbed the tube of lube, coated his condom-covered dick with a generous amount of the viscous liquid and wiped his hand clean on the damp washcloth he'd retrieved from his own bathroom while Jaylynn had been showering.

"More!" Jaylynn demanded as she wriggled her hips.

Cael groaned as he clasped one of her hips with one of his hands. Ajay met both of his brothers' gazes and nodded as he moved in closer behind Jaylynn. He gripped her other hip and the base of his dick. "Take a big breath for me, honey," he ordered between panting breaths.

Jaylynn inhaled and held the air in her lungs. Ajay aligned the head of his cock to her star and began to push in.

The air exploded from her lungs as she moaned. He growled as the head of his dick penetrated her tight muscles.

"Oh god, oh god, oh god," she gasped.

"Look at me, baby," Brax commanded.

She turned toward Brax and he devoured her mouth. Cael nodded at him as he began to rub light circles around her clit with the tip of his finger.

Ajay groaned as her ass clenched around the head of his cock before loosening again. He slowly, carefully pressed in another inch. Inch by excruciating, pleasurable inch, he forged his way deeper into her back entrance until he could go no further. Her ass flexed around his length convulsively and she shivered. "You okay, honey?" he asked. "Am I hurting you?"

"Yes! No. I don't know." She sucked in a breath. "It's a good pain. Don't stop, Ajay. Please, don't stop?"

"I won't, honey. You're fucking amazing, Jaylynn."

"I need you, too, baby," Brax rasped out.

She turned toward Brax and licked her lips when she noticed he was up on his knees beside her. When she saw his hand caressing up and down his cock, she whimpered. When she just continued to stare at Brax's dick, Ajay wondered if she was too innocent to realize what his brother wanted, but quickly pushed that thought aside when her muscles clenched around his dick.

"Fuck, sweetness, you feel so fucking good. You're so wet your cum's dripping from my balls." Cael groaned and bucked his hips up.

Jaylynn leaned toward Brax, clasped his wrist and pulled his hand from his cock. She wrapped her much smaller hand around his shaft and swirled her tongue over the head. Brax growled, tipped his head back and threaded his fingers into the hair at the back of Jaylynn's neck and head.

"Yeah, baby. So good. I love that sexy mouth," Brax said hoarsely.

Ajay wanted to move, but they needed to give Jaylynn time to get comfortable as she pleasured Brax. She pumped her hand up and down Brax's cock, opened her mouth and sucked him in. From the grunting noises Brax was making, she was doing everything right.

Ajay closed his eyes and gripped the base of his dick hard when it twitched and throbbed. Jaylynn was so fucking sexy sucking on Brax's cock, he couldn't watch any longer because he was in danger of coming too soon.

"Fuck yeah, baby." Brax gasped.

He opened his eyes before thinking about what he was doing and when he saw that Jaylynn had a steady rhythm going as she bobbed her head up and down over Brax's cock, he couldn't stay still any longer. He met Cael's gaze and nodded.

* * * *

Jaylynn was stuffed full of cock and she loved it. She couldn't believe how wonderful it felt to have Ajay's cock in her ass. She'd had no idea how sensitive, or how many nerve endings were back there until now.

For a while there, she'd thought she was going to have to ask Ajay to stop. Her ass had burned with pain as he stretched her muscles, but the pain had quickly waned when Cael had started caressing her clit.

She moaned when Ajay withdrew to the tip and as he stroked back into her pucker, Cael retreated from her pussy. She suctioned her cheeks as she took Brax's cock as deeply into her mouth as she could without choking, and when she pulled back to the tip, she whirled her tongue around the head. Each time she rubbed her tongue over the underside of Brax's dick where shaft and crown met, he trembled, and she knew that was a sensitive spot, so she made sure to lap at it again and again.

They started off slow, as one withdrew the other surged back in and she continued to pump her hand up and down Brax's shaft, squeezing firmly to enhance his pleasure. The molten heat centered low in her belly moved outward, spreading to every corner of her body. Her muscles tightened more, the tension growing with each stroke of Cael's and Ajay's cocks in and out of her pussy and ass, and yet, she also felt languid as the desire melted her from the inside.

Jaylynn pushed down over Brax's cock, taking it in as far as she could. When she felt the tip of his dick nudge the back of her throat, she swallowed and drew air in through her nose. To her surprise the muscles in her throat loosened and she was able to take the crown of Brax's cock down her throat. Not very far, but enough that she could hear him growling and groaning. His fingers tightened in her hair. The small stinging pain in her scalp sent her aching lust up another notch.

"Fuck," Ajay groaned. "Her ass is so fucking hot and tight. When she clenches around me I swear it's firmer than my own fist."

Jaylynn moaned. She was amazed that hearing them talk dirty had her arousal climbing even higher. Her internal walls clenched convulsively, and juices leaked from her pussy.

"Fuck yeah, sweetness," Cael panted. "Cover my cock in your cream." He surged into her pussy and ground his hips against hers, his pubis rubbing against her engorged sensitized clit, causing her to ripple around both their dicks.

Ajay drove hard and fast into her ass and as he pulled back, Cael shoved into her pussy. The friction of their dicks massaging along the walls of her ass and cunt, sending her another step up the steep slope toward climax.

Jaylynn drew back to the tip of Brax's cock, taking time to lave the underside before taking him back in. He groaned and as she retreated again, he started rocking his hips. "Love that sexy mouth, baby. Love that sexy little body. I love you, Jaylynn."

Emotion rushed into her heart, filling her soul with so much love, tears welled and rolled down her face. She didn't stop to brush them away, or even acknowledge them, but concentrated on showing her men how much she loved them in return. Jaylynn began to move her hips, eliciting a grunt from Ajay and a groan from Cael. She moved her pelvis forward and back, up and down in an erotic dance as she tried to enhance her men's pleasure.

This time when she took Brax's cock back into her mouth, she changed up the pace, bobbing her head faster, pumping her hand rapidly as she gripped him tighter.

"Fuck yeah, Jaylynn. Just like that." Brax gasped. "I'm getting close."

"Same," Ajay groaned.

"Three," Cael said through clenched teeth.

Jaylynn hummed as she took Brax's dick down her throat and paused. He seemed to hold his breath and when she swallowed around him, sucking at the head of his dick, he growled. Her legs began to tremble as the pressure inside grew hotter, higher. She was racing toward the peak of the slope with no way to stop the culmination. Nor did she want to, but she did want her guys coming with her.

She reached out with her free hand, cupped Brax's sac in her palm and gently rolled his balls. A deep grumbling groan started low in his chest and bubbled up out of his mouth.

Ajay retreated from her ass and stilled. Cael withdrew from her pussy and shoved a hand down between their bodies. She quivered when Cael pressed the tip of a finger onto her clit and then Ajay and Cael began to shuttle their cocks in and out of her star and cunt, faster, harder and deeper, both at the same time. One moment she was nearly empty and the next she was stuffed full. There was no way she could keep up the pace with her rocking hips, so she held still and gave herself over to the loves of her life.

Jaylynn bobbed back down over Brax's cock and this time she gently squeezed his balls. He tugged her back to the tip of his dick before she could take him down her throat, but then he pulled her back onto him. He didn't push her down as far as she'd been going nor did he hurt her. Honey flowed from her pussy in a continuous stream and the muscles in her pussy and ass grew tenser and tenser. The walls gathered closer and closer together and she knew she was about to topple.

Brax was groaning continuously now and as he stroked back into her mouth, Cael pinched her clit between his finger and thumb.

That was all it took to send her hurtling over the edge.

Her scream of completion was muffled by Brax's dick and his own roar of ecstasy. Her whole body shook and shivered. Her internal muscles clamped down hard around the two cocks still pistoning in and out of her ass and pussy before releasing and clenching down again.

A kaleidoscope of colors burst in front of her eyes as her body, heart and soul went soaring up into the heavens.

Ajay thrust deep into her ass with a yell as he climaxed. Cael shunted deeply into her pussy on a long low growl as he started to come. She felt every twitch and pulse of their dicks as they emptied their seed into her holes. She gulped quickly, swallowing Brax's seed as it shot over the back of her tongue and down her throat. Cream gushed from her cunt, the bliss so intense she felt as if her whole body was convulsing.

Jaylynn floated on a cloud of euphoric nirvana, her body as light as a feather as she felt her spirit reach out toward her men's. For the first time in a very long time, she felt connected to another person, people on a primary and transcendent level.

Brax pulled her mouth from his cock and slumped down onto the bed beside her. He caressed a hand over her head and down her back. Cael and Ajay smoothed their hands over her arms, back, and sides. She flopped down onto Cael's chest, still panting heavily as she tried to regain her breath.

Brax, Ajay, and Cael were finally hers.

She was home, where she was meant to be and had dreamed of since she was eighteen.

Jaylynn could still barely believe that this was real.

She was going to do everything she could to make her men happy. They'd spent years fighting for hers and the rest of the population's benefit. They'd put their lives on the line and she could do nothing but the same. They held her heart in their hands and she held theirs in hers.

She would never do anything to betray them or hurt them.

A frisson of alarm raced up her spine, but she quickly pushed it away.

This wasn't the time to think bad thoughts. This was a time of reconnection, happiness, and loving.

It was a time for joy.

Chapter Fifteen

Jimmy had never known such fury. He was so angry he was trembling. He'd followed Jaylynn and the Rhodes brothers back to their place from town, being sure to keep plenty of distance between his vehicle and theirs. After making sure no one was about, he'd parked his truck at the end of the street and jogged back to scope out their property.

The fuckers had a nice place with lots of land and landscaped gardens with trees planted strategically for privacy. That had aided him in keeping out of sight while he reconnoitered. The house was big and looked as if it hadn't been built long ago. Not a weed was out of place and there was a wrap-around deck. That would have made it difficult for him to figure out which bedroom was Jaylynn's if they all hadn't been so occupied fucking.

There was an angry fog over his eyes and the urge to move right now was strong, but he concentrated on breathing deeply and evenly, his fists clenched so tight his knuckles ached. A few moments later his ire receded to manageable proportions and the fog dissipated from his gaze.

Making sure to stay out of sight from the windows, he circled the house looking for weak spots. He wished he had his sniper rifle or any gun for that matter, but maybe it was a good thing he didn't. He'd have been shooting up the place if he did and that wouldn't do. Tipping his hand before he'd formulated a plan would likely get him arrested or killed. The Rhodes men were trained soldiers and had to have weapons of some kind locked away in the house.

Jimmy shielded his eyes, covered them from the glare of the late afternoon sun and looked for the optimal place to watch and lie in wait.

He didn't care if it took days to make his move, because he was determined to get what he wanted. Jaylynn under him. He couldn't believe what a slut she was, nor that she was doing all three of those fuckers at the same time. Those bastards had corrupted his innocent woman, but he was going to make them pay. After he'd dealt with them he would deal with her.

He was going to beat the promiscuity right out of her and when he had her docile, submissive, he would show her what it was like to fuck a real man. He didn't need anyone else helping him with his woman because he was more man than those assholes would ever be.

Jimmy kept to the trees and shadows as he made his way back toward the road and his truck.

Jaylynn wouldn't know what hit her. He was going to kill those pricks and she would turn to him for comfort in her grief, but he wasn't going to show an ounce of compassion. He was going to punish her for leaving him and giving something that was meant to be his to those motherfuckers. Her innocence was supposed to have been his.

She was his woman and he wasn't giving up until he had her back.

* * * *

Cael glanced at Jaylynn from the corner of his eye as she walked toward him. He smiled as he surreptitiously watched the sexy sway of her hips, her natural sensuality. She had no idea how much she affected him and his brothers just by existing.

"Hey, Cael."

"Hey yourself, sweetness."

"Do you want some help?" she asked as she knelt beside him.

"Only if you want to." He met her gaze and immediately felt himself drowning in her stunning jade green eyes. His dick twitched and began to fill with blood. He shifted on his knees, trying to give his cock more room as it grew.

"I love gardening." She started pulling at the weeds.

"I remember seeing you working in the garden in Fort Worth."

Jaylynn snorted. "There was never that much to do unless you, Brax, Ajay, and Seb were on deployment. Y'all used to do things before I even knew they needed to be done."

"We were only trying to help, sweetness, to lighten your load. You were always so busy."

Jaylynn shrugged. "I liked being busy. I hated having nothing to do because it gave me too much time to think."

Cael sat back on his haunches and frowned. "Why is thinking such a bad thing?"

"It isn't, but it made me realize how lonely I was." She sighed and glanced at him before turning back toward the garden, pulling another weed.

"We hated leaving you, Jaylynn."

"I know, but it wasn't your fault. You were doing your jobs the same as Seb was."

"We were. We wanted to hire a nanny or babysitter for you when you were underage, but Seb wouldn't hear of it."

She smirked at him. "That's because I kicked up a stink. I told him if he brought someone else into our home, I'd make their life a living hell. I feel guilty about that now, being older and maybe a little wiser, but I didn't see the need. We were already struggling financially trying to pay off our parents' debts as well as live ourselves. It would have been a waste of money since I was more than capable of looking after myself."

"You always were mature for your age."

She shrugged again. "I did what I had to, Cael, the same as anyone else would have."

"No, sweetness, you did way more than that." He stood and held his hand out to her. "Let's get you out of the sun, Jaylynn. You're going to end up getting burned."

She took his hand and rose. "I've never burned."

"That may be, but you don't know what damage the sun is doing to your skin. You might regret that later in life. We don't want you getting skin cancer when you're older." Cael strolled with her toward the gazebo. There was a small bar fridge which was stocked with drinks. In the center of the pavilion was a bar counter with cupboards underneath. There were also bench seats around the circumference with padded cushions and other cushions scattered about. It was a perfect place to be on warm spring days to relax and socialize, but Cael had something else in mind.

He wanted to make love with Jaylynn out in the open air but away from prying eyes. Their nearest neighbors weren't that close and there was an abundance of plants and trees screening for added privacy.

He guided her up the steps to the gazebo and after seeing her seated walked toward the fridge. "What do you want to drink, sweetness?"

"Is it too early for a glass of wine?" she asked.

"No, it's going on 4:30 p.m."

"I didn't realize it was so late."

Cael grabbed himself a bottle of beer after pouring Jaylynn a glass of white wine. She was so damned beautiful. The sparkle was back in her eyes, the dark smudges of exhaustion were gone, and she'd regained some of the weight she'd lost. Whenever she looked at him and his brothers, there was love and happiness in her gaze. He suspected he probably looked the same way. His brothers certainly did.

"Here you go, sweetness." Cael handed her the glass as he sat beside her.

"Thanks." She took a sip and sighed.

"What are Ajay and Brax doing?"

"They're preparing food for a barbecue. I offered to help but they shooed me away."

"You needed to rest, Jaylynn, and it's done you the world of good."

She nodded. "You're right."

"What?" Cael cupped his ear and canted it toward her.

She giggled and shoved his shoulder. "Don't make me repeat it. I might choke."

Cael laughed as he wrapped an arm around her shoulders and pulled her tighter against him. She glanced up as he looked down. "I love you so damn much, sweetness."

"I love you, too, Cael."

He lowered his head and brushed his lips over hers. She moaned and opened to him, their tongues curling and gliding with carnal delight. When they were both breathless, he lifted his mouth from hers and they both gasped for air.

"Are you happy, sweetness?" Cael asked as he cupped her cheek and stared deeply into her eyes.

"Yes, I am."

A shadow flashed across her gaze but was quickly gone again. "What is it, Jaylynn? What's wrong?"

When she lifted the wine glass to her lips, he dropped his hand from her face.

"Sometimes I feel guilty."

"Why?"

"Because Seb isn't here. I know he'd want me to be happy, but sometimes the guilt and grief just creep up on me. He never got the chance to find someone to love or have a life with. He'll never know what it's like to hold his baby in his arms."

"I understand, sweetness, but you're right, he would want you to be happy. He'd hate it if you spent your life all alone with no one to love you or for you to love in return." Cael sipped his beer. "He knew about us."

She frowned at him. "What do you mean?"

"Seb knew we wanted you to be our woman not long before he died. We promised him that we'd wait before dating you, to give you a chance to experience life. You were just about to finish up at culinary school. We were devastated when we got home to find you gone."

"I'm sorry, Cael. I..." She frowned as she thought about what she wanted to say. "I didn't know or think you liked me that way. As I've told you before, I had a huge crush on you, Ajay and Brax when I was a teenager, but I never once suspected you even saw me. I always thought you and your brothers saw me as your friend's, Seb's, pesky little sister. And I was right. It broke my heart to see you bringing women home." She held up her hand when he would have spoken. "I now know you were, are healthy sexual men and were just living your lives. I can't fault you for that. After everything with Seb's death, everything felt different. With Jimmy pestering me, as well as the memories, I just couldn't stay."

"I wish you'd come and talked to us, sweetness. We might not have wasted a year apart."

"I think we needed that time away from each other," she said before taking another sip of wine. "I'd come to depend on you all and while I was capable of doing everything for myself, I think I started taking you for granted. Whenever you were home, you and the others were always there, mowing the lawns or lending a helping hand. When I left Fort Worth I only had myself to rely on. You say I was mature for my age, maybe I was, but truly being on my own, all alone, made me grow up even more. It also made me realize that what I felt for you, Brax, and Ajay wasn't just a schoolgirl crush, but was something much deeper.

"Even though I was in a lot of emotional pain, it was my own doing and it made me open my eyes. I think if I hadn't made a clean break my feelings for you and your brothers would have remained weak, a shadow of what they are now."

"You're so fucking amazing, sweetness."

She shook her head. "No, I'm just me, but I'm glad you think so."

"Drink your wine, Jaylynn," Cael said as he drained the last of his beer, rose and walked toward the recycle bin.

She drained her glass and stood, intending to wash it out in the sink, but Cael met her halfway, removed the glass from her hand and placed it on the counter away from where they were standing. He grasped her hips and lifted her up, plonking her ass on the edge of the bar.

Cael nudged her legs apart and moved in between them. He cupped her face, gazed deeply into her eyes and lowered his mouth to hers. Jaylynn instantly opened to him, tangling her tongue with his as she wrapped her arms around his neck and her legs around his waist.

He groaned, and she moaned when his hard cock pressed against her hot mound. Cael tilted his head, delved into her mouth and kissed her voraciously. He pushed his hands up under her shirt and caressed over the warm soft skin of her back. She whimpered and arched her hips toward his, grinding her pussy against his hard cock. He broke the kiss and as he began to lick and nibble his way down her neck, he inched her shirt up higher and higher. He lifted his mouth from her skin and whipped the shirt up over her head before dropping it to the side.

"Fuck, you're beautiful," Cael rasped out as he traced the top edge of her bra with the tip of his finger. He watched, mesmerized, as goose bumps formed on her skin and her nipples hardened. He glanced up and bit his lip when he saw how she'd tilted her head back with her eyes closed. She'd braced her weight by resting on her hands behind her. Her long auburn hair was a shining cascading waterfall of dark silk. Her cheeks were flushed, her lips red and kiss-swollen and her cheeks were tinged pink with passion. He kissed over the top of her breasts and then drew her lace covered nipple into his mouth, lapping and sucking on the sensitive tip until she cried out, before switching to her other nipple.

Cael feasted on her breasts until she was writhing with need. He finally lifted his mouth and flicked the front clasp of her bra open. He caressed the straps from her shoulders before skimming his hands down over her breasts, torso, and belly toward the waistband of her jeans. After tugging the button open, he lowered the zipper, hooked his thumbs into the edge of the denim and pushed them over her hips. Jaylynn lifted her ass from the counter, making it easier for him to pull them lower down her thighs. He knelt on one knee, tugged her shoes and socks off and then removed her jeans.

He followed the creamy expanse of her toned, shapely legs up to her green silk covered mound and licked his lips. Saliva pooled, and he swallowed quickly, yearning for a taste of her sweet honey.

Jaylynn pushed up on her hands and peered down at him. She closed her eyes and gasped in a breath before opening her eyes again. "I need you, Cael."

"And you'll have me, sweetness, but first—" He cut himself off and he gripped the seam of her panties and tugged sharply. The material tore, and he pulled the scrap out from under her ass and stood. Cael scooped her up into his arms and carried her to one of the bench seats before lowering her down with her ass on the edge of the cushion. As he knelt, he wrapped his arms around her thighs and spread her legs wide.

Cael was so hungry for her, he dove right in, shoving his head between her legs and lapped at her hot, wet cunt. He growled as her sweet honey coated his tongue and she groaned as he dipped the tip into her entrance, her hands caressing over his head before clutching at his of hair. He licked, sucked and ate at her until she was sobbing with pleasure. He shoved his tongue into her pussy, fucking her with it. When she started rocking her hips as she tugged on his hair and pressed her cunt harder into his mouth, he realized she was right on the precipice.

He licked his way up to her clit and stroked two fingers into her hot, wet pussy. She cried out as she bucked against him and her legs trembled in his hold. Cael pumped his fingers in and out of her cunt, fast, hard and deep while lashing her clit with his tongue. When he heard her stop breathing he opened his mouth over her sensitive nub, caged the bud gently between his teeth and flicked it with the tip of his tongue firmly and quickly.

Jaylynn screamed as she careened over the cliff. Her muscles clenched and released around his fingers over and over. When the last contraction faded, he withdrew his fingers from her cunt and sucked them clean. He stared at her with awe as he started to strip off. When he was naked, he picked her up and sat down on the cushion before turning her in his arms until she was facing him and lowered her to his lap. She met his gaze as she reached down to grip his cock and align it with her dripping entrance. Cael held his breath as she sank down over his hard, aching dick and released it on a groan as she enveloped his length, taking every inch of him inside of her until he was root deep.

His dick twitched and throbbed and Cael hoped he could hold out long enough for Jaylynn to orgasm again.

* * * *

Jaylynn could tell that Cael was keeping his lust on a leash when she noticed how hard he was clenching his jaw and how taut his muscles were. However, she didn't want him holding back. He'd already given her an explosive orgasm and didn't need another to be satisfied. She'd be gratified seeing him orgasm even if she didn't come again.

With determination in her heart to make him lose control, she flexed her internal muscles and began to move. She started out slowly, savoring each and every liquid slide of his cock as the friction of their flesh rubbing together sent pleasure pooling low in her belly. As she got into a rhythm she picked up the pace. She undulated her hips, shifting up and down over his hard cock, moving forward and back, using her internal muscles to grip his cock and heighten his pleasure.

Cael groaned and leaned forward, taking one of her nipples into his mouth to suckle on it firmly. His hands caressed down her ribs, over her hips before stopping to grip her ass cheeks. He lifted and lowered her, pumping his own hips as he thrust his dick in and out of her pussy. She combed her fingers into his hair as she licked and sucked on his neck.

He released her nipple, lifted his head and met her gaze. "Stop squeezing me, sweetness. You're going to make me come."

"That's the whole idea," she panted. Jaylynn lowered her mouth back to his neck and kissed her way down toward his chest. She lapped at his nipple, his rumbling groan vibrating against her lips. She scraped the small hard nub with the edge of her teeth and then bit down.

Cael's grip on her ass cheeks tightened as he roared. He lifted her up higher on to her knees and then powered in and out of her pussy, hard and deeply. She gasped and moaned as the pressure inside her grew as the friction heated her insides.

Cream dripped from her pussy and the liquid desire pooling in her belly began to spread out. Her legs started shaking and it was all she could do to hold on. She clung to Cael's shoulders, worried if she let go she'd fall from his lap.

He pistoned his dick in and out of her cunt, building the carnal tension higher and higher. The coil inside began to get tauter and tauter and the walls of her pussy grew closer and closer together.

Cael shifted both of them and when he shoved into her again, the head of his dick rubbed over her G-spot. She cried out and shook as she went racing up the slope toward ecstasy.

Jaylynn flexed her internal muscles, keeping her pussy tight around Cael's cock as he shunted in and out of her cunt.

Just as she thought she was about to beat him to the finish line, she felt his cock get hotter, expand more and twitch inside of her. He covered her mouth over his, kissing her with a passionate fervor that sent them both careening to the stratosphere.

Her scream of rapture was muffled by his mouth as she quivered and shook. He shouted into her mouth as his cock pulsed and twitched as load after load of cum spewed from the tip of his dick.

Jaylynn didn't remember leaning into Cael, but became aware of her breasts pressed to his chest and her cheek resting on his shoulder as she tried to catch her breath. He ran his hands up and down her back, occasionally squeezing her ass cheeks, before skimming his hand over her skin again.

He threaded his fingers into her hair, massaging her scalp and the back of her neck. She groaned at the caress and while she wanted to meet his gaze, she was so satiated with contented repletion, she didn't have the energy or will to move.

Cael wrapped his arms around her, kissed the top of her head and hugged her tight. She hugged him back and hoped that they would have many more special loving moments in the years to come.

Cael, Ajay, and Brax were her world and she would do anything for them.

When the hair on the back of her neck stood on end, she pushed the disconcerting feeling aside. There was no reason for her to feel unsettled.

She was where she was supposed to be. In Cael's loving embrace.

Chapter Sixteen

"When are you guys supposed to start your new jobs as deputy sheriffs?" Jaylynn asked after swallowing the food she'd been chewing.

They were all sitting outside on the deck, eating the delicious barbecued food Ajay and Brax had prepared and cooked. She'd eaten more than she usually did, but she couldn't resist the marinated ribs, potato salad, steak and tossed salad.

Brax glanced at his brothers before meeting her gaze. "We can start whenever we want."

Jaylynn frowned. "How come? I'd thought you would have had an official start date. I've seen your uniforms hanging up in your closets."

Ajay shifted his gaze from her down toward his plate. Brax glanced skyward as he tipped his bottle of beer up and took a drink. She caught a sheepish look on Cael's face before he quickly looked away.

"What aren't you telling me?" She gazed from one to the other and back again.

Brax shrugged as he placed his bottle back on the table before picking up his knife and fork again. "We asked our new boss, Sheriff Luke Sun-Walker, to delay our start date."

"You what?" Jaylynn shoved to her feet, leaned her hands on the table beside her plate and scowled at all three of them. "What the hell did you do that for?"

"Don't get your panties in a twist, honey." Ajay pointed his beer bottle at her. "We had a good reason for the delay and Luke had no qualms about waiting."

"It was because of me, wasn't it?" She straightened and threw her hands into the air. "I would've been fine."

"That's bull and you know it," Ajay snapped. "You were so fucking run down you had convulsions. There was no fucking way we were leaving you by yourself. You could have fucking died, Jaylynn. Do you even get that?"

She sank back down into her chair with a sigh. Ajay was right. She could have died. From what she'd been told, her temperature had been way too high and if they hadn't been able to bring it down she might have ended up with permanent brain damage. "I do," she finally answered as she stared into Ajay's eyes. "I'm sorry." She met Brax's and Cael's gazes before meeting Ajay's again. "I'm sorry for making you worry. I'm sorry for not looking after myself, and I'm sorry for leaving without telling you or writing a note."

Ajay relaxed and then pushed to his feet. He stalked around the table and stopped beside her, holding his hand out to her. She took it and rose with his help, quirking an eyebrow at him questioningly. "I need some time alone with you, honey. Brax and Cael are going to clean up. Do you want to take a bath with me?"

She looked at Brax and Cael. "Are you sure you don't want help cleaning up?"

"We're fine, baby," Brax answered. "Go spend some time with Ajay."

She nodded and let Ajay lead her inside. He guided her through the kitchen, living room, down the hallway toward the bedrooms and into the bathroom.

"Take your clothes off, Jaylynn," Ajay commanded as he bent over the spa bath, put the plug in and turned the water on.

Jaylynn began to remove her clothes. Ajay turned to watch as he started stripping. He was naked before her and from the hungry look in his eyes, as well as the erection he couldn't hide, he needed her as much as she needed him. He gripped her hand and steadied her as she stepped into the bath and sank into the rapidly rising warm water. Ajay sat beside her.

"Did you and Cael have a good time in the gazebo today?"

She blushed, smiled and nodded.

Ajay grinned, winked and lifted her into his lap with her back pressed to his front. She sighed with contentment as she rested against him. He reached toward the shelf, grabbed a loofah, the shower gel and started washing her.

She turned to gaze up at him over her shoulder. "Why didn't you tell me about your job?"

"We were too worried about you, honey, and we weren't sure you trusted us anymore."

Jaylynn got off his lap, turned and then straddled his thighs. "I'm sorry I hurt you, Ajay. It was never my intention to do that. I trust you." She palmed his cheeks. "I trust all of you and I always have. And I'm sorry if I mucked up your plans for your job."

Ajay shrugged. "You're way more important to us than a job, honey. I love you so fucking much, Jaylynn. It nearly killed me to see you so sick."

She nodded. "I understand because I'd feel the same way if I saw any of you in the same condition I was. I promise I'll never do that to myself again."

"That's good enough for me, honey."

Ajay dropped the loofah into the water, gripped the back of her neck and pulled her toward him. His mouth opened over hers and his tongue licked inside to twirl around hers. She moaned and kissed him back passionately. He groaned, squeezed her ass and tugged her crotch against his hard cock.

They kissed and kissed and kissed until she was in danger of passing out. She turned her head and sucked air into her lungs as Ajay licked and nibbled his way down her neck toward her breasts. She drew back slightly and arched her breasts up toward him, silently begging for his touch, his mouth, anything he wanted to give her.

He smoothed his hands over her back, arms and shoulders before cupping and kneading her breasts. He rolled the nipples between his fingers before pinching and plucking them. Jaylynn caressed over his chest, ribs and washboard belly toward his hard dick. She wrapped her hand around his shaft and pumped it up and down.

"Fuck, honey. You drive me so fucking wild."

"You. Me," she said breathlessly, incoherently. She was too caught up in what he was doing to her and she was doing to him to make any sense. All her guys drove her insane with need.

"I can't wait any longer, Jaylynn. I need inside you, now."

She didn't get a chance to respond, because Ajay lifted her up against his chest, spun her around until she was facing the side of the tub. "Hold on tight, honey."

She gripped the rim of the bath as Ajay nudged her thighs wider and held her breath when she felt the head of his cock at her entrance.

* * * *

Ajay was so hungry for his woman, he felt desperate. He sucked air into his lungs, trying to rein his hunger back, but it didn't work. He dipped a finger into her cunt to make sure she was wet and ready and growled when his finger came away soaked. He grabbed the base of his cock, aligned it with her pussy and drove in with one powerful surge.

Jaylynn gasped and for a moment he thought he'd hurt her, but when she pressed her ass back against him, he knew he hadn't. Ajay wrapped an arm around her waist, grasped her shoulder, drew back and shoved in again.

He set up a firm, quick rhythm of advance and retreat, gliding his cock in and out of her hot, humid pussy, quickly and deeply. She reached back with one hand and squeezed one of his ass cheeks, her hand sliding over his skin as he drew back before thrusting forward again.

"Oh!" Jaylynn moaned. "So good. You feel so good, Ajay."

He growled in agreement as words were beyond his capabilities. When he felt the warm tingles at the base of his spine, he realized he wasn't going to last. Ajay pulled out of her pussy just in time to turn the water off. He'd been so caught up in her, in loving her, he'd completely forgotten the water was still running to fill the bath. He shifted away from Jaylynn, reached down for the plug, lifted it and drained some of the water out. He glanced at the floor to see that there was already water all over the place.

Jaylynn sank down onto the seat and turned to face him. She gazed over the edge of the tub and grimaced when she saw the soaked bathmat and the pools of water. "Thank god you remembered to turn the tap off, or we might have flooded the place. Brax would have had apoplexy."

Ajay threw his head back and laughed. Every now and then Jaylynn came out with words not many people used anymore. She'd always found a few spare minutes to read before she went to sleep, and she still did, but she hadn't read much of anything lately. He and his brothers kept her occupied by making love with her and she almost always fell asleep quickly after having an orgasm or two.

"Don't let too much water out," Jaylynn said, bringing him back to the present. Ajay shoved the plug back in and moved toward her. Without saying a word, he grasped her waist, lifted her out of the tub, lowered her ass onto the tiles, spread her legs and shoved his face into her pussy. "Oh!"

Ajay growled as he licked and lapped at cream, sucking on her folds before shoving his tongue into her creamy cunt. His groan joined her moan as he fucked her with his tongue. He hooked his arms around her legs, pulled her closer to his mouth as he tipped her hips up and delved his tongue in deeper.

"Oh, oh, oh," Jaylynn gasped, and she dug her fingernails into the skin of his shoulder. He glanced up toward her and hummed when he saw she had her eyes closed. Her cheeks were rosy with passion and her lips were parted as she panted shallowly. Her breasts swayed with each breath she took, and her nipples were hard and a darker hue from being engorged with blood.

Ajay tried to ignore his throbbing cock as he ate her out, but it was getting harder and harder—pun intended—with each passing second. As he lowered his gaze back toward her pussy, he noticed her belly muscles jumping and her legs started trembling. She was close to orgasm, but he wanted, needed to feel her coming on his cock. He lifted his mouth from her cunt, shifted, released his hold on her legs, lifted her from the rim of the bath and pulled her back down toward his lap.

Jaylynn looped her arms around his neck, hooked her legs around his waist and tried to impale herself on his dick. She almost succeeded. If he hadn't been in the process of turning around he might already be buried deep inside of her. As soon as his ass hit the seat, he adjusted her on his lap, gripped her ass and slammed in deep and hard.

She screamed as she orgasmed. Her cunt rippled around him, gripped him hard before releasing and clenched down hard again.

Ajay panted as he shuttled his hard, throbbing dick in and out of her wet cunt. Molten lava pooled deep and low in his belly as he drove his cock in and out of her like a man possessed. And he was. He was obsessed with showing her how much he loved her. Determined to have her orgasm again before he climaxed.

Still keeping a firm grip on one of her butt cheeks, he caressed a hand up her back and tilted her upper body away from him. He immediately lowered his head toward her chest, drew a nipple into his mouth and suckled firmly on it. She writhed over him and he quickly switched to her other breast.

The walls of her cunt began to tighten, letting Ajay know she was on the verge of climaxing again, before the other one had even finished. He scraped the edge of his teeth over her hard, sensitive little nipple and then bit down.

Jaylynn's mouth opened on a silent scream as she shot straight back up into the heavens. Hot, wet cream bathed his cock and gushed from her cunt.

"Yes," Ajay shouted. "Fuck yes, honey. Come all over me." He surged into her twice more and on the third time he drove in deep with a roar. "Fuuuck!"

His whole body jolted and twitched as fire boiled in his balls before erupting up his shaft and out the tip of his dick. He ground his hips into hers, prolonging their ecstasy as long as he could. Aftershocks shook them both as they panted for air and tried to calm down from such a nirvanic high. He wrapped his arms around Jaylynn, holding her close, caressing up and down her back as she shivered convulsively, continuously.

Finally, when the last shudder waned, and their breathing slowed, Jaylynn lifted her gaze to his. Tears welled and trailed down her face as she stared into his eyes. He was about to ask her if he'd hurt her, but she wrapped her arms around his neck and hugged him tight. "I love you so much, Ajay. That was so much, so special."

"I didn't hurt you, did I, honey?"

"No. I don't know why I'm crying," she sobbed. "It was just…so beautiful."

Ajay rested his forehead against hers, closed his eyes when tears burned and swallowed audibly around the emotional constriction in his throat. "Yeah, it was," he rasped out. "I love you, honey."

"I love you, too, Ajay." She pressed her lips to his, kissing him, softly, lovingly but passionately.

Ajay had no idea what he'd done to deserve Jaylynn, her love, but whatever it was, he was glad.

His life would be so empty without her in it.

Chapter Seventeen

Jaylynn smiled at Phoenix. "Thanks for the all clear, doc."

Phoenix chuckled and took her outstretched hand. Instead of shaking it, he sandwiched her hand between both of his. "Will you please promise me that you'll work your normal hours and not take on everyone else's shift?"

Jaylynn tried to keep the grimace in her mind from showing on her face, but she wasn't sure she pulled it off when Phoenix's smile changed to a frown. "I can't promise not to work extra shifts, Phoenix. I'll cover for anyone in need. What if someone calls in sick and there's no one else to fill their shoes?" She tugged her hand from his and held up a finger when he opened his mouth to speak. "However, I can promise that I won't be working twenty-hour days, for weeks on end like I did. Believe me, I've learnt my lesson."

"That's good to hear, Jaylynn. We were all so worried about you."

"I know. Thanks for the concern, but I'm fine now."

"You can call me, Axel or Cam if you start feeling ill again. I don't want you putting a visit off if you aren't feeling right. Okay?"

"Okay." She nodded.

"Do you promise, Jaylynn?" Phoenix asked.

"I promise."

"Good. Now get out of here so I can get some work done."

"Sir. Yes, sir." Jaylynn saluted with a grin on her face and then laughed with Phoenix.

"Scoot, young lady."

She waved good-bye and headed out of Phoenix's office and the hospital. She was on her own for a change, since Brax, Ajay, and Cael had been called into the sheriff's office for a meeting. She was hoping that they'd be able to start their jobs as deputies, very soon. Although she hadn't asked it of them, she still felt guilty over them taking extra time with her instead of working, but the decision had been out of her control.

She smiled as she walked down the street toward the diner, listening to the birds chirping and savoring the warmth of the sunshine's rays. It was a beautiful, clear spring day and the perfect weather had put a spring in her step, but that wasn't the only reason. She was happy for the first time in every aspect of her life, now all she needed to do was get back to work. Jaylynn needed to earn money of her own. She hated being a mooch, even if her guys didn't see her staying with them that way. She'd always paid her own way, and while she'd probably never earn as much money as her men, she wanted to at least contribute to the household finances.

When a top displayed in a shop window caught her eye, she stopped to look at it. Thankfully, the price tag was also visible, and she sucked in a surprised breath. It was expensive, but realized why when she saw the designer label. She turned away from the window and continued walking. She browsed as she passed shop windows and was just about to cross the narrow alleyway running up beside the hardware store, when she heard a woman cry out in pain.

Jaylynn didn't stop to think, she just reacted. She turned down the alley and jogged to the other end. When she saw a man and woman in the shadows, she slowed her pace. That was until she realized the guy was hitting the lady. "Hey! What the hell are you doing?"

Smack.

She cringed as the man's fist connected with the woman's jaw. The poor lady's head bounced back against the wall behind her and she went slumping down to the ground. Jaylynn put on a burst of speed and when she was close enough, she shoved the guy as hard as she could in the side. He snarled angrily as he turned toward her.

Before she could raise her arms, or do anything else to protect herself, his fist slammed into her cheek and right eye and she went flying. Pain exploded in her face and head, and her vision blacked out. She hit the ground with a hard thud, her head bouncing on the pavement. Jaylynn drew a deep breath, hoping like hell she didn't pass out or that the bastard didn't hit her again.

When her eyesight finally cleared she glanced about looking for the man who'd hit her, but he was nowhere to be seen. She hadn't even gotten a look at his face because he'd been wearing a Stetson which had shadowed his features, plus the lighting in the alley hadn't been great to begin with.

Jaylynn groaned as she rolled over to her hands and knees, ignoring the gravel digging into her flesh, and started crawling toward the unconscious woman. She gasped when she saw how bruised and swollen the other woman's face was and her lower lip was split, bleeding profusely.

She sat back on her haunches, dug into her purse for the clean handkerchief she put in there this morning and pressed it to the woman's lip. While her face was swollen, she looked familiar to Jaylynn. She'd seen her in the diner a time or two, but she was always alone. Keeping the cloth pressed to the lady's lip, she dug into her purse again, searching for her cell phone but couldn't find it. When she thought back to where she'd last seen it, she realized she'd forgotten to unplug it and bring it with her.

Jaylynn gazed toward the street and when she saw someone standing at the entrance to the alley, she yelled. "Hey, I need some help."

She sighed with relief when she realized it was Cindy hurrying toward her.

"Oh my god. What happened? Are you all right, Jaylynn? Do you want me to call an ambulance? I need to call the sheriff," Cindy said quickly.

"Take a breath, Cindy. I'm okay. It's her I'm worried about."

Cindy squatted down next to her as she swiped a finger over her phone. "Violet, is Wilder still in the diner? Can you send him to the alley next to the hardware store? We'll need a doctor, too. Shyann Bowler and Jaylynn are hurt. It looks as if someone hit them. Thanks."

Jaylynn tried to keep her expression blank, but it was difficult when her face and eye felt as if it was on fire and throbbing like a bitch. Her head was pounding, too, and she knew she was going to end up with a black eye. She just hoped the headache wasn't a sign of a concussion, but most of all she wished she'd seen the asshole's face. If she had she would have been able to press charges. Maybe when Shyann came around she'd be able to tell the sheriffs who'd hurt her.

"What the fuck?" Wilder shouted as he sprinted toward them. He skidded to a stop and knelt on the pavement. He grabbed the radio on his shoulder and called for help. "Are you okay, Jaylynn?"

She nodded and immediately gasped when her aching head protested. When she bit her lip, she whimpered. She hadn't realized her lip was swollen, too, until then.

"Who hurt you, honey?" Wilder asked as he ran his hands over the back of the unconscious woman's head. "She's fucking bleeding. Where the hell are the docs?"

Jaylynn glanced toward the alley entrance when Wilder did and was relieved to see, Dr. Phoenix Carter and Dr. Camden Brown hurrying toward them.

"What the hell is going on?" Phoenix asked as he and Cam took in the scene. "We need the ambulance and a stretcher." Phoenix carefully examined the unconscious Shyann and then carefully lifted her into his arms.

Cam nodded since he was already talking on his cell phone. "The paramedics are on their way." Cam held his hand out to Jaylynn. When she clasped it, he helped her to her feet. She swayed when she got dizzy and Cam swept her up into his arms.

"I can walk. You don't have to carry me."

Cam shook his head and just kept walking. Wilder was asking Cindy questions and the young woman answered. Just as Cam got to the entrance of the lane, the ambulance pulled up. The paramedics, Raiden and Brig Tremaine, who were fairly new to Slick Rock, got out, hurried toward the back of the van, and opened the doors.

"What have we got?" Brig asked.

"Two women who were assaulted by some fucking asshole," Phoenix said angrily. "This one's been unconscious ever since being hit. We'll do an MRI when we get her to the hospital."

"Jaylynn!" Brax roared her name.

She turned at the sound of his voice and saw him, Ajay and Cael sprinting toward her. They looked angry enough to chew nails. If she wasn't hurting so bad, she would have been as angry as they were. She'd never been hit by anyone before and hadn't realized how much it hurt. Her heart went out to all those women and kids who put up with abuse on a daily basis. She couldn't understand how someone could want to hurt anyone weaker than they were.

* * * *

"Brax, Ajay, Cael, you need to go. Jaylynn's just been hurt," Sheriff Damon Osborn said after entering the office. "She and another woman are down on the ground in the laneway between the hardware store and the lingerie shop."

Brax's heart flipped in his chest as it missed a beat before slamming painfully against his sternum. Sweat broke out on his brow and he clenched down hard on his teeth to prevent the roar of fury building in his chest from escaping.

Brax shoved to his feet, brushed passed Damon and raced out of the Sheriff's Department. He didn't need to look back to see if his brothers Ajay and Cael were behind him. He could literally feel them breathing down his neck. When he saw the ambulance parked on the main street close to the alley entrance, his knees nearly buckled.

"Jaylynn!" he shouted. If he hadn't reached out to steady himself on the brickwork and added a skip, he might have gone down. He was about to turn the corner but stopped abruptly when he saw Cam carrying Jaylynn. Ajay and Cael bumped into him, but he didn't care. He glanced at the woman Phoenix was carrying, and while he hated that she was battered and bruised, his first concern was for his woman.

"Baby," he whispered in a hoarse voice when he saw her red swollen face and eye. Her lips were pulled into a tight line and she was squinting. He knew her head had to be killing her. "Give her to me," he ordered as he moved closer to her. Cam passed her over without quibbling.

Brax lowered his forehead to hers and breathed in her delectable scent. His racing heart slowed somewhat, but he wanted answers. He wanted to know who the fuck had hurt her. When he had the fucker's name he was going to hunt the bastard down and beat him to within an inch of his life. "Who hurt you, baby?"

"Is she all right? We need to get her to the hospital," Damon said.

Brax hadn't realized the other man had followed him and his brothers, but he should have expected it. All the men of Slick Rock were protective of the women and when they heard what had happened in their town, they were going to be as livid as he was.

"Who hit you, honey?" Ajay asked angrily.

"The questions can wait," Cam said. "We need to get Jaylynn and Shyann to the hospital so we can check them over."

Brax swallowed around the lump in his throat and nodded, before carrying her into the back of the ambulance. He gazed at the paramedics. "Make sure you look after her."

"We will."

"I don't need to go in the ambulance." Jaylynn sighed. "I can walk perfectly fine."

"Do as you're told, baby." Brax pointed at her. "You've just recovered from being sick."

"We'll be with you soon, sweetness," Cael said as he nudged Brax aside so he could see her.

"Do everything the doc tells you to, honey," Ajay ordered.

Brax almost smiled when Jaylynn rolled her eyes at them, but he was too angry. Especially when his woman ended up gasping with pain. If the paramedic hadn't closed the doors right then, he would have climbed into the back with her. He didn't give a shit about protocol. That was his woman in the back of the ambulance, hurt.

"Did you find out who hurt them?" Damon asked Wilder.

"No. Jaylynn called out to Cindy as she was walking along the street but there was no one about by then," Wilder explained.

Brax glanced about. "Where's Cindy now."

"I sent her on her way. She couldn't tell us anything. I'm damn glad that she heard Jaylynn calling for help. If she hadn't, I'm not sure she would have been able to get help herself," Wilder said. "When Cam helped her up, she looked as if she was going to pass out. Plus, she wouldn't have left Shyann alone while she was lying unconscious on the ground."

"Was there any evidence left behind?" Damon asked as he stared up the lane.

Wilder shook his head. "Nothing. Maybe the docs can get some DNA swabs from Shyann and Jaylynn."

"I fucking hope so." Damon scrubbed a hand down his face.

"We're going to the hospital to be with Jaylynn," Ajay said before he turned on his heel and began jogging back up the street. Cael followed.

"I'm going, too. Call me if you find out anything," Brax said.

"I will," Damon replied. "I won't be far behind you."

Brax nodded and raced after his brothers. He needed to see Jaylynn and make sure she was all right. His gut was a big knot of anxiety and the back of his neck was itching. That didn't bode well at all. He learned to never discount his internal alarm system. When that started pinging it usually meant trouble wasn't far away.

"Who the fuck would hit a woman?" Cael asked in a growly voice just as Brax caught up with him and Ajay.

"When I find out, he's a dead man," Ajay replied angrily.

Brax didn't say anything as he and his brothers entered the hospital. He bypassed the reception area and headed toward the emergency triage section. He hurried toward Cam when he spied him coming out of a curtain-enclosed bed. "Is Jaylynn in there?"

"Yeah." Cam rubbed the back of his neck. "I've given her a shot of painkillers and an icepack for her cheek and eye, but she's going to end up with a hell of a shiner."

"What about the other woman?" Cael asked as he came to stand beside Brax.

"Phoenix said she's just regained consciousness, thank god. She's got a severe concussion and is going to be out of it for a while. She's sick to her stomach and very disorientated. I'm hoping she'll be on the road to recovery in a few days to a week," Cam explained.

"Did you ask who hit her?" Ajay asked.

Cam nodded and sighed. "She said she doesn't remember."

"Fuck!" Ajay spun away and began to pace.

"Ajay," Jaylynn slurred loudly. "Keep your…voice down. No s-s-swearing. Kids."

Brax nodded his thanks to the doc and strode toward the curtain. He slipped between the gap and stared at Jaylynn. She was pale and had her eyes closed. She was holding an icepack to her cheek and eye. He walked toward the head of the bed, bent over and kissed her uninjured cheek. "How are you holding up, baby?"

"I'm okay. Have you heard how Shy…Shy…Shyann is?"

Brax brushed her hair back from her forehead. "Cam just got word that she's awake. She's got a bad concussion and is sick, but she should be fine in a few days to a week."

"Do you know Shyann, Jaylynn?" Cael asked as he moved to the other side of the bed. He bent over and kissed her on the forehead.

"No, not really. I've seen her a few times in the diner, but other than that…" Jaylynn shook her head and groaned.

"Don't go moving too much, honey," Ajay stated as he sat on the bed near her hip. He quickly shoved to his feet when she winced. "Did I hurt you? I'm so fucking sorry, Jaylynn."

"It's not you, Ajay. You d-didn't hurt me."

Brax knew something was wrong when she squeezed her eyes tightly closed as if she was in agony. He pushed the nurse call button and flung the curtain aside. When he spied Cam across the room talking with a nurse, he beckoned him over.

"What's up?" Cam asked.

"Jaylynn's in a lot of pain."

Cam frowned as he walked closer to the bed. "Isn't the painkiller working, Jaylynn? Is your head still hurting?"

"Not my head, the back of my hip is."

"Close the curtain," Cam commanded.

Brax and Ajay tugged the curtain closed.

"I'm going to lower the head of the bed and if you can, I want you to roll over onto your stomach. Okay?"

"Hmm," Jaylynn acknowledged.

Once the bed was lowered, Brax and Ajay helped Jaylynn roll onto her belly since she was having trouble moving.

"Shit! She's bleeding." Cael pointed at Jaylynn's denim covered hip. Her jeans were soaked with blood.

"Nurse!" Cam shouted. "Get a trolley and bring it to me, now!"

"How the fuck did you miss that?" Ajay snarled.

Cam met Ajay's gaze. "I asked her if she was hurt anywhere else and she said other than numerous aches and pains from being hit and landing hard on the ground, she was fine."

"And you believed her?"

"Calm down, Ajay." Cael placed a hand on Ajay's shoulder and squeezed.

Ajay sighed and rubbed a hand over his face. "Sorry."

Cam nodded and then turned toward the nurse as she wheeled a trolley in.

"Oh. That doesn't look good," the nurse said as she handed Cam a pair of surgical scissors. "Why didn't we see this before?"

"That's what we need to find out," Cam said as he cut Jaylynn's jeans away.

Brax gasped when he saw the long deep cut in Jaylynn's hips just above her ass. Blood was seeping in a steady trickle from the wound.

"I need a magnifying glass with more light," Cam lifted his gaze briefly toward the nurse. "I think there's glass in her flesh."

Brax and his brother shifted out of the way as the nurse scurried away. She was back moments later with a large magnifying glass and a stand with wheels. She placed it above Jaylynn's hip and turned the bright white light on, before pulling latex gloves on. While she'd been away, Cam had donned gloves and cleaned as much of the blood away as he could. Thankfully, Jaylynn hadn't flinched or whimpered. The pain medicine the doc had given her had put her to sleep.

"I can see a sliver of glass," Cam murmured and held out his hand. The nurse placed a pair of large tweezers in his palm. Cam poked around in the inch long cut and pulled out a long shard of glass. Brax had so many questions, he didn't know where to start, but decided to keep quiet until the doc was finished treating Jaylynn.

He watched avidly as Cam cleaned and then sutured the cut. The nurse covered the stitches with an antibiotic ointment and then a waterproof bandage and then tugged the covers up over Jaylynn. Cam turned toward him and his brothers as he removed the gloves and dropped them into the dish.

"I'm not sure we would have ever known that glass was in her if she hadn't called your attention to the fact she was in pain. I'll check with the paramedics, but I'm sure they would have noticed if there had been blood present on her jeans and the gurney. I suspect the glass worked its way in deeper as she shifted around and cut into her flesh."

"Why wouldn't she have known it was there," Ajay asked.

Cam frowned as he pondered the question. "She was already hurting. She probably thought she was bruised from her hitting the ground."

Brax nodded.

Ajay offered the doc his hand. "I'm sorry for getting angry at you. I was just…angry over the situation."

"Don't worry about it." Cam shook Ajay's hand.

"When can we take her home?" Cael asked.

"As soon as she wakes up and the paperwork's done," Cam answered. "I need to know if she's had a recent tetanus shot. If not, I'll give her one before she leaves as well as some antibiotics to stave off infection."

"Thanks, Cam." Brax and then Cael shook his hand.

"No worries. I'll be back after I check on our other patient."

Brax hoped they could take Jaylynn home soon, but he had a feeling it would be hours before he carried her in the front door.

Chapter Eighteen

"Can we go home now?" Jaylynn winced as she shifted onto her side. She was tired and hurting. She'd answered all of Wilder's, Damon's and her men's questions, and could tell they were frustrated. She wished she'd seen the asshole's face so she could give the sheriff and deputy a description, but she hadn't and wasn't about to lie.

"Soon, sweetness," Cael murmured before kissing her cheek.

"That reminds me," Ajay piped up. "Cam wanted to know the last time you'd had a tetanus shot."

Jaylynn frowned as she tried to remember.

"From the frown, I'd say you have no idea," Cam said as he walked around the curtain.

"No, I don't. Sorry."

"Doesn't matter, because I'll give you one now."

"Do you have to?" Jaylynn whined. She didn't have a phobia against needles, but she wasn't a fan either.

"I do." Cam circled his finger in the air. "Roll over, Jaylynn."

With a sigh she rolled to her back and glanced toward the curtain to make sure it was closed as Cam tugged the blanket and sheet down. He swiped a wipe over her hip, the opposite side to her injury, then inserted the needle and plunged the medicine into her body. She was about to pull the sheet back up, but Cam stopped her. "Not yet. I need to give you some antibiotics." He held up another hypodermic. Jaylynn tried to tune out the sting as she thought about Shyann. Even though she didn't know her, she was worried about her and decided to go and visit with her before going home with her guys. "All done. You can open your eyes now." Cam patted her shoulder.

She opened her eyes and rolled to her side, glad the covers were already covering her bare skin. "I'm going to need some clothes."

"Enya's on her way with some. I called her and asked her to pick you up something."

"Thank you, Camden."

"You're welcome, Jaylynn. No strenuous activities and if that headache persists come back to see me. Okay?"

"Okay."

"Good. I'll see you all later." Cam hurried away.

The nurse arrived with the paperwork and she signed it. Just as the nurse left Enya walked around the curtain. "How are you feeling, Jaylynn? God, your poor face. Do you know who hurt you?" She hurried toward her, gave Jaylynn a careful hug and held up a shopping bag. "I bought you a couple of pairs of jeans, some underwear, and a shirt. I think I guessed the right size."

"Thanks, Enya. I really appreciate it. I didn't really see who hit me, and I'm okay."

"You're not coming back to work now, I hope." Enya frowned. She turned and glanced at Brax, Ajay, and Cael. "Hi, guys. Sorry, I didn't mean to be rude."

"Hi, Enya," they replied simultaneously.

"Thanks for getting Jaylynn something to wear," Brax said. "How much do I owe you?"

"Nothing," Enya answered. "Friends don't need to be repaid." She met Jaylynn's gaze again. "So, work?"

"No," she sighed with reluctance. "Cam gave me a couple of days off to heal, but I'll see how I feel."

"No, you won't." Enya pointed at her.

"I won't?" Jaylynn quirked a brow.

Enya shook her head. "Doctor's orders are doctor's orders, girlfriend."

"But I—"

"No buts," Enya said and then smiled. "I'm just glad you're going to be okay. How's Shyann doing?"

"Not so good, from what I hear." Jaylynn flung the covers aside, grabbed the shopping bag, pulled the clothes out and started dressing. She bit the inside of her cheek when the denim rubbed over the back of her hip and bandage covered wound, so she wouldn't gasp or cringe with pain. "I'm going to go visit with her."

"I'll come with you."

"You're tired, honey." Ajay stepped into her path, blocking her way.

"I am, but I'm not going to leave that poor woman here all alone without finding out how she is." Jaylynn glared at Ajay determinedly.

"She'll be fine, Ajay," Enya said. "I won't leave her side."

"We won't be long." Jaylynn hooked her arm into Enya's and hurried out. "Do I look as bad as I feel?"

"Worse," Enya whispered back.

Jaylynn shrugged. "I'll live."

Enya smiled. They stopped outside the room the nurse told them Shyann was in and after making sure no one else was visiting, Jaylynn led Enya toward the bed. Shyann had her eyes closed, but must have heard them coming or sensed their presence.

"Hi, Shyann, I'm Jaylynn and this is Enya. We've just come to make sure you're all right?"

Shyann nodded, groaned, closed her eyes and clutched her head. When Jaylynn saw tears seeping out from beneath her eyelids her heart hurt for the other woman. "Thank you," Shyann whispered.

"You saw me?" Jaylynn asked.

"Just before he hit me and knocked me out."

"Who was he?" she asked.

Shyann shrugged. "He introduced himself as Gavin Redpath."

"How do you know him?" Enya asked. "Have you seen him before?"

"I met with him by accident a couple of times over the last few days. I go to the café across the street from the diner for coffee and to use their internet. He showed up every time I was there. He always sat next to my table, close to the window and stared across the street."

"At the diner?" Jaylynn asked and shuddered as a shiver of alarm raced up her spine.

"Yeah. Today, he sat at my table and laid on the charm. He was asking about all the women working in the diner, who the owners were and the like. I didn't tell him anything. I just smiled politely and shook my head, playing dumb, you know. I quickly finished my coffee, grabbed my things and left." Shyann paused to draw in a ragged breath. "I didn't know he'd followed me until it was too late. I even changed my usual walking route because he scared me. That was a mistake I won't be making again. I went around the block to the narrow street behind the diner and the other shops. He grabbed my arm and dragged me into the alley."

"What was he after?" Enya asked.

"Information." Shyann closed her eyes and swiped at the tears on her cheeks. She opened her eyes again. "He told me that I needed to get him all the diner's employees' names and personal information. Of course, I refused. That's when he started hitting me."

"Why didn't you tell the sheriffs?" Jaylynn asked.

"He told me if I didn't keep my mouth shut, he'd come back and kill me. He said he knew where I lived and wouldn't have any trouble getting to me." Shyann trembled and wrapped her arms around her middle as she drew her legs up closer to her body. "He rattled it off as if he'd memorized it."

"That's not good, Shyann." Jaylynn rubbed her shoulder. "We need to tell the sheriffs. Enya and I will stay with you if you want."

"Would you?" Shyann whispered her question.

"Yes," she and Enya replied at the same time.

"Us women have to stick together," Enya stated.

"I've never had a friend before," Shyann murmured.

Jaylynn and Enya glanced at each other.

"I didn't really either until I came to Slick Rock. This is a good town with good people in it, Shyann. I hope we can be friends, too," Jaylynn said.

"I'd like that," Shyann said as her heavy eyelids lowered. "So tired."

"Go to sleep then. I'll be here when you wake up," Enya said.

Jaylynn wanted to stay, too, but had a feeling her guys wouldn't be happy if she did, especially after being beaten. She was tired but after hearing Shyann's story, she was also full of adrenalin.

Enya grabbed hold of two chairs and carried them closer to the bed. "Why would a man be asking for a list of our names and all our details?"

"I don't know, but I don't like it."

"I don't either." Enya frowned.

"Jaylynn, are you ready to go?" Brax asked in a soft voice after entering the room and glancing at the sleeping Shyann.

"No."

Brax knelt down beside her. "What do you mean, no?"

Jaylynn and Enya explained what Shyann had told her.

"Stay in this room and don't move," Brax ordered as he shoved to his feet. "I'll be back."

Enya giggled after Brax had left. "Did he just sound like Arnie?"

Jaylynn smiled. "Sort of."

"If he had the accent, he would have had that line down pat," Enya said.

"I agree, but I think he'd be offended if I compared him to the famous actor. He's an old man now. At least compared to my guys he is."

Enya nodded.

Jaylynn couldn't stop frowning even though Enya had tried to lighten the mood. She had a bad headache, her face and eye were hurting, and she was worried about Shyann. Plus, she couldn't shake the feeling that she knew the man who'd hit Shyann and her. Trying to remember who he reminded her of wasn't cutting it either. No matter how hard she tried to picture the guy who'd slammed his fist into her face, it didn't help. She'd been scared and angry when she'd found the asshole beating on Shyann and hadn't even thought about the consequences of stepping in to try and stop him. However, if she had to do it again, she would. If that bastard had beaten Shyann while she'd been down on the ground unconscious, he could have killed her.

"Are you okay, Jaylynn?" Enya asked.

"I'm fine," she answered even though she was anything but fine.

Enya shook her head. "You don't have to lie to me. I can see that you're in pain."

Jaylynn shrugged. "Not as much as Shyann is, but I was frowning for another reason. I can't get the incident out of my head. Even though I didn't see the guy's face or eyes, I can't shake the feeling that he's familiar somehow."

"Maybe he's been to the diner to eat," Enya suggested.

Jaylynn nodded. Enya was probably right. Other than the women she worked with, their partners and now her guys, she didn't really know anyone else. She'd seen a lot of faces since she'd been living in Slick Rock and working at the diner. There were more than a few regulars, so it was possible that was the reason the asshole wasn't so much of a stranger to her.

So why was she having trouble convincing herself of that, too?

She gazed toward the doorway as Brax entered and sighed with relief when Wilder followed him into the room. Both men knelt on the floor next to her and Enya, while Wilder asked his questions in a quiet voice. The more they explained, the angrier the deputy looked.

"I'll have both of your statements typed up and bring them to you sometime later today or early tomorrow for you to sign them." Wilder shoved to his feet as he turned his phone off the recording app. "Rest up and do as your men say, Jaylynn. We don't want you getting sick again."

Jaylynn nodded and forced a smile but rolled her eyes at Enya. The other woman giggled and quickly turned it into a cough to cover up the sound. Thankfully, Wilder was already striding out of the room.

"Let's get you home, baby," Brax said as he held out his hand.

"I don't want to leave Shyann by herself. Enya and I both promised to stay with her."

Brax dropped his hand back to his side with a sigh of frustration. He ran his fingers through his hair and spun away before turning back again. "If you could see the way you look…you're in pain, baby. No matter how hard you try to hide it from me and even yourself, it's there on your face for everyone to see. One side of your face might be bruised and swollen, but the other side is as white as a sheet. I can tell by how dull your good eye is that you've got a bad headache. You need to be in bed, Jaylynn."

"I'm fine…"

"Fuck!" Brax clenched his jaw. "What is it with women and the word fine? Us guys aren't as stupid as you think we are. When a woman says she's fine, it usually means she isn't."

Jaylynn wanted to refute that even if it was sort of true. As she opened her mouth to reply, Shyann groaned.

She and Enya rose and moved closer to Shyann.

"You don't need to stay with me," Shyann said quietly as she opened her eyes. "I'll be okay."

"Are you sure?" Jaylynn asked. "I said I'd stay and don't want to go back on my word.

Shyann blinked as if it hurt to keep her eyes open, but she met Jaylynn's gaze. "I'm sure. You were hurt, too. You need to go home with your man and rest."

"But—"

"No buts." Shyann paused to lick her dry lips. "Thank you for everything you did. I'm sorry you got hurt because of me."

"Hey." Jaylynn clasped Shyann's hand in both of hers and squeezed. "You have nothing to be sorry for. You weren't the one who hit me. That asshole did."

"You're right." Shyann gave a semblance of a smile, which turned to a grimace as she closed her eyes. "I take my apology back."

Jaylynn and Enya chuckled.

"Good for you, hon." Jaylynn glanced at the hospital table and sighed with frustration before turning toward Brax. "You wouldn't happen to have a pen and a piece of paper on you, would you?"

"No, I don't. Sorry, baby."

"I do." Enya moved to where she'd dropped her bag on the floor, bent over, grabbed it and rummaged around in it. She turned back to Jaylynn and handed them to her.

"Thanks." Jaylynn took them, leaned the paper on the table and wrote down her cell phone number. "I've just written my phone number down for you, Shyann. Please call me if you need anything. I don't care what time of day or night it is, okay?"

"Okay, thanks, but I'll be fine."

"This isn't about this situation. I like you and I think we could be great friends. I'd really like to spend more time getting to know you." Jaylynn handed the pen back to Enya.

"I would, too," Enya said as she skirted around Jaylynn. "I'm adding my name and cell phone number, but I will be staying here with you."

Jaylynn smiled at Enya before returning her gaze to Shyann. Tears trickled out from beneath the other woman's lowered lashes. "I'd really like to call you both. You don't need to stay with me, Enya."

"I know I don't, but I have nothing better to do right now. My shift at the diner is over and I would love to sit with you for a while," Enya said.

"I'd really appreciate that," Shyann replied. "But I won't be very good company. I'll probably end up falling asleep on you."

"I'll stay until you do." Enya nodded.

Jaylynn clasped Shyann's hand again. "It was great meeting you, Shyann. I just wish it was under better circumstances. Get better soon."

"Thanks," Shyann replied.

"Bye, Shyann, Enya."

Brax stepped up to Jaylynn's side, wrapped an arm around her shoulders and guided her toward the door. She was so exhausted, she ended up leaning into him and sighed wearily. She was looking forward to taking some pain pills, climbing into bed and falling asleep. "Where are Ajay and Cael?" she asked.

"We're here, sweetness," Cael said.

She turned to look at him and Ajay and tried to smile. When they both frowned at her, she knew she'd failed miserably, but this time she didn't care.

"Do you want me to carry you, baby?" Brax asked close to her ear.

It was only then that she noticed he was practically holding her up and while it was tempting, she could get wherever they were going under her own steam.

"I'll go and get the truck," Ajay said and took off at a fast clip.

By the time they got to the entrance of the hospital, Ajay was waiting in the truck just outside with the motor still running. When Brax swept her from her feet and lifted her into the cab, she didn't protest. Brax got in the back with her and Cael got into the front passenger side.

Jaylynn closed her eyes and leaned her head against the back of the seat, thankful to Brax when he put her seatbelt on for her. Once he had on his own safety belt, she leaned into his side as he once more slung an arm around her shoulders, and sighed.

She fell asleep moments later.

Chapter Nineteen

"Is she all right?" Cael asked as he turned and met Brax's gaze.

"She's asleep," Brax answered.

"When was Wilder going to contact us after searching for that asshole?" Ajay glanced in the rearview mirror before looking back at the road.

"Whenever he has something," Brax replied.

"Have you ever heard of Gavin Redpath?" Ajay asked.

"No, and neither has Wilder or any of the other deputies," Brax said. "He contacted Luke and he asked around. No one has ever heard of the fucker and if he lives in Slick Rock, his name isn't on anything."

"He could have given a false name," Cael piped up.

"Could be." Brax rubbed his chin as he stared down at Jaylynn. "Unless we catch this asshole hurting someone else, I don't hold out much hope in catching the prick and arresting him. Neither Jaylynn or Shyann gave a great description."

Cael shrugged. "I'm just glad that Jaylynn wasn't hurt worse."

"She shouldn't have been hurt at all," Ajay snapped as he slowed the truck and turned onto their street.

"I agree," Brax said.

"I do, too." Cael sighed. "But it could have ended a hell of a lot worse than it did."

"Yeah, I know." Ajay slowed the truck and turned into their driveway. Seconds later he parked the vehicle in the garage.

Cael jumped out of the front passenger seat, closed the door and hurried toward the door leading into the house. He unlocked it and stepped aside just as Brax walked up with Jaylynn in his arms. He followed his brother and their woman inside toward the bedroom.

Ajay entered the room when Cael and Brax were removing Jaylynn's shoes and socks. They went to work on the rest of her clothes until she was left in her underwear. Anger surged through his blood when he saw the white bandage covering the stitches in her hip. He hated seeing her hurt, but he was glad she hadn't been seriously injured. Cael helped Brax pull the covers up over Jaylynn and while he wanted to strip down to his shorts and climb into bed with her, they needed to talk things out. He was still full of ire and didn't want to inadvertently hurt his woman by holding her too tightly. After giving Jaylynn a last lingering glance, Cael followed his brothers from the room.

* * * *

Jimmy flexed his bruised knuckles and rubbed at the back of his neck. He hated punching Jaylynn in the face when he hadn't been ready to confront her, but he'd had no other option. He hadn't wanted her recognizing him, but he wasn't sure if she had or not. His gut was churning with rage and anxiety, but it was too late for regrets. He hadn't meant to hit her so hard, but she scared him by shouting at him. He'd been so intent on getting that other bitch to co-operate it hadn't registered that it was his woman who'd yelled at him. He'd been lucky to escape without anyone seeing him. Thank fuck he'd parked his truck in the back of the parking lot behind the diner. If he'd parked on the main street like he'd originally planned he'd probably already be in jail.

"Fuck!" He'd had the perfect opportunity to snatch up Jaylynn, but then another slut had shouted from the other end of the laneway. He'd bolted away worried someone had heard her screaming and bring unwanted attention his way. Thank fuck the bitch had seemed to be frozen in shock after yelling so loudly, because there was no way she'd have been able to see his face from such a distance as well as the lack of light.

Now, here he was sitting in the street where those assholes and Jaylynn had been holed up, waiting for them to come back home. It'd been hours since he'd parked his truck at the end of the street and he was getting impatient.

Jimmy was just thinking about leaving when a late model blue truck turned and headed his way. He'd recognize that vehicle anywhere. He slid down in his seat and peered through the windscreen. When the truck indicated and slowed before turning into the drive about two hundred yards away, he smiled for the first time that day and rubbed his hands together. He'd already checked out of the motel for a quick getaway and he was locked and loaded just in case.

Now was the time to make his move. If he didn't get Jaylynn today, he didn't think he'd ever get the chance again. Nonetheless, he couldn't move too soon. Maybe waiting a couple more hours would be better. He chuckled to himself. He'd give the bastards and his woman time to settle down and become complacent and then he'd go in. If he could get to Jaylynn without alerting those arrogant fucking Marines, his task would be that much easier. He glanced at his watch. No, an hour would have to do. If he waited longer than that, people who lived on the street were going to start arriving home from work and see him. The last thing he wanted was to have someone witnessing his abduction.

"Soon, you'll be mine again, bitch." Jimmy rubbed his hard, aching cock. "Once I've got you, I'll never let you go again."

* * * *

As soon as Jaylynn saw the big guy hitting Shyann, she knew she was dreaming. Even though she tried to convince herself to wake up, the images, feelings of fear and pain didn't stop until they'd played themselves out. She jerked upright and gasped as the stitches in her hip pulled at the abrupt, swift movement. She was covered in sweat and she was breathing heavily. Once she had her breathing back under control, she flung the covers aside, scooted to the edge of the mattress and climbed out of bed.

After using the facilities, she turned the shower on and stepped in under the warm spray. Jaylynn made quick work of washing off the sweat and grime, turned the water off and got out. She dried off, brushed her teeth and hair before heading back to the bedroom to get dressed. She'd just sat down on the edge of the bed to pull her socks and shoes on, when she felt a breeze drift over her skin. She frowned as she stood, dropping the rolled-up socks onto the bed and turned toward the window. The blind was up but she didn't think it had been earlier, before she had her shower. She walked over to the window and just as she glanced out toward the garden, she felt a presence behind her.

Just as she was about to turn, a large cruel hand clamped down over her mouth and nose and a muscular arm wrapped around her waist. Jaylynn's scream was muffled, but she wasn't giving up. She kicked back with her bare foot and ended up moaning when she hurt herself.

Her heart was pounding, and her lungs were burning from lack of oxygen and she could already feel herself starting to wilt. She was sweating and shaking with terror, but knew she couldn't give in to the fear. She reached up and back, trying to claw the bastard's face, but he somehow managed to avoid her nails as he shifted from side to side behind her. Darkness invaded her eyesight and in a last-ditch effort of desperation, she kicked out again. This time she was aiming for the wall to the side of the window, hoping the noise would alert her men that she was in trouble. Whoever had her must have seen her intent, because before her foot connected with the gyprock, her assailant spun her around.

The lack of oxygen was too much, and Jaylynn slumped into unconsciousness.

* * * *

Jimmy couldn't believe how easy it was to gain access to the house. Luck had been on his side since those fucking Marine idiots hadn't armed the security system. He'd had a lot of experience getting into places that were supposed to be impenetrable thanks to his military training. Breaking the lock on the window had almost been child's play. Getting into the house had been easy as pie. When he'd first gained entrance to the bedroom and heard someone rummaging around in the bathroom, he thought he was going to have to shoot someone. He'd hidden in the closet and kept the door slightly ajar and waited for whoever was in the other room to come out. He'd nearly given himself away by laughing when he'd spotted his woman, but he'd managed to stave off his glee. She was so fucking sexy just fresh and clean from her shower and he'd had trouble being patient as she'd dressed. He knew the jig was up when she'd frowned toward the open window, but she wasn't as smart as she thought she was.

Her turning her back to him as she walked over to the open window to investigate had given him the perfect opportunity to make his move and get what he wanted. Jaylynn in his arms.

Stifling her oxygen was conducive to keeping the other fuckers in the house in the dark. She tried to fight him, but he'd been prepared and when she passed out after he'd starved her of air, he lifted her into his arms, stepped over the sill of the large open bay window and jogged away from the house toward his truck. He wasn't about to put his quarry down to replace the fly screen and close the window, because he wanted to get away as far and as fast as he could.

He snorted with laughter as he imagined the shock and fear of those fuckers finding Jaylynn gone. Hopefully, he'd have a major head start before they came looking for her. Although he didn't think they'd even know it was him that had taken the beautiful bitch right out from under their noses.

Jimmy scanned the area as he carried Jaylynn to his truck and was happy to see that no one was about. Once he got her into the back seat of his vehicle, he secured her wrists and ankles with duct tape, slapped another piece over her mouth, got out and climbed into the front seat. After securing his seatbelt in place, he turned the key in the ignition, put the truck in gear and drove away.

He was just about to turn the corner when he saw the sheriff's car heading his way. Jimmy held his breath as he kept driving and didn't breathe easy until the cop's vehicle was out of sight. Jimmy was hoping to get to Farmington, New Mexico, before stopping at a cheap motel. He wanted to be across the state line from Colorado. When he found somewhere to stay for the night, he was going to start training his woman to be the good wife she was supposed to be.

He didn't think it'd be too hard to get Jaylynn to cooperate. All he had to do was remind her how painful it had been to have his fist in her face.

Tonight was going to be the best night of his life.

* * * *

Wilder gazed at the truck and the man driving it as he drove toward it. He catalogued the man's features as well as the make, model and license plate with a quick glimpse. He kept repeating the registration number in his mind so he wouldn't forget it. He wasn't about to take chances with anyone after what had happened to Shyann and Jaylynn. He was suspicious of seeing a Texas license plate, but since the driver hadn't broken any laws he had no reason to pull him over to check the guy and his truck out.

He pulled into the driveway, parked, turned off the ignition and got out of his truck. He rang the doorbell and waited, Jaylynn's written witness statement in hand ready for her to sign.

* * * *

"Hi, Wilder, are you here to see Jaylynn?" Cael asked after opening the door.

"Yeah. How is she?" Wilder asked after entering the house and following Cael toward the kitchen.

"You can ask her yourself soon enough," he replied as he walked toward the coffee pot and reached to the cupboard to get another mug down.

"She's fucking gone," Ajay shouted as he came to a skidding stop in the kitchen.

"What?" Brax, who was sitting at the dining room table reading over his work contract, dropped the paperwork onto the table as he shoved his chair back and stood. "What the fuck do you mean she was gone? I'm sure I heard the shower running not that long ago."

"The bedroom window's wide open, the lock's been broken, and Jaylynn is nowhere in the fucking house." Ajay slammed his fist into the wall to the side of the doorframe.

"Shit!" Wilder snarled. "I fucking saw him. Let's go."

Cael didn't bother to ask Wilder what he was talking about. He was a Marine and he'd trust him with his, his brothers' and Jaylynn's lives.

Brax and Ajay ran after them and they all piled into Wilder's sheriff's truck. Wilder didn't speak until they were out on the road heading away from Slick Rock's town center. He grabbed his radio and called in a possible kidnapping, rattled off a description of the driver, the vehicle and the license plates.

Cael's heart flipped and sweat sheened over his skin. He didn't need the despatcher's response to know who had their woman. The Texas plates had given the fucker away.

Jimmy Appleby was a dead man.

* * * *

Jaylynn moaned as she surfaced from unconsciousness.

"I'm glad you're awake, baby. We're going to have such a good life."

No! She mentally screamed in denial. She knew that voice. Jaylynn trembled on the back seat of the car and tried to stop herself from rolling off when it careened around a corner way too fast. The tires screeched and just as she started to relax, she was flung into the door, headfirst. The top of her head smarted fiercely when it hit the door handle, but that was the least of her worries. Jimmy had somehow managed to find her and now she was trussed up in the back of his truck. Her wrists and ankles were bound with duct tape and even though she'd tried to tug the tape off and loosen it, she'd only managed in abrading her skin.

She shivered as the cool night air breezed over her bare feet, arms and hands. She didn't think she was cold because of the air temperature, more because she was scared out of her ever-loving mind. Her armpits were damp with sweat and it trickled down between her breasts.

The tires squealed as Jimmy took another corner way too fast and while she tried to use her feet against the door on the opposite side of the cab to brace herself, it didn't help. She was flung from the seat, banged into the seat in front of her, landing hard and painfully on the floor. She groaned when the ribs on the right side of her body took most of the impact when they slammed into the hump separating the foot wells. The air was knocked from her lungs and she panicked when she couldn't draw in another breath.

Tears burned her eyes, but she ruthlessly pushed them away. Crying wasn't going to get her out of this situation. Neither was giving in to the fear coursing through her blood, making her body quake.

Finally, after what felt like hours the pressure on her chest let up and she gasped air in through her nose. Being able to breathe helped her control the fear, trembling and the threatening tears. When the vehicle stopped weaving and swerving, Jaylynn used her shoulder to try and push herself up into a sitting position. It was difficult with her hands tied behind her back, but she was determined and wasn't about to give up. Her first and second attempt failed. After taking a small breather to regain her breath, again, she shored up her fortitude, tensed all the muscles in her body and heaved herself up. The relief was immediate for her poor bruised ribs and while she was elated she achieved her goal, she still had a long way to go. Although she was sitting up, she was still sitting on the floor. Her aim was to get back onto the seat, but she wasn't quite sure how she was going to manage that just yet.

"Fucking assholes," Jimmy yelled.

Jaylynn startled at the unexpected sound and while she couldn't see him, since she was on the floor behind the driver's seat, she heard him banging his hands against the steering wheel or dashboard. She had no idea why he was so angry and was glad she couldn't ask. She wasn't sure she'd like his answer.

Jaylynn ignored the angry snarling coming from the front and tried to decide what to do next. If she could turn herself around— which would be near impossible in such a small space without the use of her hands—she'd hoped by getting her back to the door, she could brace her feet on the hump and shimmy her way up to the seat. However, it was going to take way too much effort and Jimmy would be alerted to what she was doing. Not that she was trying to harm him since it would be impossible. Even if she did manage to hurt him she'd be endangering herself in the process. He was speeding and if he lost control she was likely to end up seriously injured or dead. She didn't have a seatbelt on or any way to pull it across her lap and secure it in place.

Maybe she'd be safer where she was on the floor.

She closed her eyes and hung her head in defeat.

That's when she heard the sound of a siren.

Chapter Twenty

"Have you got any spare weapons?" Brax asked, his hands curled into tight fists. He couldn't believe that Jimmy Appleby had managed to break into the house and kidnap Jaylynn while he and his brothers had been there. He'd been so intent on getting her to bed, he hadn't thought about re-arming the alarm. That mistake could have cost him and his brothers everything.

"There's a locked safe in the far back," Wilder answered as he glanced in the rearview mirror at one of his brothers. "I have a Glock 9mm, a semi-automatic rifle and a .38." He gave the combination to the safe as Ajay climbed over the back seat.

Wilder picked up his radio and called dispatch. "Who's patrolling toward Egnar and Dove Creek?"

"Damon is," came the reply.

"Can you contact him and get him to set up road spikes? Our assailant is heading his way fast. I want that vehicle disabled before he hits Egnar. Tell Damon he's probably packing and he's military trained."

"Roger. Dispatch out."

When Ajay had the weapons and ammo, he handed the .38 and some bullets over to Brax in the front passenger seat. Brax would have preferred the Glock but he wasn't about to quibble over a gun. He was just glad he had something to protect himself, his brothers and hopefully, Jaylynn.

"Get ready, guys," Wilder said. "We should be coming up on this asshole soon. We're only ten miles out."

Brax checked the gun to make sure there were no bullets in the chamber and then loaded it up. He could hear his brothers checking their own guns. When he lifted his gaze, he sucked in a breath when he caught sight of taillights in the distance. They were gaining on them fast.

Either Appleby wasn't going as fast as he thought, or Wilder was traveling faster. He glanced across at the dash and smiled when he saw the speedometer. Wilder had an added advantage. He lived and worked in this county and had local knowledge of the roads. Brax hadn't realized how fast they were going because the deputy handled the vehicle and road curves with ease.

Before he knew it Wilder had the vehicle close enough to illuminate the interior of Jimmy's truck. He narrowed his eyes and tried to see Jaylynn's silhouette but all he could see was the shadow of the asshole's head and broad shoulders.

Brax turned to gaze at Wilder when the deputy backed off the gas. He was about to yell at him and tell him to keep up, but realized a moment later why he'd slowed down. The truck in front of them ran over the spikes and swerved across the road. Only the two tires on the right had been blown out and Jimmy was struggling to keep control. He veered to the left across to the wrong side of the road and when the tires hit the gravel, the vehicle started to tip.

Everything after that seemed to happen in slow motion. The truck in front teetered on the verge of the road before it started to roll toward the embankment. Brax held his breath, hoping and praying the truck would right itself or that the fucker would get control. Just as Brax thought it was going over, it bounced back down onto all four wheels and rolled down the slight incline. Wilder screeched to a halt, blue smoke billowing up from the burning rubber and as soon as it was safe, Brax unclipped his seatbelt, flung his door open and jumped from the truck. He didn't turn to see who came up beside him or who was running after him from behind, because all he could think about was getting to Jaylynn.

The front end of the truck was smashed in since it had hit a large rock and steam was hissing from under the crumpled hood and radiator. Brax slowed his approach, weapon in hand and pointing toward the vehicle in case he needed to shoot Jimmy, but no movement came from the truck. When he saw movement in his periphery and Wilder and Cael were moving toward the other side of the truck, his racing heart slowed a little, but he knew he wouldn't be able to relax until he knew that Jaylynn was all right and back in his arms. He glanced toward his brothers and the other men at the worst possible time. The bastard dove through the two front seats, his gun aimed toward the floor.

Normally Brax wouldn't have hesitated to pull the trigger, but he was worried that Appleby would kill Jaylynn even if he managed to shoot him. The trajectory of his shot could end up veering after going through glass, and he was also concerned he'd accidentally shoot the love of his life.

He was sure the other guys held off firing their guns because of the same reason as he had. None of them could see Jaylynn. If they just started shooting they could end up hitting her.

* * * *

Ajay shadowed Brax as they ran toward the crashed truck. Cael was right behind him. Wilder and Cael were coming at the vehicle from the rear passenger side. Damon was covering them all from the rear.

"He's on the move," Damon snarled. "Don't shoot. We don't know where Jaylynn is."

He'd never felt so much fear since meeting and falling in love with Jaylynn, but he was a trained soldier and was able to push his emotions aside. All that mattered was getting to her, making sure she was safe.

Brax aimed the gun toward the driver's window as he moved in closer and Ajay aimed near enough to the same spot from a slightly different angle. If Jimmy so much as moved, he was a dead man.

Cael had moved around to the front of the car, climbed onto the rock and aiming at the driver through the windscreen.

Wilder moved closer toward the front passenger window and shone a flashlight into the car. Ajay's heart stuttered when he realized the bastard was no longer in the front seat. He gazed toward the back as Wilder directed the light into the rear of the truck and his breath caught in his throat. That fucker was in the back seat with Jaylynn holding a pistol against her head. She had tape across her mouth and from the way her upper arms and shoulders were angled, her hands were either tied, or taped behind her back. The asshole had probably restrained her feet at the ankles, as well. He couldn't see her eyes very well, but from how wide they were, she was terrified. Fear for his woman tried to encroach in his heart and soul, but he quickly pushed it away before it could take hold. Now wasn't the time to be feeling. Now was the time to be that cold-hearted soldier he learned to be while in the Marines.

"Put down your weapon and let her go," Wilder ordered loudly. "You've got nowhere to go. You're surrounded."

Appleby didn't so much as flinch, just kept the gun pressed against Jaylynn's temple. His arm was wrapped around her shoulders just above her breasts. If Ajay had been certain the fucker wouldn't pull the trigger if he shot him, he would have taken him out already, but there was never any certainty when dealing with injuries or death. Everyone reacted differently, and the person being shot nearly always jerked. Jaylynn could end up with a bullet in her brain.

* * * *

Cael had the perfect headshot but he wasn't about the pull the trigger on his gun. Jaylynn was way too close to the fucker and he was scared he'd hit her instead. He could see her slight body trembling, but he couldn't react. He needed to keep his feelings at bay so if the perfect opportunity came to light, he'd be ready to take the bastard down.

"There's only two ways this can end," Wilder said in a calm voice, trying to talk the asshole down. "You're either going to be leaving here in a body bag or in handcuffs."

Cael wondered what Appleby was waiting for. He hadn't moved since he'd grabbed hold of Jaylynn and pulled her in front of him. Nor had he responded to Wilder's speech. He began to wonder if the prick was waiting for something, or maybe someone.

He tried to keep his gaze on Appleby and ignore the way Jaylynn was quaking, but it was hard to do since she was literally shielding the fucker. Cael glanced at Damon and wondered if he had a better chance of taking the bastard down without hitting their woman.

* * * *

Jaylynn could barely breathe with her mouth covered by the tape. She knew she was practically hyperventilating but she was so scared, she couldn't slow her breathing. Jimmy was using her as a human shield and had a gun pressed hard against her head. She wanted to do something to help in her own rescue but the terror coursing through her was making it hard to think straight. The trembling was so bad it felt as if she was on the verge of convulsing, but for some reason she thought of all the wars her guys had dealt with while fighting to keep their country safe.

The shaking slowed and while her breathing was still faster than normal, she managed to get enough air into her lungs so that they didn't burn as badly. She could see Wilder off to one side of the truck and Brax and Ajay off to the other. Cael was perched on the top of the rock the car had smashed into and his aim was true and steady. She thought she heard someone at the rear of the vehicle, but since she couldn't move to look, she wasn't totally sure. While she was glad that her men and the deputy were here, she couldn't understand why they hadn't already shot Jimmy.

As her panting slowed even more, her brain started ticking over. They hadn't taken a shot because they were concerned she would end up getting hurt by one of their stray bullets or because Jimmy might pull the trigger in a reflexive action. The only way the men were going to be able to take the bastard down was if she managed to get away from him, but how?

Jaylynn couldn't use her hands or feet since they were restrained. All she had left was her brain, her head. A light bulb flicked on and she knew what she had to do.

She stared through the windscreen of the truck at Cael. She couldn't see his eyes but was hoping he could see hers since Wilder was shining a light into the rear of the car. Praying and hoping he would realize what she was up to, Jaylynn winked first one eye before waiting a beat and then winked with the other.

Cael shifted on the rock, rolling his shoulders as if trying to get comfortable or to relieve the tension in his tight muscles.

"Put the gun down and get out of the truck," Wilder ordered.

"Fucking idiot," Jimmy mumbled angrily. "Does he think I'm stupid?"

Jaylynn felt Jimmy move and as he did so the pressure of the gun against her head lightened. She didn't stop to think about what she was doing, she just reacted as quickly as possible.

She drew her head forward slightly, inhaled, held her breath and snapped her head back as hard and as fast as she could. Pain slammed into the back of her head and skull as it connected with Jimmy's face. He howled as bone and cartilage crunched and his hold around her shoulders loosened. Using her feet against the hump in the middle of the floor, she pushed off and away from the bastard with as much force as she could.

Gunfire erupted around her in a loud barrage just as her forehead crashed into the window. Her vision blanked as darkness invaded and while she tried to suck air in through her nose so she wouldn't pass out, there was no stopping the rapidly approaching unconsciousness.

Jaylynn slumped against the door as she lost consciousness.

* * * *

When Brax saw Cael flexing his shoulders, he knew something was about to go down. He gave the other guys a signal just after Wilder drew the fucker's gaze when he ordered Appleby to put down his weapon and get out of the truck.

Jaylynn smashed the back of her head into Appleby's face, her aim right over his nose, and then she shoved her body to the side. He didn't hesitate to pull the trigger and neither did any of the others. The only person who hadn't shot their gun was Damon and that was because he'd moved out of the line of fire. Appleby jerked as multiple bullets slammed into his body. He and Ajay only managed to wing him in the shoulder and side. Wilder's shot was dead center in his chest, and Cael's was right between the eyes.

Jimmy Appleby would never harm Jaylynn or another human being again.

Brax spun toward the back door of the truck, but Ajay was already there. As he carefully pulled the door open, he reached in to steady Jaylynn so she didn't fall out onto the ground. As soon as he had the door wide open, Ajay carefully lifted their woman into his arms.

Tears of anger and relief burned his eyes, but he quickly pushed them aside. Jaylynn had bruises on her arms where Jimmy had grasped her viciously and there was another forming on her forehead where she thumped it into the window. The imprint of the gun muzzle was embedded in the skin of her temple as well as bruising, but she was still breathing, and she hadn't been shot.

Ajay carried Jaylynn away from the truck and sank to his knees. Brax hurried over and crouched next to them. Cael wasn't far behind. When he raised his hand to brush the hair back from her forehead, Brax realized his hand was shaking, but he didn't care if anyone saw what state he was in. All he cared about was Jaylynn.

"I thought you might want this," Damon said.

Brax looked up, nodded and swallowed around the emotional constriction in his throat as he gratefully took the knife Damon held out toward him.

"Did she get shot?" Cael asked as he lifted her arms up so Brax could slice through the tape wrapped tightly around her skin.

"No," Ajay replied hoarsely. "She just hit her head twice that we know of. First into the fucker's face and then on the window. I think the last hit knocked her out."

"I've already called for the paramedics," Damon said. "They should be here any minute."

"Thank you," Brax said as he glanced at first Sheriff Damon Osborn and then Deputy Wilder Sheffield. If it hadn't been for these two lawmen, they might never have gotten Jaylynn back. He quickly pushed that thought aside. He didn't want to think about what that fucker would have done to her, stolen from her.

Brax cut the tape around Jaylynn's ankles and tugged it off. He winced at the red welts left on her abraded skin. Cael was trying to very carefully and gently remove the tape across her mouth. Ajay held her cradled in his lap, propping her upper body up with one arm and his chest while he massaged the blood back into first one arm and then the other.

While Brax wanted to take her from his brother and hold her tight, he didn't want to jostle Jaylynn around and end up hurting her. She'd been through hell tonight. First being kidnapped from their house, then in a car wreck and finally, she'd witnessed a shooting. He just hoped that she wouldn't end up with PTSD or other emotional scars after what she'd endured. However, if she needed counseling and suffered nightmares, they'd be with her each step of the way. He and his brothers knew how to deal with the effects of war and emotional scars.

Brax had been so intent on staring at Jaylynn, on touching her, he'd only vaguely been aware of a siren coming toward them. He gazed toward the road when flashing lights drew his attention and sighed with relief that the paramedics were finally here.

Just as Raiden and Tane Tremaine hurried down the slope carrying a gurney, Jaylynn moaned and opened her eyes.

Tears of relieved joy rolled down his face when he gazed at her painfilled, hazy, green eyes. He hated that she was hurting but was ecstatic that she'd woken up.

"Thanks," she whispered, a smile curving her lips up as her eyelids fluttered closed again.

"You don't need to thank us, honey." Ajay kissed her forehead, away from the bruise and lump. "We'd do anything for you."

"Ajay's right," Cael said. "We love you, Jaylynn. We'd die for you."

"Love you, baby," Brax said in a hoarse voice.

"Same," she replied softly. "Love…y'all. Die, too."

"What have we got?" Tane asked as he and Raiden lowered the gurney to the ground near Jaylynn's feet.

Brax explained and after the paramedics made sure Jaylynn didn't have any serious injuries, he and Cael steadied Ajay as he rose with her in his arms. Ajay gently placed her on the portable stretcher and stepped back as they lifted the gurney and started up the hill. As much as Brax and, no doubt, Ajay and Cael wanted to go with them, there was only room for one of them. He nodded at Cael. Cael nodded his thanks and jogged up the slope after the medics.

Brax just hoped that he and Ajay didn't have to hang around the crime scene for hours on end. He needed to be with the love of his life.

Epilogue

"We think we figured out why Appleby wanted the list of employee details from the diner," Cree said.

"Why?" Jaylynn asked.

"We think he was looking for a way to get to you. You'd been off sick, and he was getting frustrated," Wilder took over the explanation.

Nash jumped in. "We think he was going to try and use one of the other women as bait or blackmail them into helping him get his hands on you."

Jaylynn met Shyann's gaze across the table. "I'm sorry he used you to get to me."

Shyann waved her hand in the air. "Pfft. I've already told you, you have nothing to apologize for. He was an asshole."

"Yes, he was." Jaylynn nodded.

"Stop it," Enya snapped as Phoenix leaned in for another kiss.

Jaylynn laughed as she watched Enya slap Phoenix's chest. The man and his friends were so in love with their woman, they wouldn't leave her alone to eat the delicious barbecue food she and her men had made and cooked.

It had been just over a week since she'd been abducted by Jimmy Appleby and while she still had a few mottled bruises on her flesh from the accident, she was mostly recovered from all her injuries. She'd spent three days and two nights in the hospital recovering from a brain injury after using her head to get away from Jimmy and hitting it against a window, and she was lucky enough to have no lingering, persistent headaches.

Brax, Ajay, and Cael had once more delayed starting their new jobs as deputy sheriffs to be with and look after her while she was convalescing, and she'd loved every minute they'd spent with her. However, she was looking forward to getting back to work at the diner and she knew her guys were excited about starting a new venture in their working lives.

Jaylynn glanced about and smiled. She was happy, in love and accepted by all the wonderful people sharing the meal. Delta was talking to her guys, Major, Ace, and Rocco, in sign language. The men had become so proficient, Jaylynn couldn't keep up, but she was practicing so she would be more fluent.

Wilder, Cree, and Nash were sharing tidbits of food with their wife, Violet. Her eyes were sparkling so vividly with happiness, they looked as if they'd turned to a mauve hue.

They'd also invited Shyann Bowler as well as the paramedics, Raiden, Brigg and Tane Tremaine. Shyann was sitting between Brigg and Raiden with Tane on Raiden's other side, and while the shy woman kept her gaze lowered toward her plate, she was blushing and watching the three men from the corner of her eyes. From the way the Tremaine brothers were watching the quiet woman, they were enamored.

Brax drew her gaze when he wrapped an arm around her shoulders and kissed her cheek. "You're doing an awful lot of sighing, baby. Are you okay?"

She nodded, leaned up and kissed him on the lips. "I'm wonderful. How could I not be? I have three amazing men whom I love with my whole heart and some amazing friends."

Brax smiled and pressed his forehead against hers. "Just think, if we hadn't taken Nash up on his offer to come and live here, we might not be together."

"It's amazing how our choices brought us together again," Jaylynn said.

"It was meant to be, honey." Ajay kissed the top of her head before shoving his chair back and walking a few steps away. Brax removed his arm from around her shoulder, stood and moved to stand beside Ajay.

She turned when Cael pushed his chair away, rose and walked to stand on the other side of Brax. Just as she was about to ask them what they were doing, Brax rushed over to her and held his hand out. She took his hand as he helped her to her feet and didn't release it until he was once more standing between his two brothers and she was in front of them. As if one of her guys had given the others a signal, they all went down on bended knee.

Jaylynn's heart flipped before pounding hard and fast inside her chest. The chatter in the background slowed and then stopped altogether. Ajay and Cael reached out and grasped a hand each. Brax cleared his throat nervously. "Jaylynn, we're so glad you're in our lives. We loved you as a sister, and now we love the woman you've become. I love you so damn much, baby, and want to spend the rest of my life with you. Will you please marry me?"

Tears stung her eyes and while she tried to blink them back they wouldn't be contained. She was so happy she wanted to shout with joy.

Ajay squeezed her hand. "I love you, Jaylynn Freedman. Please, marry me?"

"You're our shining star, sweetness," Cael rasped out. "Without you there'd be no light in our lives. I love you, Jaylynn. Would you please marry me?"

Tears were rolling down her face and her vision was blurry. She opened her mouth to reply but nothing came out. When she saw the nervousness on her men's faces her heart melted. "Yes! I love you all, so very much. Yes, I'll marry you."

The people behind them erupted into cheers and whistles. Brax slid a ring onto the third finger of her left hand. She looked down to see a large emerald surrounded by smaller diamonds in a gold setting. "It's so beautiful," she whispered.

"Not as beautiful as you are, baby," Brax said as he and his brothers stood. She was about to tell her men how much she loved them again, but Brax cupped her face between his hands and slanted his mouth over hers. She kissed Brax with all of her love and passion, before kissing Ajay and Cael.

She had no idea how long she stood there as they all hugged her at once, but she was too intent on savoring their love, their strength, and their heat. Finally, her men released her and guided her back to the table.

They laughed with their friends for another couple of hours until their guests started departing. Jaylynn and the other women had cleaned up the dishes so now there was nothing much left to do before heading to bed. It wasn't late yet and while it was still too early to turn in for the night, she wanted to make love with her men.

She snuck away to the bedroom while her guys were putting the last of the glasses and mugs in the dishwasher and took a quick shower. By the time she came out of the bathroom, her men were waiting for her, naked.

"Come here, baby?" Brax held his hand out to her and it was only then she noticed that she'd stopped moving. They were so scrumptious to look at, they scrambled her brain. Jaylynn hurried toward Brax and laced her fingers with his. He wrapped an arm around her waist, lowered his head and kissed her hungrily.

Jaylynn moaned and kissed him back.

Ajay pressed his front to her back, caressing his hands up and down her sides before moving up to cup and knead her breasts.

Cael knelt at her side, skimmed his hands up and down her legs, before nudging them farther apart. The first lick of his tongue through her folds and over her clit had her knees buckling.

Brax broke the kiss and Ajay swept her from her feet before carrying her to the bed. He lowered her down onto the mattress near the end, stepped between her legs, tested her wetness and as he covered her body with his, pressed his hard cock all the way into her pussy.

Jaylynn groaned as her nerve endings came to life and wrapped her arms around his neck. She pressed her lips to his and kissed him wildly, passionately. Ajay tangled his tongue with hers as he rolled them over. She gasped in a breath as she lifted her mouth from his, bent her knees and braced her hands on his chest.

A whimper of need escaped from her parted lips when Brax caressed cool moist fingers over her star before pressing them inside, pumping them in and out, and stretching her muscles.

Ajay broke the kiss before reaching up to pinch and pluck at her nipples. Brax withdrew his finger from her ass, and when she felt the broad bulbous head of his hard cock against her star, she inhaled deeply.

Brax pressed firmly with his cock until he breached her ass and she groaned as air exploded from her lungs. He began to rock his hips, slowly working his way deeper in her back entrance, until, finally, his pubis was against her butt cheeks.

Jaylynn turned toward Cael. He was up on his knee, cock in hand as he stared at her hungrily. He opened his mouth to speak, but she didn't give him to time to voice whatever he was about to say. She leaned over to the side, lapped at the head of his dick and then took him into her mouth.

Brax and Ajay began to pump their hips, sliding their cocks in and out of her ass and pussy. She took more of Cael's dick into her mouth, started bobbing her head as she wrapped her hand around his shaft and pumped her hand up and down.

She was so full of lust and love she was already on the way up the slope toward the peak. Each time Ajay and Brax drove into her pussy and ass, they increased the pace until their bodies were slapping against hers.

Jaylynn suctioned her cheeks as she bobbed back down over Cael's cock and when the head bumped the back of her throat she reached over with her free hand, cupped his balls and rolled them gently.

Liquid desire pooled low in her belly as the tension began to invade her muscles, the pressure growing fast. She tried to stave off the impending orgasm, but Ajay had other ideas. He released one breast, reached down between their bodies and pinched her clit.

Jaylynn flew toward the stars. Her whole body shook and shivered as she came. Her internal muscles clamped down tight around the two cocks in her ass and cunt before releasing and clenching down again.

Cael threaded his fingers into her hair and groaned as he started coming. She hummed just before his cum shot out of his dick, over the back of her tongue and down her throat. Jaylynn gulped and swallowed quickly.

Brax started grunting each time he shuttled his cock in and out of her ass and he roared just before he shoved deep, grinding his hips into her ass cheeks as he came.

Ajay shouted as he drove his dick deeply into her pussy, his fingers digging into her waist as he filled her pussy and womb with his seed.

After giving Cael's cock a final lick, Jaylynn collapsed on top of Ajay and panted with a smile on her face.

She was happy and in love and had so much to look forward to.

Although it had hurt, and she'd doubted her choice to move away from Fort Worth and the men she'd loved from afar, it had turned out to be the best decision of her life.

She had no idea if her choices were the reason she was now realizing her dreams, or if fate had had a hand in sending the men she loved her way, but now that she had them, had their love, she was going to hold on to it with both hands and never let go.

Jaylynn had everything she'd ever wanted and imagined that Sebastian and her parents were smiling down at her from the heavens. They would be happy for her that she was happy, in love and loved in return.

Her choices had brought her full circle.

THE END

WWW.BECCAVAN-EROTICROMANCE.COM

Siren Publishing, Inc.
www.SirenPublishing.com

CPSIA information can be obtained
at www.ICGtesting.com
Printed in the USA
BVHW04s1428130418
513333BV00009B/44/P